I
MUST
betray
YOU

ALSO BY RUTA SEPETYS

I MUST *betray* YOU

RUTA SEPETYS

PHILOMEL BOOKS

PHILOMEL BOOKS
An imprint of Penguin Random House LLC, New York

First published in the United States of America by Philomel Books,
an imprint of Penguin Random House LLC, 2022

Library of Congress Cataloging-in-Publication Data is available.

Printed in the USA

ISBN 9781984836038 (Hardcover)
1 3 5 7 9 10 8 6 4 2

ISBN 9780593524152 (International Edition)
1 3 5 7 9 10 8 6 4 2

LSCH

Edited by Liza Kaplan. Design by Ellice M. Lee. Text set in Bembo.

In memory of the brave Romanian students.

December 21, 1989

BENEATH THE GILDED FRAME

SUB RAMA POLEITĂ

They lived in darkness.

Breathing shadows.

Hands plunged deep within their pockets, hiding frozen fingers balled into fists.

They avoided the eyes of others. To look into the face of fear brought risk of getting trapped in its undertow. But somehow—invisible eyes—they were forever upon them. Even in the darkest darkness.

Watching.

Always watching.

Romania's perpetual sense of surveillance.

That's how it's been described: the burden of a secret storm.

This is not recited from memory.

There was a student, a young man in the capital city of Bucharest. He wrote it all down.

Then feared it was a mistake.

We speak of mistakes—some believe that Dracula is the most frightening character associated with Romania. When they learn the truth, will it haunt them?

Dracula is fiction, with no real connection to Romanian history. But there was once a real bloodthirsty monster living in a castle in

Romania. He remained in his tower for twenty-four years. While Dracula chose specific victims, this other monster chose to be evil and cruel . . .

To everyone.

He denied them food, electricity, truth, and freedom.

The citizens of Romania were stoic and resilient, but they suffered a terror of tyranny.

How many, you ask?

Twenty-three million people.

Names and history, largely unknown. Then—

A metal box. Found next to a grave. Inside was a manuscript.

This is how one boy told the story.

Din biroul lui

Cristian Florescu

BUCHAREST, ROMANIA
1989

1

UNU

Fear arrived at five o'clock.

It was October. A gray Friday.

If I had known? I would have run. Tried to hide.

But I didn't know.

Through the dim half-light of the school corridor I spotted my best friend, Luca. He walked toward me, passing the tedious sign shouting from the concrete wall.

New Men of Romania:

Long live Communism—the bright future of mankind!

At the time, my mind churned on something far from communism. Something more immediate.

School dismissed at 7:00 p.m. If I left at the right moment, I'd fall into step with her—the quiet girl with the hair hiding her eyes. It would feel coincidental, not forced.

Luca's tall, thin frame edged in beside me. "It's official. My stomach's eating itself."

"Here." I handed him my small pouch of sunflower seeds.

"Thanks. Did you hear? The librarian says you're a bad influence."

I laughed. Maybe it was true. Teachers referred to Luca as "sweet" but said I was sarcastic. If I was the type to throw a punch, Luca was the type to break up a fight. He had an eagerness about him, while I preferred to evaluate and watch from afar.

We paused so Luca could talk to a group of loud girls. I waited, impatient.

"*Hei*, Cristian," smiled one of the girls. "Nice hair, do you cut it with a kitchen knife?"

"Yeah," I said softly. "Blindfolded." I gave Luca a nod and continued down the hall alone.

"Pupil Florescu!"

The voice belonged to the school director. He lingered in the hallway, speaking with a colleague. Comrade Director shifted his weight, trying to appear casual.

Nothing was ever casual.

In class, we sat erect. Comrade Instructor lectured, bellowing at our group of forty students. We listened, stock still and squinting beneath the sickly light. We were marked "present" in attendance but were often absent from ourselves.

Luca and me, we wore navy suits and ties to *liceu*. All boys did. Girls, navy pinafores and white hair bands. Embroidered badges sewn onto our uniforms identified which school we attended. But in the fall and winter, our school uniforms weren't visible. They were covered by coats, knitted mufflers, and gloves to combat the bitter cold of the unheated cement building.

Cold and dark. Knuckles aching. It's hard to take notes when you can't feel your fingers. It's difficult to concentrate when the electricity snaps off.

The director cleared his throat. "Pupil Florescu," he repeated. "Proceed to the office. Your father has left a message for you."

My father? My father never came to school. I rarely saw him. He worked twelve-hour shifts, six days a week at a furniture factory.

A slithering knot coiled inside my stomach. "Yes, Comrade Director."

I proceeded to the office as I was told.

Could outsiders understand? In Romania, we did as we were told. We were told a lot of things.

We were told that we were all brothers and sisters in communism. Addressing each other with the term "comrade" reinforced that we were all equal, with no social classes to divide us. Good brothers and sisters in communism followed rules.

I pretended to follow rules. I kept things to myself, like my interest in poetry and philosophy. I pretended other things too. I pretended to lose my comb, but really just preferred my hair spiky. I pretended not to notice when girls were looking at me. And this one—I pretended that studying English was a commitment to my country.

"Words are weapons. I'll be able to fight our American and British enemies with words, not only guns."

That's what I said.

Our weapons course was called Preparing Youth for Defending the Country. We began training with guns at age fourteen in school. Is that old or young compared to other countries? I remember jotting that question in my secret notebook.

In reality, my desire to speak English had nothing to do with fighting our enemies. How many enemies did we have, anyway? I honestly didn't know. The truth was, English class was full of smart, quiet girls. Girls I pretended not to notice. And if I spoke English, I could better understand song lyrics that I heard illegally on Voice of America broadcasts.

Illegal, yes. Many things were illegal in Romania—including my thoughts and my notebook. But I was convinced I could keep everything hidden. After all, blankets of gloom are thick and heavy. Good for covering things, right?

I proceeded down the dark hallway to the office.

I was an idiot.

I just didn't know it yet.

2

DOI

I entered the school office. The old, brittle secretary glanced at me, then looked to her lap. No eye contact. She pointed a shriveled finger toward the director's office.

My stomach curled, tighter.

A windowless box. Smoke-stained ceiling. The stale, suspended tang of moldy paper. Hanging above the director's plain, blocky desk was a portrait in a golden frame. Identical portraits decorated all of Romania—classrooms, train stations, stores, hospitals, and even the front of books.

Him.

Nicolae Ceaușescu.

Our beloved leader. Our hero. Maverick of the grand Communist Party of Romania and vampire to the necks of millions. Illegal metaphor? Absolutely.

The new portrait depicted our hero with blushing cheeks and wavy, thick brown hair. He and his wife, Heroine Mother Elena, had guided the country of Romania for twenty-four years. I didn't linger on the picture that showed a much younger version of our leader. Instead, my eyes pulled to the stranger seated below the portrait.

Mid-thirties. Unbroken line of an eyebrow. More scalp than hair. Hands each the size of a tennis racket and shoulders extending well beyond the width of the chair.

"Close the door," instructed the man.

I closed the wooden door but did not sit. I was not told to.

The stranger peeled through a file in front of him. A photo clipped to the upper edge of the folder showed a young man with messy dark hair and pale eyes. And that's when the floor of my stomach collapsed.

Sitting a meter away was not just a hulking man with one eyebrow and paddles for hands.

No.

This man was executioner, black rider, and spy. He was an agent of the Securitate, Romania's fearsome secret police. Within his grasp sat a file and a photo.

Of me.

"They say there's one Secu per every fifty Romanians," my sister Cici once warned. "There are twenty-three million Romanians. Do the math. Securitate agents, they're everywhere."

We called them "the blue-eyed boys." Nickname aside, they were generally easy to spot. In Romania, if your family was lucky enough to afford a car and could wait five years until one became available, you knew what you were getting. There was only one brand of car—Dacia. They came in a few colors like white, blue, or green. But the secret police, they drove black Dacias. A young man in our apartment block drove a black Dacia. I watched him from our balcony. I was intrigued from afar.

The man in front of me drove a black Dacia. I was certain of it. But I was not intrigued.

I was scared.

The agent leaned back, bullying the metal chair he sat upon. His eyes drilled silent holes through me, splitting the walls of my confidence. He waited, and waited, allowing the holes to fill with fear.

His weight suddenly shifted. The front legs of the chair clapped to the floor. He leaned across the desk, exhaling the dead nicotine that lived on his pasty, yellow tongue. His words still haunt me.

"You're Cristian Florescu," he said. "And I know what you've done."

3

TREI

He knew what I had done.

What had I done?

The truth was, most Romanians broke the rules someway or another. There were so many to break. And so many to report that you had broken them.

A songwriter wrote negative lyrics about life in Romania. He was committed to an insane asylum.

A college student was discovered with an unregistered typewriter. He was sent to prison.

Complaining aloud could get you arrested as a "political agitator." But I hadn't complained aloud. I did most things quietly. Secretly. So what had this agent discovered?

Was it my homemade radio antenna? The jokes I composed? Was it the travel guide?

I bought English language stuff on the sly, through a neighborhood trader named Starfish. Reading English contraband bolstered my vocabulary. My last purchase was a handful of pages torn from a travel guide printed in England. Foreign travel guides and maps were often confiscated from visitors. Reading those pages, I learned why:

Abysmal conditions in Romania.

Nicolae Ceauşescu. Ruthless leader. Megalomaniac.
Everyone under surveillance.

Worst human suffering of any country in the Eastern Bloc.

And this one—

Romanian people are intelligent, handsome, and welcoming,
but forbidden to interact with foreigners. Imagine a madhouse
where the lunatics are running the asylum and the workers
are punished for their sanity. Best to avoid Romania. Visit
Hungary or Bulgaria instead, where conditions are better.

The note about surveillance—it was true. Everyone was a possible target for surveillance. She, Mother Elena Ceauşescu, even decreed that balconies of apartments must remain fully visible. The Communist Party had a right to see everything at all times. Everything was owned by the Party. And the Ceauşescus owned the Party.

"Nice for them. They don't have to live in a block of cement," I once sneered.

"Shh. Don't ever say that aloud," gasped my mother.

I never said it again, but I wrote about it in my notebook.

My notebook. Wait. Was this about my notebook?

The agent motioned for me to sit. I sat.

"Do you know why you are here?" he asked.

"No, Comrade Lieutenant."

"Comrade Major."

I swallowed. "No, Comrade Major, I don't know why I'm here."

"Let me enlighten you then. You have an impressive stamp collection. You sold a vintage Romanian stamp. The transaction was with a foreigner and you accepted foreign currency. You are now guilty of illegal trafficking and will be prosecuted."

A chill flashed across the back of my neck. My brain began to tick:

The old stamp.

The U.S. dollar bill.

That was two months ago. How long had they known about it?

"I didn't sell the stamp," I said. "I gave it to him. I didn't even find the—"

I stopped. It was illegal in Romania to say the word "dollar."

"I didn't find the . . . currency . . . until several days later when I opened the album. He must have slipped it in without me seeing."

"How did you come to interact with an American teenager in the first place? Interaction with foreigners is illegal. You must report any contact with foreigners immediately. You are aware of that."

"Yes, Comrade Major. But my mother cleans the apartments of two U.S. diplomats. That is on record."

But there were things that were *off* record. At least I had thought so. I had met the son of the U.S. diplomat while waiting for my mother. We became friendly. We traded stamps. We talked. I glimpsed a peek at his notebook—and decided to start a notebook of my own.

"Your mother cleans the apartments of U.S. diplomats. How did she get that job?"

"I think . . . through a friend?" I honestly couldn't remember. "I met the American while waiting for my mother. I often walk her home. My mother has a hard time seeing in the dark. It's frightening for her."

"You're claiming you engaged in illegal currency activity with an American teenager because your mother is afraid of the dark? Your mother's handicap has nothing to do with your crime. But punishment *will* extend to your entire family."

A crime? My entire family?

But I had never accepted the dollar. It just . . . appeared.

How did he even know about it?

The pleading refrains of my mother and sister appeared in chorus.

Don't tell anyone—anything.

Remember, Cristian, you never know who's listening.

Please, don't draw attention to our family.

I stared at the agent in front of me. A shivery sweat glazed my palms and an invisible moth flapped in my windpipe. In Romania, the Securitate carried more power than the military. This man could destroy us. He could put our family under increased surveillance. He could ruin my opportunity to attend university. He could have my parents fired. Or worse.

The agent leaned forward, placing his massive flesh rackets on the desk.

"I can see you've absorbed the severity of the situation. I'm told you're a strong student, talented, an observer among your peers. I'm feeling generous today."

He was letting me off with a warning. I exhaled with gratitude.

"*Mulțumesc.* I—"

"You're thanking me? You haven't heard my proposal yet. It's simple and, as I said, very generous of me. You will continue to meet your mother and walk her home. You will continue your interactions with the son of the American diplomat. And you will report details of the diplomat's home and family to me."

It was not a proposal. It was an order, and one that compromised all principles of decency. I'd be a rat, a *turnător*, secretly informing on the private lives of others.

I could never tell my family. Constant deception. I should refuse. But if I refused, my family would suffer. I was sure of that. And then, amidst the silence, the agent made his final move.

"Say, how is your *bunu*?"

Șahmat. Checkmate. The simple mention weakened me.

He knew about my grandfather. Bunu was a light, full of wisdom and philosophy. Bunu knew of my interest in poetry and literature. He encouraged it. Quietly.

"They steal our power by making us believe we don't have any," said Bunu. "But words and creative phrases—they have power, Cristian. Explore that power in your mind."

The stamp collection was Bunu's treasure. It had been our secret project for years.

We had other secrets. Like Bunu's leukemia. It stormed upon him so quickly.

"Don't tell anyone," begged our perpetually nervous mother.

We didn't have to. Anyone could see that an energetic, healthy man had suddenly turned gray and shriveled. He lifted the frying pan and his wrist snapped.

Paddle Hands cleared his throat. "It's a generous proposal. We'll work together. You give me information and I give you medicine for Bunu. He won't suffer."

And that's how it began.

I was Cristian Florescu. Code name "OSCAR."

A seventeen-year-old spy.

An informer.

|| OFFICIAL RECRUITMENT REPORT OF "OSCAR" ||

Ministry of the Interior

Department of State Security

Directorate III, Service 330

TOP SECRET

[15 Oct. 1989]

For the informative supervision of American diplomat Nicholas Van Dorn (target name: "VAIDA"), we were referred by Source "FRITZI" to Cristian Florescu (17), student at MF3 High School. Florescu's mother works as housekeeper to Van Dorn and has access to the family. Florescu was described to us as intelligent, quietly observant, with strong facility for the English language. He also has access to Van Dorn's apartment and family. Approached Florescu on school grounds and used guise of illegal stamp trading as basis for recruitment. Florescu appeared wary but agreed to provide information as OSCAR when medication for his grandfather was presented as an option. OSCAR will be used to:

-interact with Van Dorn's son, Dan (16)

-determine schedule patterns of the Van Dorn family

-determine who frequents the residence

-provide detailed mapping and layout of the Van Dorn residence

-ascertain general attitudes of the Van Dorns toward Romania

4

PATRU

Guilt walks on all fours.

It creeps, encircles, and climbs. It presses its thumbs to your throat.

And it waits.

I left school, grateful for the two-kilometer walk to our apartment block. But with each step I took, guilt and fear transformed into anger.

What sort of human being preys on teenagers and uses a sick grandfather as a bargaining chip? Why didn't I refuse and tell him to drive his black Dacia straight to hell? Why did I give in so quickly?

The agent had a file. Who informed on me? I threw a quick glance over my shoulder into the shadows. Was I being followed?

I didn't yet know the truth: many of us were being followed.

Night pooled with a scattering of clouds. The sky slung black and empty of light. Tall, ashen buildings towered together on each side of the street, lording over me. Living in Bucharest was like living inside a black-and-white photo. Life in cold monochrome. You knew that color existed somewhere beyond the city's palette of cement and charcoal, but you couldn't get there—beyond the gray. Even my guilt tasted gray, like I had swallowed a fistful of soot.

Perhaps it wasn't as evil as it felt? I would be spying on an American family only, not fellow Romanians. Romanian spy novels depicted the Securitate as defenders against evil Western forces. But if the stories were realistic, the agents were predictable. Maybe I could outwit them.

Yes, that's actually what I thought. I could beat the Securitate.

But how could I manage the guilt? It wouldn't dissolve overnight. My family would know something was wrong.

I could fool my parents. My father was always gone, working. In recent years he felt more like a shadow than a man. Mama was always distracted and worried, constantly making lists. I think she actually made lists of things to worry about. But I wouldn't be able to fool Bunu. And I certainly couldn't fool my older sister, Cici.

So, I invented a story about exams.

University exams were highly competitive. Thirty students would compete for four spots to study education. Seventy students for just one spot in medicine.

"Philosophy," nodded Bunu. "Soul nourishment. Sit for a spot in philosophy. You see, communism is a state of mind," he would lecture, tapping at his temple. "The State controls the amount of food we eat, our electricity, our transportation, the information we receive. But with philosophy, we control our own minds. What if the internal landscape was ours to build and paint?"

Bunu spoke often of vibrant what-ifs. I pondered them in my notebook. How could we paint or sketch creatively? If the West was a box of colorful crayons, my life was a case of dull pencil leads.

My family knew I wanted to go to university. I'd pretend I was upset because the available spots for philosophy had been cut in half. Cici would roll her eyes.

"You take it all too seriously, Cristi," she would say. "Many Romanians have advanced degrees and no use for them now. It can be dangerous to be considered an intellectual. I wish you'd let it go."

I thought my story would work. I'd pretend to be worried, say I was busy studying for exams. They wouldn't ask questions.

But Bunu always asked questions.

What if he figured it out? He would never understand how I could become an informer. A traitor. I was worse than the cancer that was eating him.

And then I heard the footsteps.

My question was answered.

I *was* being followed.

5

CINCI

I took a breath, listening closely. I risked a glance over my shoulder. A shadowy figure lingered nearby. A girl. Carrying a large stick tucked beneath her arm. And then her quiet voice emerged, saying hi.

"*Bună.*"

"*Bună.*" I nodded.

She stepped closer and suddenly, we fell into step.

My pulse tapped.

Liliana Pavel. The girl with the hair hiding her eyes. The girl I wanted to "coincidentally" catch up with after school. I had created a grand plan with precision timing, but it evaporated after the meeting with Agent Paddle Hands.

Liliana lived in Luca's building and also studied English. She was quiet, smart, a mystery beneath brown bangs with a clever sense of humor. When my responses carried an irony that Comrade Instructor didn't catch, Liliana did. Her efforts to hide a smile, they gave her away.

Most students loitered in groups, but Liliana often wandered somewhere to read. Her folders were covered with hand-drawn flowers and zodiac signs. Sometimes—the way she looked at me—it felt like she could read my mind. And I liked it.

Our apartment blocks faced each other at the tail of a dead-end street. Liliana's father managed a grocery supply—an extremely desirable job in a city where most people were starving.

Unlike some chattering girls, Liliana didn't speak to just anyone and everyone. When we were younger, she once paid attention to me. I was standing amidst a group on the street and out of the blue she walked up to me and gave me a piece of *Gumela*.

"It's for you," she said. My buddies snickered.

I was secretly elated but didn't want my friends to know.

"It's just gray gum. It turns to sawdust in your mouth," I had said with a shrug.

I was an idiot back then too.

I still remember the sad look on her face. It had taken until now, two years later, for her to approach me again. Should I apologize for being a jerk about the gum? Nah, she probably didn't remember.

We walked in silence, the darkness punctuated by the occasional tap of the stick Liliana carried. She pointed the stick, gesturing.

"What's the English word for these?"

"Streetlights," I said. "But guess what, in other countries I think they actually work."

She laughed.

The streetlights in Bucharest weren't illuminated. Too costly. Romania was rich in resources, but for several years, our "hero" exported all of our resources to repay the country's debts. As a result, electricity and food were rationed.

We passed a long, snaking line of people in front of a State-controlled shop. They stood, huddled against the cold, clutching their ration cards and waiting for some scrap of food that no other country wanted.

"Russia gets all of our meat. Isn't that unfair?" Luca once asked. "We get nothing but the patriots."

The feet of slaughtered pigs and chickens were sometimes available in the shops. We called them "patriots" because they were the only part of the animal that remained in Romania. Dark humor, it entertained us.

I pointed toward the shop. "Daily ration of delicious patriots, right?"

"Patriots . . . and that *Gumela* you love so much," said Liliana.

She looked at me, serious, then broke out laughing.

I laughed too and shook my head. "Sorry, I was a jerk."

She gave me a wordless nod. And then a smile.

I tried not to stare but stole glances as we walked. Her purple scarf, it wasn't something you could buy. Did she knit it herself? Should I ask? I knew that beneath the scarf was the necklace she always wore— a brown suede cord with a silver charm. Her hair fell in soft, loose waves, hanging just above her shoulders.

Liliana looked at the food line, grimacing. Over the past few years, the feeling of darkness had grown beyond electricity. To me, the darkness felt poisonous, leaching into everything. Did she feel it too?

She flashed a look over her shoulder and spoke below her breath. "My father said that Bucharest used to be called 'Little Paris.' There were trees everywhere, lots of birds, and even Belle Époque architecture. Do you remember what the city used to look like?" she whispered.

"I remember some parts. My *bunu* used to have a house. He said that Bucharest was once a luxury stop on the Orient Express."

"Really?"

I nodded.

It was happening. I was walking home with Liliana Pavel. We were having a conversation. If I could speak freely, I'd say, "Yeah, Bunu said that after visiting North Korea, Ceaușescu decided to bulldoze our city to build 'the House of the People' and cement apartment blocks. Our beloved leader destroyed churches, schools, and over thirty thousand private homes, including Bunu's. What do you think of that?"

But I couldn't speak freely.

No one could.

"I wish our neighborhood had more trees," said Liliana. "I miss the birds."

Trees appeared in parks and on large boulevards where they could be shared by all. Families, like our family of five, were herded into one-bedroom, ashtray-sized flats. I looked at the cement apartment blocks we passed. Some weren't even finished. They had no doors, no elevators, no stair railings. Similar concrete hulks loomed around the city, gray staircases to nowhere. Concrete walls gave birth to concrete faces.

But no one discussed it.

Everyone will live together! Everything is collectivized, shared by the Party! was the mantra. When Ceauşescu spoke the words, he sliced the air with his hand. The *Aplaudacii*, his faithful supporters, clapped and clapped. Those applauding men, did they shiver when a cold wind whisked through their hollow hearts and abandoned souls? I searched for English words to describe the *Aplaudacii*. I put them in my notebook: Bootlicker. Butt-kisser. Fawner.

Liliana grabbed my arm, yanking me from my thoughts.

"Cristian! Oh no!"

6

ŞASE

Stray dogs stalked a young girl across the street.

"Don't run!" I called out. I grabbed the stick from Liliana. A scream tore through the darkness.

I was too late.

The animals lunged at the girl, growling wild and guttural. She frantically swiveled her torso, holding her small fists protectively in front of her neck. Teeth landed, found anchor, and ripped. The sound, it still lives in my ears.

I ran and pressed in front of her, trying to block the dogs.

"*Culcat,*" I ordered, extending the stick for the gnashing dogs to bite, speaking low to subdue them. Others rushed to join our circle, stamping their feet. The dogs, eventually outnumbered by the group, ran off to search for easier prey. Frantic chatter ensued, arguments about the strays.

"If we don't kill them, they'll kill *us*!" wailed a woman.

"It's not their fault," snapped Liliana.

Stray dogs. They were everywhere. And Liliana was right. It wasn't their fault.

When the regime bulldozed the city, dogs were lost and left to the streets. Starving and wild, the poor creatures drifted and hunted in packs. The month prior, our teacher's baby was mauled to death in her stroller. Some people, like Liliana, carried sticks for protection.

The young girl's coat now hung in shreds. Her wool mitten lay on the ground, splashed in blood.

"Were you bitten?" Liliana asked.

"I don't care about a bite," sobbed the girl. "My mother stood in line for months to get me a coat. Now it's ruined. What if she's angry?"

"She'll understand. We'll walk you home," said Liliana. She looked to me. I nodded.

Liliana's hand grazed the torn edge of my jacket. "They got you too," she whispered. "You okay?"

Her touch on my jacket. Her concern. Suddenly, the dogs, my coat, and the meeting with the agent—it all faded into the background.

"I'm fine. You okay?" I asked. She nodded.

We said nothing after leaving the girl at her building. I wondered if Liliana's thoughts mirrored mine. Being eaten by wild dogs—did kids in other countries have to worry about that?

We turned onto our street and I recognized the bowlegged silhouette.

Starfish.

He was a few years older and wore black-market Levi's, Adidas, and concert T-shirts from the West. Sometimes he wore black boots with silver studs. It wasn't illegal to wear clothing from the West, but it was difficult to get. And very expensive. And very cool.

When people asked Starfish where he got his clothes, he shrugged and said, "I know someone." I tried to find an English word to describe Starfish and found this one: operator.

He lived in my building. We called him Starfish because he had lost an eye and the thick stitches pinching his eye socket closed left a scar shaped like a crooked star. Beside him trotted our community block dogs, Fetița and Turbatu. Liliana's building fed Fetița. We fed Turbatu. But for some reason, the dogs loved Starfish best.

We stopped in front of our apartment blocks.

Mine on the right.

Hers on the left.

"Video night," whispered Starfish. "Saturday. My place. You in?"

"We have school," replied Liliana.

"You have school during the day," said Starfish. "This is tomorrow night. Are you coming?"

I couldn't see Liliana's face through the darkness. I took a chance.

"Yeah, we're coming," I said.

"Okay, I'll add you to the list. Ask your pretty sister."

"Ask her yourself," I told him.

"Bring your money. Five *lei* each," said Starfish. He walked off, disappearing through a seam of black with the dogs.

I had never seen Liliana at a video night. Maybe her parents knew someone with their own videocassette player? A video player wasn't illegal, like a typewriter. But it was expensive and hard to get. The cheapest video player cost thirty-five thousand *lei,* half the price of a car. Most families needed a Dacia more than a video player.

"You don't have to go tomorrow," I told her.

"Okay. But . . . what if I want to go?" she said. "Can I go with you?"

Did she really just say that? I tried to search her expression through the shadows. "Sure. Meet me outside at nine o'clock."

We stood, feeling others nearby, but unable to see them. I was alone with Liliana, in a private wrapper of darkness.

"Cristian," she suddenly whispered. "Do you ever wonder . . . if any of it's real?"

"If what's real?"

"The things we see in videos—in American movies."

It was an odd question. Or maybe it felt odd because I had wondered the same thing but never had the courage to say it out loud. But it also felt . . . suspicious somehow. Too honest.

And then I was angry again. Not at her—at myself.

For months I'd been trying to talk to Liliana Pavel. We were finally alone, talking, agreeing to see each other on Saturday night and instead of being elated, I was suspicious?

Bunu was right. Communism is a state of mind.

But video nights were an escape. Gathering secretly to watch American movies dubbed into Romanian—it felt dangerous and exciting, like winning a forbidden prize. The worlds we saw depicted in the movies were oceans away. And the incredible lives we saw on-screen were all make believe.

They were, weren't they?

7

ȘAPTE

Ocean fish! No meal without fish!

The electricity in our building was on.

The television health advisory for ocean fish crackled behind closed doors. Since meat wasn't available, we were advised to eat ocean fish. But we didn't have fresh fish, just fish bones to make watery soup. Did that count? I paid little attention to the television. The English travel guide summed it up correctly:

> *Romania has one TV channel. And one brand of TV set. The State broadcasts only two hours of bland television per day, mainly propaganda and salutes to Ceaușescu.*

I trudged up the concrete stairs to our top-floor apartment. Life in an apartment block felt like living in a cement chest of drawers. Each floor equally divided into boxes of families. I climbed the steps, slapped with the smell of kerosene and unwanted information.

First floor—A hungry baby crying.

Second floor—A drunken man screaming at his wife.

Third floor—A chain pulling to flush a toilet.

Fourth floor—A grandpa with leukemia coughing.

Just as you could be certain of lack of privacy, you could also be certain that the building administrator reported to the Securitate.

After all, the Party had a right to know *everything*.

Everything was owned by the Party.

And the Party kept track—of *everything*.

"Bugs, bugs all around," lamented Bunu. "Philips inside and outside."

Philips were listening devices and rumored to be everywhere: hidden in walls, telephones, ashtrays. So all families followed the same mantra:

At home we speak in whispers.

The constant threat of surveillance clawed at our mother. Her hands shook. Her eyes darted. Her figure resembled the cigarettes she smoked. I looked up English words and phrases to describe her and wrote them in my notebook: Jittery. Distressed. Flustered. Freaked out.

Being around Mama was like living with a grenade. On the rare occasion the pin was pulled, she'd explode, say awful things, and then cry afterward. In our family photo, our mother peered in a different direction, as if she saw something no one else did. She constantly begged us to whisper, to keep everything secret.

I should have listened to her.

But back then, I felt so clever. Didn't realize I had confused intellect with arrogance. Serious mistake. And the first of many. But I *was* wise enough to whisper.

Our small apartment box housed four "whisperers" and Bunu.

Bunu refused to whisper. If the librarian thought I was a bad influence, she needed to meet my true hero, Bunu. I admired his bravery. I also admired his ingenuity. Because of Bunu, we had an illegal sofa wedged in our small alcove of a kitchen.

"I don't care if it's against the rules," announced Bunu when he moved in. "Five people in this tiny space? I need a place to sleep and the kitchen is the warmest."

With a sofa in the kitchen, we had less than a foot of clearance to stand at the two-burner stove and the tiny cast-iron sink, or listen to the radio.

With the exception of the kitchen sofa and Cici's Ileana sewing machine, our communist apartment was the same as everyone's. The living area consisted of an oval table with chairs, a narrow buffet cabinet, and a sofa that folded open. Before Bunu moved in, my mother and sister slept in the bedroom and I slept with my father on the folding sofa. When Bunu arrived, he argued that the arrangements were all wrong.

"Couples should sleep together. Gabriel and Mioara, take the bedroom. Cicilia has her own schedule for sewing, so she will take the folding sofa. I will sleep in the kitchen."

"If Cici's getting the sofa, where will I sleep?" I asked.

"Ahh," said Bunu, wagging a finger. "A young man needs his own space for things, doesn't he?"

I did but hoped Bunu wouldn't elaborate and embarrass me. He didn't. Instead, he negotiated with my parents and that's when I got my own "space." Next to the front door, every apartment had a closet. One narrow crack of a closet for the entire apartment.

"If we're creative, we can reorganize so Cristi has his own room."

My own room. Yes, that means I lived in a closet.

Crouched in a closet, is more like it.

I noted the arrangement in my notebook:

- *One sick, yet feisty grandfather on an illegal sofa in the kitchen.*
- *Closet contents moved and unlawfully covered on Mother Elena's balcony.*
- *One teenager camped out in a closet making radio antennae, writing illegal jokes, thinking about Liliana Pavel, and hiding a secret notebook of reports and opinions about Romania.*

The transgressions made me think of the Securitate agent. These were the type of things I'd probably have to report about the American family. Things I myself was guilty of.

Yes, I was guilty.

And walking up the stairs that day, I suddenly realized—

I knew who had informed on me.

8

OPT

You're late," whispered my mother. "Your jacket. Cristian, what happened?"

"A pack of dogs attacked a little girl. We walked her home," I replied.

"*We?*" said Cici, turning from her sewing machine. "Who is *we?*"

I ignored her query. I stepped to the kitchen to check on Bunu and hear the daily joke.

"How are you today, Bunu?"

I didn't have to ask. Bunu was a strange mix of gray and green. His voice was a murmur.

"I'm doing very well," he lied. "In fact, I've had some good news from Bulă." A grin crept across his face.

Joking about the regime was illegal and could ferry you straight to Securitate headquarters. But people told jokes anyway. In a country with no freedom of speech, each joke felt like a tiny revolution. Some jokes were relayed through a fictional character named Bulă.

My grandfather waved me forward for the joke. The blue veins in Bunu's hand now lived above the skin instead of beneath it.

I leaned in.

"Good news." He smiled. "Bulă says Romania is repairing the country's tanks—both of them."

Our laughter was momentary. The ration of breath left Bunu

coughing, hacking so deeply my parents came running. The cough, it sounded painful and evil, like wild dogs were living inside Bunu, barking and tearing through his innards. How did this happen? Bunu had been so fit and healthy.

"Did you take the iodine tablets? All of them?" asked my father.

"Gabriel," Bunu wheezed. "What's happening to me . . . it's not from Chernobyl."

"Cristian, go to the wardrobe. Quickly! Count the cartons of Kents," instructed Mother as she bent a trembling knee to my grandfather.

Kents.

Kents were Western cigarettes.

Kents were used as currency. For bribes. For trade. For the black market.

We needed Kents for a lot of things: seeing a doctor, gratuities for our schoolteachers, bribing the apartment administrator. If you're sick and Kentless, you're out of luck. But use your Kents wisely. Do you really need stitches—or that toe? Save your Kents for what really matters. I once opted to go Kentless for a filling. Instead of using Novocain, the dentist put his knee on my chest while he drilled and wrenched. The socket became infected and my face was swollen for a month. My psyche is still swollen. Definitely bribe the dentist.

How many Kents did kids in other countries need for the dentist or for their teachers? Did others buy Kents in a hotel gift shop like we did? I had written those questions in my notebook.

Merchandise had value. We had Romanian *lei*, but what could you do with Romanian currency when there was nothing in the local shops to buy? The shelves were always empty, but the apartments of doctors and dentists probably looked like a well-stocked store.

I headed to the wardrobe in my parents' room, but I already had the count. A recent notation in my notebook reported our family bribe inventory—three cartons of Kents, two yellow packages of Alvorada coffee, one bar of Fa soap, and one bottle of Queen Anne whisky. Russian vodka was worth something, but we didn't have any. We traded our vodka for an X-ray last year when my father had pneumonia and was coughing up blood.

"You should have drunk the vodka," Bunu told my father. "Better than medicine."

Even my sister dabbled in the black market. Cici worked at a textile factory. After hours, she made clothes and mended things for others. She had a particular talent for copying designs from the West German Neckermann catalogs. On occasion, Cici traded her sewing for black market contraband. She had a locked box hidden under her folding bed that contained a host of unusual and banned items.

Bunu's coughing ceased. And then the retching began.

The sound, it was excruciating. A heaving of jagged glass.

I stood in my parents' room, thumping my forehead against the wardrobe. Bunu's suffering, it made my own chest heave and ache. The thought of losing Bunu terrified me.

But it was temporary.

I'd give the agent the information he wanted.

The agent would give me medicine to cure Bunu.

I had made the right decision. Hadn't I?

I was smart. A great pretender. What if I turned the tables? What if I secretly spied on the agent, somehow gathered information that put me a step ahead? I'd know the game and outplay him.

That's right, I thought I could outwit Paddle Hands.

The very idea—was it blazing ignorance or blazing courage?

In hindsight, a bit of both.

Ignorant courage, blazing.

9

NOUĂ

The shadows followed me into the closet, onto my bed of rugs, and across the night. But I made it through school on Saturday without thinking of agents, spying, or Bunu.

I thought of video night.

What films had some thick-fingered truck driver smuggled across West Germany, through Austria and Hungary, into Romania? We never knew when videos might arrive. Most illegal movies from the West were dubbed into Romanian by the same woman. No one knew her name, but more than twenty million people knew her voice. She brought us into a secret, forbidden world of inspiration.

"So, see you tonight?" Liliana asked that day at school.

"Yeah, meet you at nine," I told her.

It was happening. Liliana Pavel was going to video night.

With me.

I arrived home from school and saw Mirel, a Roma boy in my building, standing on the sidewalk.

Roma families lived on the first floor, in ground-level apartments. Without moving his head, Mirel gestured with his eyes. I nodded to him, as if in greeting, but sending a private acknowledgment.

The Reporters.

The second floor and upper apartments had balconies, like ours.

And on the balconies perched the "Reporters"—women who watched all comings and goings and chattered constantly.

I listened closely. One of the Reporters was gossiping. About me. Her voice carried from above.

"Quiet, but he speaks English, you know. Handsome if he'd comb his hair."

I recognized her voice without looking—the woman with the drooping face. Unlike the other Reporters who wore stiff lines of age and exhaustion, this woman wasn't old. Her baby had been born prematurely and died in a hospital incubator when Ceaușescu turned off the electricity one night. Within a matter of days, her young features drooped twenty years. Cici always wanted to help her. I wanted to write a poem about her. The woman with the fallen face.

The electricity was on when I arrived home, so I opted for the elevator to our fourth floor. The fickle elevator doors rattled shut, presenting a new display of communist poetry inscribed on the metal:

VIAȚĂ DE RAHAT

Life is like shite.

I laughed. Most of the time it was. But not tonight.

My parents were still at work and Bunu was snoring in the kitchen. Cici was sitting at her sewing machine, creating a blouse from an old curtain.

"Starfish hopes you'll be at video night," I whispered. "I told him he'd have to ask you himself."

"I can't," she replied over her shoulder. "I'm going to the Popescus'. Their son has a suit that needs altering."

Their son, he probably also had eyes for Cici. My twenty-year-old sister was tall and pretty, with long legs, black hair, and gray eyes like mine. People said we looked alike. To me, she resembled an exotic doll, the kind that's collectible, not the kind that's dragged around. Cici mended clothes for fellow workers and neighbors. She doted on the elderly people in our building and they adored her.

I did too.

Pretty girls like Cici generally had an attitude. They used their beauty as a strategy. But Cici didn't. My sister was suspicious and watchful, but she was also fun and kind. She'd wedge into the kitchen with me, and together, we'd illegally listen to music I'd hotwired from Voice of America. She'd beg me to translate the song lyrics and then she'd whisper-sing all the wrong words. She had a hard time understanding English and it made me laugh. And when I laughed, Cici laughed.

And when Cici laughed—really laughed—it felt like the sun was singing. Blue sky, pure joy uncorked. I imagined that's what freedom felt like. You wanted it to go on forever.

But today Cici wasn't laughing. She sat motionless at her sewing machine and her shoulders began to tremble.

"Cici?"

She turned slowly to face me. Her eyes were rings of red, her cheeks stamped with splotches from crying.

"Cici, what—"

She quickly shook her head.

And put a finger to her lips.

10

ZECE

Cici, what's wrong?" I whispered.

She raised a hand to stop me. She grabbed her pillow from the sofa and put it over the telephone. She then placed a book on top of the pillow.

Rumors claimed that Romanian telephones were all constructed with built-in listening devices. When whispering wasn't enough, we put a pillow over the phone, just to be sure. We'd usually put the radio on as well, but ours was malfunctioning.

Cici sat back down. I pulled a chair from the table so she could whisper in my ear.

But she didn't whisper. She looped her arms around my neck. And cried. What had upset her? She finally raised her face to mine, tears streaming down her cheeks.

"Oh, *Pui*," she whispered.

Pui. Little chick. It was her nickname for me. I looked at my sister's tear-streaked face and took a guess. "Examination at the factory?"

She paused, awkward and averting her eyes, then nodded and returned to my shoulder, crying.

I didn't know what to say or how to make it better, so I just let her cry—as she probably did during the examination with the "baby police." Women were periodically checked for pregnancy at their place of work. The makeshift gynecological exams by medical inspectors were disgusting and humiliating, not to mention unsanitary.

Ceaușescu wanted to increase the population, to breed more work-ers. Population growth meant economic growth. If you were childless, you were taxed.

Everyone knew Ceaușescu's decrees:

The fetus is the property of the entire society!

Heroic women give children to the homeland!

Anyone who avoids having children is a deserter!

Mama had only managed to have two children. She felt guilty about it.

"Fertility under state control? That's an abuse of human rights!" Bunu would wail. "How can families take care of multiple children with no electricity and so little food? Cristian, there is no happy ending here."

Bunu was right. Some infants were put in orphanages where families were assured they'd be cared for and raised properly as good comrades. Would they? Were conditions in the orphanages better than the cement apartment blocks? I pondered those questions in my secret notebook.

"Oh, *Pui*." Cici drew a breath, gathering strength. She wiped her eyes. "I'm sorry."

"Stop. You have nothing to be sorry for."

What could I say to my sister? What could I say to my own mother who had to suffer the same indignity? Their bodies were owned by the State. I couldn't promise that things would get better. In the last few years, they had gotten worse. I couldn't intervene or help. But I wanted to take the pain away. So I leaned in to her ear.

"Hey, have you heard? Bulă says Romania is repairing the country's tanks—both of them."

Cici looked at me with her gray-blue eyes. She paused, as if suspended. And then she laughed, the laugh I loved, and swatted my shoulder.

Slowly, her smile faded. She pulled a deep breath. "Promise me you'll never change. Promise, *Pui*. We have to stay close."

She stared at me with such a desperate, imploring look. My stomach cramped with guilt. If Cici knew that I had become an informer?

She'd hate me.

She'd never speak to me again.

But what choice did I have?

I swallowed. I think I managed a small smile.

"Of course," I whispered. "I promise."

Deceit. Treachery. Hypocrisy.

I lied to my sister. The person I loved most.

But at the time, I didn't blame myself for any of it.

I blamed Him.

11

UNSPREZECE

8:50 p.m.

I waited in the stairwell. Early. Anxious. Maybe a little nervous.

My sister could tell I was energized about something but didn't pry.

"There's no hot water. The shower will be freezing. Do you want me to boil some water?" she had asked.

"No, save it for Bunu."

I showered under the freezing tap. At least the water was running. It could be switched off at any time. I reshuffled and forked my hair using my fingers. No comb necessary.

"Luca called," said my sister.

I nodded but said nothing. I had been dodging Luca. And he knew it.

Cici brushed her hands across my shoulders and sent me off with a whisper.

"Be careful. Don't say too much around Starfish. You can't trust him."

While standing in the stairwell I spied the Securitate agent who lived in our building. He tramped down the stairs wearing a long black coat, leaving behind a phantom of cigarette smoke. The black leather coat, the black Dacia. Secret agents—they weren't very secret.

I waded into the blackened street, mining the darkness for Liliana.

My hair was still wet, but I was accustomed to the cold. I hoped it wasn't obvious, showering and all. I also hoped she hadn't changed her mind.

She hadn't. She stood in front of her apartment block, waiting for me. The night clouds suddenly shifted, dropping a pale glow of moonlight.

"*Bună*," I said.

"*Bună*."

Fetița, her building's block dog, sat next to her.

"Someone fed her?"

"Apparently. Otherwise she'd be eating my shoe. She's a good amulet. Most people are scared of her."

"I'm not scared of her."

"Yeah, because your building's dog is a wolf!" She laughed.

"He's not a wolf."

"Turbatu? Well, his name's pretty intimidating."

Turbatu. The rabid one.

"Yeah." I scratched at some nonexistent itch in my wet hair. "I guess he scares people off."

"Hey, I brought something," she said, exposing her jacket pocket.

I leaned in close to see. Being so close to Liliana . . . I had to force myself to focus. I could barely see the can, but I saw the white letters.

No. It couldn't be.

Coca-Cola.

"What?!" I whispered. "Is it real? Where did you get it?"

"My dad got it at work. Someone traded it to him. He gave it to me for Christmas."

"Aw, we can't drink your Christmas present."

"Why not?" said Liliana. "Have you ever tasted it?"

I shook my head. There were lots of things I'd never tasted.

"Have *you* tasted it?" I asked.

"No," she said. "But the characters in movies, they're always drinking it, so I thought it would be fun."

A real Coke. And she was going to share it with me.

I looked to the balconies. It was late for the Reporters, but I couldn't be sure. "Well, we can't open it here. Not even with a guard dog," I said.

"Right. Where should we go?"

We walked around the side of her building, Fetița following. We found a shadow and slid down, huddled next to each other against the cold cement wall.

Liliana opened the can. It released a *shusssshh* that made the dog bark. We laughed. She offered the can to me.

"No way. You first. It's your Christmas present. You've been waiting ten months."

She took a sip. I squinted to watch. Her bangs fell over her brow, but I could see her eyes flutter closed. I waited.

"Well?" I finally asked.

Her eyes popped open and a smile pulled across her face. "*Uau!* It's really great. Sweet but sharp. Definitely worth the wait." She handed the can to me.

I took a swig. It fizzed and popped. A revolution on my tongue. I didn't have words. I just laughed. And Liliana, she laughed with me.

"If you could try anything," she asked, taking another swig, "what would it be?" She passed the can back to me.

"A banana," I replied without hesitation. "Have you ever had one?"

"Yes," she squeaked, trying to muffle a burp and giddy laughter from the Coke.

"My parents tell me we had bananas when I was little," I said. "But I don't remember. When I was thirteen, a girl had one at school. I could smell it across the room. After that I begged for a banana constantly.

It's kind of a funny story." I took a sip of the Coke and passed it back to Liliana. The sugar and bubbles—it was too amazing.

"What happened?" she asked.

"Well, my mom tries to make holidays special, you know? So, she went to great lengths for my fifteenth birthday."

"To get you a banana." Liliana nodded.

"Well, not exactly. She couldn't get a banana. But she somehow got black-market shampoo from West Germany . . . that smelled like a banana."

"Ohhh . . ." She bit her lip.

"Exactly. But I made a big fuss and"—the Coke was definitely going to my head—"I'll tell you a secret."

Liliana waited, eyes wide.

"That shampoo smelled so good"—my voice dropped to a whisper—"I drank some when no one was looking, just to say I had tasted a banana."

"Oh, Cristian."

"I know, embarrassing. If you ever tell anyone, I might have to kill you."

"Don't worry. I might not survive this Coke!" She laughed.

I often think about that moment, reliving its perfection in my head.

Liliana. A real Coke. Banana shampoo.

Sometimes we don't recognize life's perfect moments.

Until it's too late.

|| INFORMER REPORT ||

[17 Oct. 1989]

Cristian Florescu (17), student at MF3 High School.

Observed Friday evening with Liliana Pavel (17), in 3rd sector, Salajan. After meeting in the street, the two quickly proceeded to a hidden spot where they engaged in clandestine discussion and the sharing of illegal items.

Advise monitoring.

12

DOISPREZECE

We couldn't stop laughing, drunk on contraband and sugar. By the time we got to video night there was little room to move.

"You're late," whispered Starfish. "Movie's starting. You'll have to stand in the back. Is your sister coming?"

"No, she's not coming. What's the movie?" I asked.

"First movie is called *Die Hard*."

I leaned over and whispered to Liliana. "*Die Hard*. Bulă says they're making an action film about Romania. It's called *Live Hard*."

We laughed and Starfish told us to shut up. I wanted to brush Liliana's hair from her face so I could see her eyes when she laughed. But I didn't.

Over thirty people sat, crammed in the small, musty living room. Girls in the front, guys in the back. I spotted Luca among the boys. Arriving late had worked in my favor. I could stand against the wall, next to Liliana. In the dark, amidst the glow of the small television, I felt the press of her arm against mine. Did she feel it?

Video nights were forbidden. The Securitate could burst in at any time and haul us to headquarters. That only increased the excitement. The nervous energy in the room buzzed like a fizzy static over my entire body. I looked around. How did this video network function? It had to be big business. Who was duplicating the tapes and secretly distributing them to neighborhood operators like Starfish? Starfish was probably making more money in one night than most Romanians made in a month. I once spied the Securitate agent in our building with a handful of videos. Had they been confiscated from a video night somewhere, or were they his own?

Everyone sat, hypnotized by the screen and the woman's voice coming from it, speaking the dubbed Romanian translation. No one cared that the copies were poor and grainy. We'd watch four movies per night and be blissfully bleary-eyed by morning.

Liliana leaned in to whisper. "She's replacing the swear words. Can you hear it? She's using 'Get lost' for all the swears."

Her mouth was so close to my ear. Liliana smelled like flowers— the type you smell on the air in spring but can't find when you look for them. That smell, the press of her arm against mine, it made it difficult to concentrate and look at the TV. I wanted to look at her instead. But Liliana was right. The woman dubbing the English into Romanian was replacing the swear words.

"If you listen closely," I told her, "sometimes you can also hear forbidden English words like 'priest' or 'God.'"

She nodded then touched my hand. "Look! They're drinking a Coke."

"Be quiet or leave!" said a girl next to us.

We laughed but stopped talking. We didn't want to be kicked out.

When I watched the movies, I generally tracked the plot. The stories were far-fetched yet fascinating. But Liliana absorbed detail. I decided to watch the film as I imagined she was watching it. And I noticed something.

Choice.

Options.

The characters in foreign movies had both.

In Romania, jobs were assigned. Apartments were assigned. We had no choice.

But the characters in movies, they made their own decisions—what to eat, where to live, what kind of car to drive, what type of work to pursue, and who to speak to. They didn't have to stand in line for food. If they turned on a faucet, hot water rolled out. If they didn't like something, they complained out loud. It was crazy.

But crazier—the interactions. They looked at one another for extended periods without diverting their eyes.

There was an ease between them. Unspoken comfort.

They weren't worried they might be standing next to an informer. Like me.

13

TREISPREZECE

Dan Van Dorn. Son of American diplomat Nick Van Dorn.

A chance acquaintance had become my assignment.

The diplomatic apartments my mother cleaned were near the U.S. Embassy on Strada Tudor Arghezi. The Van Dorn family had arrived four months prior, in June.

After reading the criticisms in the British travel guide, I often wondered what foreigners thought of Romania. The regime claimed that our beloved leader was respected in the West—considered a maverick of the Eastern Bloc—because he disagreed with the leadership of the Soviet Union. We saw reports of Ceaușescu being invited to meet with American presidents. We were told Americans admired our hero and Heroine Mother.

So when I'd caught a peek at Dan Van Dorn's notebook shortly after we met, I was surprised. He was working in the living room while I sat nearby, waiting for my mother.

"Homework?" I asked.

"Nah, notes for my college admissions essay."

"What's the essay about?" I asked him.

"Romania. But the essays are a waste of time. I know I'm going to Princeton."

"You've already been accepted?"

"No, but my dad went there. He'll arrange it," said Dan casually.

He'll arrange it. What did that mean?

I was curious to see what notes for a U.S. college essay looked like, so when he used the bathroom, I glanced at his notebook. I expected it to say that Romanians descended from Romans and Dacians. Or maybe something about Transylvania and our castles. But that's not what it said.

Romania—Serious:

- *Fear induces compliance. Nonconformists put in mental institutions.*
- *Amnesty International reports human rights abuses.*
- *Population is fed propaganda and kept in a state of ignorance by Ceaușescu and his wife (who have a third-grade education).*
- *One U.S. ambassador resigned because Washington refused to believe reports that America has been outfoxed by Ceaușescu.*

Romania—Funny:

- *Romania received a shipment of twenty thousand Bibles from the U.S.—Ceaușescu turned them into toilet paper.*
- *The President of France reports that the Ceaușescus stole everything from their diplomatic suite in Paris—lamps, artwork, even the bathroom faucets!*
- *After the looting in France, Queen Elizabeth removed valuables from Buckingham Palace in fear that the Ceaușescus might steal them during their stay. The Queen knighted "Draculescu" anyway.*

That's all I'd had time to read.

At first, I was offended. Evil American. But the words, they circled my conscience. *Human rights abuses. Propaganda. Ignorance. Draculescu.*

After seeing Dan's notebook, that's when I decided to start a notebook of my own. I wrote in small type, in English. And I kept it hidden. Deep beneath my mattress of rugs, I had lifted the edge of the vinyl flooring to create a secret hiding pocket. At night in my closet, I filled the notebook with thoughts and feelings. I tried to use creative phrases and questions like Bunu had suggested:

DO YOU HEAR ME?
RECITING JOKES,
LAUGHING TO HIDE TEARS OF TRUTH
THAT WE ARE DENIED THE PRESENT
WITH EMPTY PROMISES
OF AN EMPTIER FUTURE.

The list in Dan's notebook—I thought about it constantly. I had even tried to ask Bunu about it a couple months prior when he was well enough to take some air outside.

"*Salutare*, ladies!" Bunu had called up to the Reporters from the sidewalk. He lowered his voice and laughed. "An old man says hello. They'll chew on that for at least thirty minutes, eh? Crazy country . . ."

That was my opportunity.

"Speaking of crazy, I heard some jokes that claimed some crazy things."

Bunu's thin wrinkled face turned toward mine. "What kind of things?"

"That the Ceaușescus stole stuff during their visit to France. Oh, and that they turned Bibles from the United States into toilet paper."

Bunu spoke while staring straight ahead. "You heard those things in jokes, you say?"

I didn't reply. I held Bunu by the arm as he shuffled very slowly down the sidewalk. When he spoke, the usual twinkle was absent from his voice.

"Don't repeat those 'jokes.' Ever. Do you hear me, Cristi? Not to anyone. Not to your sister, not to a friend, and especially not anywhere in public."

Was he implying what I thought he was? I had to know.

"Bunu, has Ceaușescu outfoxed America?"

My grandfather stopped on the sidewalk. His frail hand reached for mine, and his cold, thin fingers squeezed, trembling against my palm.

He looked me straight in the eye.

"You're smart, Cristian. Wisdom—thank god that's something this country can't take from you. But trust no one. Do you hear me? No one. Right now there is no such thing as a 'confidant.'"

His words. They return to me often.

I remember walking with Bunu, thinking about trust. Who in life could we truly trust? What remains unseen, hunting through the shadows?

I had no idea then that within a few months I'd be an informer and Bunu's words would ring so true.

I could trust no one.

Not even myself.

14

PAISPREZECE

After two visits and two weeks, I still hadn't seen Dan.

I waited for Mama in the hallway, outside the Van Dorns' apartment. I hadn't heard from Agent Paddle Hands, but if I wanted medicine for Bunu, I needed something to give him when I did. And finally, that evening Dan poked his head outside the door.

"Hey, Cristian. I thought you might be here. Come in. Your mom's waiting for my parents."

The Van Dorns' apartment occupied nearly the entire floor of the building. It was a lemon bath of bright light warmed by the power grid of the U.S. Embassy down the street.

Antique furniture. Tall bookshelves spilling with forbidden books: Müller, Blandiana, Pacepa. Expensive foreign paintings. Color photos in frames laddering the shelves. In America, photos were developed in color? Did all Americans have expensive, forbidden things—and hired help to dust them?

"You want something to drink?" asked Dan.

Of course I did. I wanted something to eat too. "No thanks."

"I have to show you these new stamps," he said.

Stamps. That's what started the trouble in the first place. I followed him down the hall.

Dan didn't live in a closet. He had his own big bedroom, the size of our living room. On the wall was a poster of a band called Bon Jovi and a sports jersey with an autograph. He noticed my glance.

"Dallas Cowboys. Texas. American football."

"Texas? I thought you're from New Jersey," I said.

"I am. But my godfather is from Dallas. I'm named after him." Dan gestured to a framed photo on the shelf. "His oil company is a corporate sponsor for the Cowboys."

I had no idea what that meant but pretended like I did. In the picture, Dan and Mr. Van Dorn were standing in an enormous sports stadium next to a glamorous dark-haired couple. They all looked relaxed and carefree, like the people we saw in movies.

While Dan retrieved the stamp, I scanned the room, making mental notes:

- Second floor, large apartment. Desk beneath bedroom window. Desk lamp. Leather jacket on chair.
- Bon Jovi poster. Dallas sports jersey. Rich godfather oil sponsor.
- Music player labeled SONY WALKMAN. Stacks of cassette tapes.
- Bookshelf with books and binders.
- White sweatshirt with the word BENETTON. Several pairs of sports shoes, all different brands.

In Bucharest, we had one shoe factory, Pionierul, so most people had similar, boring shoes. My eyes lingered on a pair of red, white, and black sports shoes. Puffy leather. I moved closer to make out the words: *Air Jordan.*

"Here it is," said Dan, interrupting my inventory.

He brought over a sheet-block of four U.S. stamps.

"The U.S. Postal Service released these this year. Dinosaurs. But look closely. This one's labeled 'brontosaurus' but it's an apatosaurus. They made a mistake, so it's collectible. It could be worth a lot."

"The post office in America makes mistakes?"

Dan nodded. He then tapped his chest and pointed to the ceiling.

"Sometimes," he said, increasing his volume. "But U.S. government agencies do their best." He grinned and then directed his voice to the light fixture on the ceiling. "But boy, the U.S. could sure learn a lot from Romania!"

He had a leather jacket, a Walkman, Air Jordans, and something else.

Intel.

Dan Van Dorn knew he was under surveillance.

15

CINCISPREZECE

My breathing tripped and stumbled.

Light fixtures on the ceiling. Were they bugged? Was ours bugged? Why hadn't I thought of that? The light fixture made more sense than the telephone. You couldn't put a pillow on the ceiling. How often did the Securitate access apartments to install devices?

Voices filtered from the hallway.

"I think your parents are home," I said.

I followed Dan out of his room. Mama stood in the foyer, speaking with Dan's mother.

"Hey, buddy." Mr. Van Dorn gave a light punch to Dan's shoulder. "And you must be Mioara's son. What's your name?"

"Cristian. Pleased to meet you."

Mr. Van Dorn nodded slowly, evaluating me.

"Nick Van Dorn. Pleased to meet you too. Your English . . . it sounds pretty good, Cristian."

The way he said it, there was hesitation—a question or curiosity behind it.

"His English is definitely better than your Romanian, Dad." Dan laughed. His mother made a comment, but not in English. She spoke another language to Dan.

Mr. Van Dorn leaned in, sheepishly. "My Romanian's pretty bad.

My wife gets us by though. She's got a gift for Romance languages."

I nodded. Mr. Van Dorn had done his homework. Some people assumed Romanian was a Slavic language because of our proximity to Slavic countries. But Romanian is a Romance language, like French or Italian. Bunu could speak all three.

I remained quiet, casually trying to make note of things for Agent Paddle Hands.

Van Dorn set his hand on his wife's shoulder. Her fingers instinctively moved to join her husband's. Their affection, it was natural, effortless, and absent the constant tension that surrounded my parents' interactions. When was the last time my parents held hands? It sometimes felt like they tried to avoid each other at night and by morning, carried the fatigue of it.

Mr. Van Dorn carried fatigue of a different sort. His blue suit was crisp, but he didn't seem as well rested and smooth-faced as most Americans. He probably spent long hours at the U.S. Embassy and long nights with his wife. The way he casually kissed her fingers, it had the look of it.

He caught me watching and hiked an eyebrow. I quickly looked away.

The heat crawling up my neck, was it visible?

Mr. Van Dorn turned to face me, his expression sincere. "It's nice of you to walk your mother home. It's rough in Bucharest at night, huh?" he asked.

"No, it's not rough."

He nodded. Extended eye contact. Evaluation. It felt so uncomfortable, but I willed myself not to glance up at the light fixture.

"No. You're right, Cristian. Bucharest's not rough. Just a little . . . dark," said Mr. Van Dorn.

• • •

"You don't have to come so often," my mother whispered once we were out on the street. "It's much too far. It could be dangerous. I'm authorized to interact with foreigners, but you're not." She threw a nervous glance behind us.

"The wife. She's not American, is she?" I asked.

"No, she's from Spain."

"What do they think of Romania?"

"How would I know?" said my mother. "I'm just cleaning their toilets."

"The husband. He seems . . . tired."

Her head snapped to me. "He's a very good man."

Interesting.

If she was just cleaning their toilets, how would she know that?

16

ŞAISPREZECE

A gift? Why do you need a gift?" whispered Cici the next day. "Someone shared something with me. I want to return the favor."

"Was this *someone* a girl? Who is it?" pressed my sister.

I bit back the grin I felt emerging. "Liliana Pavel."

"Ooh! Lili's nice. Smart. What did she share? Study notes?"

I shook my head and dropped my voice beneath a whisper. "A Coke."

Cici stared at me. She blinked. She mouthed the words. "A Coke?"

I nodded. "It was her Christmas present."

"A Coke."

"Shh . . ."

Cici would understand. I had to "reciprocate"—that was the English word. I couldn't let Liliana share her Christmas present and not give something back. But what could I offer? To rig their TV antenna to get signals from Bulgaria? Not exactly on par with a Coke.

Cici shot a glance to make sure Bunu wasn't looking. She reached under the sofa and retrieved her locked box. She opened it on her lap, contents obscured by the lid. I moved to sit next to her, but she motioned for me to stay put.

"What kind of things does she like?" asked Cici.

I shrugged. "I don't know. What would a girl want?"

"Honestly, these." Cici held up two narrow tubes wrapped in white paper.

"What are they?"

"They're called tampons. Instead of wadding up old cotton or cheese cloth for your period, you use these. Way more efficient."

"Come on, I can't give her those." Disgust raised my volume level.

"You asked what a girl would want." She rooted around in the box and displayed another option. "Chocolate?"

"Definitely!"

"And what are you going to give me?"

I pulled her farther from the light fixture above so I could whisper in her ear. "I have an American dollar. But foreign currency, it could get you in trouble."

Her eyes flashed with alarm. "Of course it could. Where did you get a dollar?"

"It's a long story."

"I'll take it. I'll keep it locked in the box. Maybe we can trade it for medicine for Bunu." Cici looked at me, displeased. "A Coke and a dollar. What's going on, *Pui*?" she whispered.

"Nothing," I assured her. "Just good luck and bad luck."

Cici nodded slowly, suspicious. "Just remember, *Pui*, good luck comes at a price. Bad luck is free."

Her statement. I should have written it down, thought about it. But I didn't.

Once my transaction with Cici was complete, I went to the kitchen to check on Bunu. He was off the couch, examining our broken radio.

"I need some air," said Bunu. "Help me out to the balcony."

I helped him outside and stood, shivering.

"We need that radio," said Bunu. "I hate missing the reports."

"You know what I hate? The cold. I'm tired of warming bricks in the stove for bed."

"I don't blame you," replied Bunu. "This hardship, it hasn't always been this bad, you know."

I rolled my eyes.

"It's true. When Ceauşescu assumed power in the sixties, things were fairly moderate; conditions actually improved for several years."

"What changed?" I asked, rubbing my hands together for warmth. "The debt?"

"Yes, the need to pay the country's debts, but something else." Bunu moved closer. His voice dropped to a rare whisper. "Building a cult, a cult of personality. Are you familiar with those terms?"

I shook my head.

"Listen, Ceauşescu may be near illiterate, but even I can admit that he's a statesman and a mastermind. He's slowly made people believe that he's a god and we must follow him, blindly. And think about it, Cristi, he starts with toddlers. The little ones are just four years old when they're indoctrinated."

Falcons of the Fatherland. That's what the communist toddler group was called. And in second grade, children became Pioneers and wore a red neck scarf. No one questioned it.

"Four years old. It's cunning. More than a communist dictatorship. Remember that."

I nodded. I would add that to my notebook.

"But now—on to more important things. The conversation you had with Cici. Who is *her* and what can't you give her?" A gleam appeared in his eye. "Got yourself a girlfriend, have you?"

I stared at him.

"Please. I might be dying but I'm not deaf yet, Cristian."

My stomach clenched. If Bunu heard our whispers from the kitchen, what did the microphones pick up from the ceiling?

17

ŞAPTESPREZECE

Compulsory volunteering.

That's what they called it. An oxymoron. How could it be considered volunteering if it was mandatory? Students were required to devote themselves to helping the great golden era of Romania. Sometimes, that meant raking a thick field or sorting through boxes of vegetables outside the city. That's what we were supposed to be doing that morning during "Harvest Day" season.

The largest and best produce was sorted for export. The deformed and mealy produce held for Romanians. We called them "bean potatoes" because they were so small.

Luca and I were sent to a field to collect cartons of produce. I took a breath, trying to steady myself. I had been ignoring Luca, pretending he didn't exist. But walking alone with him, I could no longer pretend. And suddenly, I was more upset than I realized.

Luca had informed on me. I was sure of it. He was the only one who had known about the American dollar.

"What's wrong with you?" he asked.

I stopped walking and faced him. "No. What's wrong with you, Luca? I thought we were friends."

He gave me an odd look, like he was hurt but trying to pretend he wasn't. Nice guys like Luca were terrible at lying. I shook my head and continued walking.

Luca and I had been friends since we were ten. He planned to sit for the exam in medicine. He was smart and would probably pass. I wanted him to pass. Luca was kind. He'd make a great doctor who wouldn't turn away the Kentless. He never—ever—struck me as a rat.

But maybe they got to Luca through some weakness, just as they had gotten to me. Or maybe they convinced him that informing was his patriotic duty to the homeland. I was OSCAR. What was Luca's code name? I should have listened to my sister.

"I don't know," Cici had said. "There's just something about Luca. He's so eager. Asks a lot of questions. Am I too suspicious?"

We were all too suspicious.

And that's how the regime undermined everything. In my notebook, I drew a diagram of the Securitate—a monstrous apparatus with huge spinning tentacles planting doubt, spreading rumors, and casting fear. I remember my father and Bunu fighting about it.

"You do realize what they're doing, don't you, Gabriel?" Bunu asked. "Mistrust is a form of terror. The regime pits us against one another. We can't join together in solidarity because we never know whom we can trust or who might be an informer."

"Stop this talk," said my father.

"You see, even out here in the street, you're paranoid to be speaking with your own father! You've become a man without a voice. Mistrust. It's insidious. It causes multiple personality syndrome and rots relationships. At home, you're one person, speaking in whispers. Outside, on the street, and standing in lines at the shops, you're someone else. Tell me, who are you?"

Bunu's question lingered. *Who are you?*

I thought I knew. I had always been myself with Luca. Until now.

Now I hated him for informing on me, not only because it resulted in my being forced to spy for the Secu, but also because it ended the first true friendship I had.

We arrived at the field.

"Wait, I think we went the wrong way," I said.

"No, this is it," said Luca.

This couldn't be it. Could it?

Moments of profound realization are memorable, especially when they involve your own stupidity. Romania was full of beauty and natural resources. The majestic Carpathian Mountains, the Black Sea, the lush Transylvanian countryside. I had seen them myself as a child. And for the past several years, our national TV bulletins showed chest-high crops, thick and wondrous. If you waded into the fields, you might never return.

The field in front of us was not a field. It was a scrubby lot of weedy plants. An emaciated cow moaned in the dirt. A carpet of flies feasted on the animal's corrugated rib cage.

No.

I wanted the fields they showed during our pathetic two hours of television. I wanted the lush crops and enormous produce. Of course I didn't believe everything they told us, but I *had* believed the fields were overflowing. I not only believed it, I needed it to be true.

We were told Romanians made sacrifices, but we had so much to be proud of. The country needed more children because we needed more workers for our bountiful crops. Life was difficult, but I found comfort that nature hadn't turned its back on us.

I looked at the scrawny field in front of me. Even nature had betrayed us. But maybe that's what happens when you roll cement over grass, remove the trees, displace the birds, and starve the dogs. You're punished.

But the person responsible—he wasn't suffering.

We were.

Our hero, Draculescu, sat in his cardboard castle wearing a hollow crown, surrounding himself with clapping men who bowed to him as the Golden Man of the Carpathians while his people suffered, starved, and lived in terror.

I blinked, trying to stop myself. The thoughts alone warranted a death sentence.

I turned my back to Luca and the field. Dormant anger stirred, a scream inside me that I didn't know existed. Tightness gripped the bottom of my ribs. The tightness rose, hot, and spread into full-blown fury.

Nature was betraying me.

My friend was betraying me.

Life was betraying me.

"Cristian, you're mad at me. I can explain—"

I whirled around and threw my fist.

I punched my very best friend.

18

OPTSPREZECE

You think you know someone. And when you realize you're wrong, the humiliation steals something from you. Your mind becomes a thick forest of dark thoughts and you wonder— what else am I not seeing? But I couldn't figure it out. Who was I angrier with? Luca or myself?

I ignored his bruised face and the way people stepped back when I passed through the halls at school. I told myself it didn't matter. They didn't understand. Besides, I was focused on Liliana. I wanted to walk home with her and give her the chocolate.

"Pupil Florescu."

Damn it.

The school director flagged me in the hall. He stood, making idle chatter as the students filed out of the building. I saw Liliana approaching so I looked to my feet and spoke of exams. "Thank you, but tutors are very expensive, Comrade Director. My parents don't have the money." As soon as Liliana passed, I stood silent, waiting.

He handed me a piece of paper with an address. "Around the corner," said the director.

I looked at the paper. A "host location." I had read about them in the spy novels. Sometimes the Securitate used a nearby apartment for meetings. The "host" was usually an adult informer who allowed access to their apartment while at work. Good. If I had to meet with the agent, I preferred being away from school grounds.

I lingered until all the other students had left, worried that someone might see me. I rechecked the address on the paper and set out onto the darkened street. The wet, blowy cold slid beneath my jacket. I shivered. A drone of Dacias buzzed by, weary brake pads shrieking. An old red bus spit fumes as it rumbled around the corner. Head down, I walked to the stone monster of an apartment block.

Up the stairs. Second floor.

The door was open a crack.

The agent sat at a table smoking. His wisps of remaining hair were slicked with a greasy pomade. He yawned. The cigarette burned, a white toothpick in his huge hands, and the smoke climbed like a curious spirit toward the ceiling. The rank of major, yes, but an agent assigned to teenagers? He had to be second rate. I could outmaneuver him, couldn't I?

"Close the door and sit down."

I did as I was told. I took a breath and reviewed my plan. In the Romanian spy novels, people talked too much when they were nervous. That always tipped off the agents. They gave too much, gave their own opinions, and gave themselves away in the process.

I would be calm. I would speak sparingly. I would be in control.

Or so I thought.

"Have you visited the target?"

"Yes."

"Were you inside his home?"

"Yes."

The agent pushed a sheet of paper across the table to me. "Draw the plan of the apartment."

I began to sketch the layout of the Van Dorns' apartment, purposely crude and simplistic. Walls. Doors. Windows. I worked quickly, hoping to leave quickly.

He watched me and alternated sucking on his cigarette and his fingernails. The agent's neck was thick, his body bulked by beer and the black market.

"The teenager's room. Identify it on the plan."

I noted it.

"Identify and notate any electrical devices you saw and where they were situated."

"Electrical devices?"

"Fixed devices like lamps, telephones, and televisions. Also, portable devices like cameras or radios."

I noted what I remembered. If they had bugged the Van Dorns' apartment like Dan suspected, wouldn't the agent already know where the phone and lamps were located?

"Now, what other details did you observe?"

I was prepared. I had written everything down in my notebook, reviewed it, and decided in advance what I would tell him: things that weren't a secret or that wouldn't interest him. I pinched my brows together to appear deep in thought. I began to recite.

"The mother speaks Spanish to her son. The father appears tired. The son has blond hair and blue eyes, sports shoes called Air Jordans, a leather jacket, and a shirt that says Benetton. He likes American football—"

"What is the interaction like between Van Dorn and his wife?"

The visual of Van Dorn's hand joining with his wife's flashed in my mind. Affectionate. Connected. It felt private, none of the agent's business. Why did he care?

I shrugged. "I don't know. They interact like parents, I guess."

"When will you be there again?"

"I'm not sure when my mom will be working."

The agent flipped open the folder in front of him. "Thursday."

"Well, then I'll go Thursday. But sometimes Dan isn't there."

"Then figure out a way to see him more often. He goes to the American Library to read magazines from the States. Ask him to take you. Make note of what he's reading. And next time you're at the apartment, see if the father has a desk somewhere. Observe what's on it."

I remembered his desk. Against the wall in the living room.

I said nothing.

"Anything else?" said Agent Paddle Hands.

"Yes, the medicine for my *bunu*."

"Right. I'll see about that."

"When?"

"When I see about it." He thrust a sheet of paper at me. "Write it down. Everything you just told me."

I stared at him. Write it down? He wanted an official, handwritten statement? Of course. That way he had proof. Proof of my traitorous testimony versus something he made up.

He placed a pen in front of me. "Write it down and then sign the bottom of your statement."

I paused, thinking, then picked up the pen and began writing. I wrote a simple list, bullet points, and slanted my letters to the left instead of the right to disguise my handwriting. The agent stood and stretched. He lit another cigarette and walked slowly about the room. I peered over the paper while writing, secretly observing him.

"I'm finished, Comrade Major."

He leaned over me. The heft of his smoky frame pushed in close. I smelled the oily pomade in his hair. Musk over sweat. Disgusting.

"You forgot to sign it." He pointed to the bottom of the page.

"Oh, sorry." I scratched an illegible string of scribbles. Impressive. Kind of artistic.

And then the meeting was over.

I exited the apartment, filing through my mental notes:

The agent didn't smoke Carpați, Romanian cigarettes. He smoked

BTs, Bulgarian cigarettes. He wore no wedding ring. His fingernails were meticulously clean and buffed. Odd on such enormous, knuckled hands. Peeking from the pocket of his black leather jacket was a piece of paper with a word we all recognized—Steaua.

Our national team. The agent was a soccer fan.

Many Westerners couldn't find Romania on a map, but we knew that some associated our country with athletics. Although gymnastics and tennis had taken Romania to the Olympics, no team from a communist country had ever won the most cherished prize in European soccer. Not until Steaua București.

The agent's large mitts—perhaps Paddle Hands fancied himself a goalkeeper? Regardless, I now knew more about him: BT cigarettes. Unmarried. Steaua.

I knew how to proceed.

|| OFFICIAL REPORT ||

Ministry of the Interior   TOP SECRET

Department of State Security   [28 Oct. 1989]

Directorate III, Service 330

Discussion with source OSCAR at host meeting house near MF3
High School. OSCAR's behavior was appraising, smug. Thinks
he has the upper hand. Provided the following information
on target VAIDA:

    -hand-drawn diagram of VAIDA's apartment

    -locations of fixed and floating electronics

    -son's interests

    For further documentation, OSCAR is now tasked with the
     following:

    -trying to accompany VAIDA's son to the American Library
     to collect further information

    -guiding us to VAIDA's desk in the home

NOTE: Recent informer source report states that OSCAR had a
physical altercation with his friend and fellow student Luca
Oprea. Recommend increased surveillance.

19

NOUĂSPREZECE

Fahrenheit și Celsius, două căi de a măsura același lucru.

Fahrenheit and Celsius, two ways of measuring the same thing.

I wrote that translation in English class. Spring and summer were pleasant in Bucharest. But winter drew near and the cold would get colder. There was no set schedule for electricity. No announcements to help us prepare.

"This never knowing, it weakens us," Bunu would say. "It's a form of control. They know exactly what they're doing."

When the power snapped off in the winter, the dark was instantly deep. The windows became a glaze of ice inside and out. Even when the electricity was on, the temperature in our apartment rarely rose above 12 degrees Celsius, which was 54 degrees Fahrenheit.

"People in other cities and in the countryside have it easier," said Cici. "They have farms, more food, less restrictions. It's the worst in Bucharest."

So why were we living in Bucharest?

I tried to describe it in my notebook:

DO YOU SEE ME?
SQUINTING BENEATH THE HALF-LIGHT,
SEARCHING FOR A KEY TO
THE LOCKED DOOR OF THE WORLD
LOST WITHIN MY OWN SHADOW
AMIDST AN EMPIRE OF FEAR.

During the day, neighborhood streets milled with people. Friends lingered together outside. After all, why sit in a smoky, freezing matchbox of an apartment when you could have fresh air and privacy on a freezing street?

Luca and I continued to avoid each other. That was fine by me. His bruised face—it cramped my knuckles and conscience. I looked for Liliana the next day after school but couldn't find her. Did she leave early? I had been carrying around the chocolate and wanted to give it to her. When I arrived on our street, she was standing on the sidewalk near her building.

"Cristian, you need to feed your dog."

"Yeah? You have anything I can feed him?"

Her response and smile surprised me.

"Sure. Follow me."

She turned and set off toward the entrance of her apartment block.

Did she really want me to follow her? I wanted to follow her.

So I did.

The electricity was off. We started up the stairs, ascending into blackness.

"My mom is terrified in a dark stairwell," I said.

"So am I," replied Liliana.

Should I reach for her hand? Before I could decide, we were on the second floor.

"Your apartment faces the street but ours overlooks the inner courtyard," she said.

"How do you know ours faces the street?"

"Because I've seen you on your balcony. Fourth floor. Watching the agent in the black Dacia come and go. Are you spying on him?"

"I'm plotting a Kent heist. He has a stash on his balcony. You in?" I joked.

She laughed.

"So," I said softly, "you've been watching me, huh?"

"That's not what I said," she replied as she opened the door. I couldn't see her face, but I could hear the smile in her voice.

I stood in the doorway of her dark, quiet apartment.

She leaned against the open door, gazing at me. A tiny silver heart hung from the suede cord around her neck, resting perfectly in the hollow of her throat. "You can come in," she whispered. "No one's here. My brother and parents are working."

I nodded and stepped inside. A match hissed. Her hand moved to light a stub of a candle. Did her family buy candles at the street markets or from the church? Centered on the table beneath a handmade lace doily was a car battery. She noticed my gaze.

"My brother rigs it to create light for homework. It's brighter than a candle." She stepped into the kitchen.

"Hey, are you hungry?" I asked.

"I thought we were feeding the dogs." Liliana returned from the kitchen and set a bone on the table. "My dad brings bones home from work."

"We are feeding the dogs. But I thought we could also share this." I removed the small chocolate bar from my pocket. "It's not a Coke, but—"

"*Uau!* I've never had that kind! Where did you get it?"

I shrugged and handed it to her. "I know someone."

She broke it in half. We stood near the table, candle glowing, eating the chocolate.

Her fingers brushed the bottom of my jacket. "The dogs tore it. You repaired it?"

"My sister did. She has a sewing machine."

"I've heard." And then it was quiet. "Do you like music?" she suddenly asked.

"Sure, do you?"

"Yes. I like . . . Springsteen's lyrics." She glanced up at me as she said it.

The candlelight danced shadowed patterns on her face and hair. My heart bumped. She was even prettier up close.

"Springsteen was born in September. He's a Libra," said Liliana.

"Oh, yeah?" I leaned against a chair. "Can you guess what my sign is?"

"I don't have to guess." She smiled. "I know." She placed her hand near the candle. On the center of her palm was a small symbol. It looked like a lowercase "m" with a comma stuck to it. "You're a Virgo."

She had drawn my sign on her palm? "Whoa, how did you know?" I asked.

"I just know."

I nodded, not sure what to say. "Hey," I whispered. "What color are your eyes?"

"Yours are a weird gray-blue color," she said.

"Weird?"

"Sorry." She laughed. "Not weird. Different. I mean, unique. They're unique."

"And what color are yours?" I repeated.

She lifted the candle from the table and held it in front of her face.

"You tell me. What color are my eyes?"

The candle flame swayed. "I can't see them through your hair," I whispered.

"You can't?"

"No."

She stepped closer to me.

And then closer.

Silence and candlelight flickered between us. I paused, then slowly brushed the hair from her eyes. A shudder of energy pulsed through me. Did she feel it? I thought something might drop from a shelf.

"Brown," I whispered. "They're brown. They're really pretty."

"You think so?"

"Yeah."

She smiled.

And then she blew out the candle.

We stood, silhouettes in the dark. Somewhere in the room, a clock ticked softly.

I gently wrapped my arms around her.

She pulled me closer and pressed against me, placing the side of her face on my chest. We held each other. Soundless yet somehow boundless. And in that quiet moment, all hardship melted away. For once, the shadows weren't gloomy. They were private. Holding Liliana, alone in the stillness of that dark apartment, feeling her breathe, it was everything.

I had everything.

I closed my eyes, held on to the moment—and for once, thanked the heavens for the darkness of communism.

20

DOUĂZECI

5:00 a.m.

Layers.

Two pair of socks. Three shirts. Hat. Gloves. Jacket. Ration card.

I pulled the woolen hat down over my ears and zipped my jacket. It doesn't take long to dress when you sleep in your clothes for warmth. Bunu's wall thermometer said the temperature in our apartment had dipped to 8 degrees Celsius, 46 Fahrenheit overnight.

I left quietly. As if in unison, the other apartment doors opened and a line of tired residents clutching oilcloth shopping bags appeared. We trudged down the cement stairs to join the sea of humanity swarming into the freezing dark—that bleak wasteland of time.

To stand in lines.

Every family had a system for the *Alimentara*, the local shop. This was ours:

I stood in line three days per week before school.

Cici stood in line three days per week before work.

Mama stood in line after work.

Our father relieved Mama in line during the evenings.

To shiver. To wait in line for absolutely everything. That's what I was used to.

That's what we were all used to.

How long were the lines in other countries?

I thought of the advice from the British travel book:

Best to avoid Romania. Visit Hungary or Bulgaria instead, where conditions are better.

How much better? Did they have blue-eyed boys and teenage informers?

The wind blew in icy breaths. A little boy shivered alone in front of me, gripping his rumpled shopping bag like a blanket. He yawned, awakening a slumber of phlegm. His cough sliced so sharp I could feel the infection in my own chest. Near him, a spindly silhouette hunched against the wind, smoking a cigarette in the cup of his hand. Ahead of the smoker was the quiet kid from my calculus class who wore a ratty brown scarf. I had finally found an English word for him: loner. An ancient, babushka-wrapped woman heaved in close by, propped up by arthritis and a cane. Age or illness was no exemption from standing in line.

If an outsider approached, they wouldn't see Romania—once beautiful, lush land of the Romans and Dacians. No. They'd see a snaking line of frosty communism, huddled against the cold on a dark street full of potholes.

I looked toward the front of the line. Luca stood behind the woman with the drooping face. Beneath the flickering lights of the *Alimentara*, the folds of her skin glowed an eerie blue. If Luca passed the university exam for medicine, he'd eventually be drinking coffee and counting Kents in the morning instead of standing in lines. He'd cure coughs, save babies from broken incubators—maybe even save women from drooping faces.

Me? I'd be a philosophical wordsmith. A poetic traitor.

My stomach murmured, reminding me it was empty.

Would there be anything in the shop today? We stood in line, programmed, never knowing. If a line formed at a neighborhood shop, most rushed to join it. Last night after three hours in line, my father came home exhausted, clutching a dented can of beans covered in dust.

"The expiration date is 1987. Two years ago," said Cici.

My father said nothing, just shrugged. My father was quiet when he was mad, quiet when he was tired, quiet when he was happy, and quiet when he was contemplating. He felt inaccessible and I hated it. He was nothing like Bunu. How could a father and son be so different?

"Your father's hungry, Cristian, literally and figuratively. Ration cards in the 1980s? We had more food during World War II," complained Bunu. "Do you see the lunacy of all this? They've got us brainwashed, standing in lines for hours, grateful for rotten beans. But what is the cost of self-worth?"

I didn't have an answer. My self-worth was temporarily detouring through the sewer.

Liliana's brother stood a few places ahead. He glanced back at me. If he was in line, that meant Liliana was still asleep. Did he know that his sister had invited me into their apartment? Did he know that I had held her in the dark? Did he know that I had thought about her all night?

I felt a tug at my jacket. I turned. Behind me was an elderly gentleman that Bunu used to play chess with. The squat man with the spongy nose.

"How's your *bunu*?" he whispered.

"He's fine," I lied.

"Good, good," nodded the bulbous face. He leaned in close. "Give him a message for me. Tell him the coffee's not as tasty as I expected. I'll come to visit him."

I looked at him, confused. His eyes pivoted to his feet.

"They're watching. The coffee, you'll tell him?"

"Sure," I said.

"You too," he whispered. "No coffee."

I turned back around. They're watching? Of course they were watching. And coffee? No one had real coffee, except for bribes. Was he referring to a bribe? Or maybe it was a joke.

Or maybe, we were all going a little bit insane.

21

DOUĂZECI ŞI UNU

November arrived. I stood in the entry of the Van Dorns' apartment, trying to ignore the burning in my fingers as they defrosted. Did the homes of all Americans feel like summer? The temperature in the apartment had to be nearly sixty-five Fahrenheit.

"Hey, Cristian," Dan called to me from down the hall. "I thought I heard the door. Come on back."

"Come on back" sounded like something we'd hear in American movies on video night. The way he waved me forward, I assumed "come on back" meant that I should join him.

The room had a large color television—certainly different than the black-and-white Romanian TVs. There was also a video player and tall stacks of VHS tapes. Connected to the video player was a cord with headphones.

"Is that how you watch videos?"

"No, family stuff." Dan pointed to the light fixture and reached for a pad and pen nearby.

He wrote: *These are videos that friends send us from home.*

I took the pad from him: *Your friends send you American movies?*

He wrote: *No, they film themselves with their video cameras.*

"Not many visitors here," he said aloud. "It's nice to see people once in a while."

Wait. Americans not only had video players and color TVs, they had video *cameras* to make their own movies? I looked at Dan, confused. The image on the screen was frozen. He handed me the headphones. I put them on and he pressed a button on the video machine.

A scene suddenly came to life. Three American guys were in a huge kitchen amidst a blaze of light. The ceiling alone had four light-bulbs. And they were all on.

"The Super Bowl is in New Orleans this year, but I wouldn't bet on your precious Cowboys, Dan."

Their voices rolled through the headphones. I heard them speaking, but my eyes were glued to the screen. Stuck to the lower right corner. Staring at a table and a large glass bowl—

Of bananas.

Not just one banana. Many bananas. Large bananas.

A woman entered the kitchen and a boy began to complain.

"Aw, Mom, you stepped in the frame. We're making a video for Dan to cheer him up."

"Yeah, apparently communism sucks," laughed another boy.

"It's not funny," said the woman. "Dan's father says it's very difficult in Romania. Hello, Dan!" she called to the camera as she circulated around the kitchen. "Tell your parents I said hello and that we miss them! Wish them a Happy Thanksgiving for us."

As the mother spoke, she opened the door of a gigantic, towering refrigerator. Even the inside of the refrigerator had a light. And then I saw it. I felt my mouth opening. The wide shelves, they were all packed. Stuffed from top to bottom.

With food.

All kinds of food. In bottles, cans, cartons, dividers, and drawers. So many colors and quantities.

Of food.

I leaned closer to the screen.

Fresh. Ripe. Just waiting to be eaten.

A pang of desperate sadness filled my chest and crawled up into my throat.

That refrigerator had enough food to feed a Romanian for an entire year.

The woman on-screen removed a cluster of Coke cans from the refrigerator. She carried it to the table, along with a plate of crackers, sliced meats, and cheese. No one pushed or lined up. The boys casually grazed at the food while continuing to speak to the camera. I stared.

The bananas. Weren't they going to eat the bananas? But the bananas remained in the bowl.

Untouched.

A hand on my shoulder. It startled me. I removed the headphones.

"Sorry, didn't mean to scare you." Dan gestured to the TV. "Cool, right? Far away but seems like they're so close."

"Yes, cool," I said, trying to swallow past the lump in my throat.

"I've gotta go," said Dan.

"You going to the American Library?"

"No, meeting my parents at the embassy." He paused, looking at me. "How did you know I go to the library?"

Damn. I was so thrown by the food. I slipped.

"Oh, all Romanians have heard of the American Library," I lied. "Seems like a place where I could practice my English."

"Sure." Dan nodded. "I was planning on going Saturday to see if they have any new magazines. You can come with me if you want. Come by after school and we'll go together."

"Okay."

I followed Dan out of the room. My head felt detached, spinning with thoughts. Liliana's question floated back to me.

Cristian, do you ever wonder if any of it's real? The things we see in American movies?

The video I saw that afternoon was not a fabricated script.
The boys on-screen were not actors.
They were real people, in a real house in the West, with real food.
It was all true.
And everything we'd been fed?
It was all lies.

22

DOUĂZECI ȘI DOI

We walked through the frozen dark toward the bus stop. Sleet ticked against my jacket and the cold crept through my shoes. My mother's eyes darted. She clutched her purse, digging her elbow into it. I felt bad for the purse.

And I wondered how much she knew.

"Dan showed me a video today," I said quietly. "His friends in America have their own video camera. They filmed a greeting at their house and sent a tape to him."

My mother said nothing.

"Did you see their color TV and video player?" I asked.

"I don't look at their things; I just clean them. It's none of my business."

My mother had worked for the Van Dorns since June. After several months, she had seen much more than I had. What did she think of the disparity? Mama had seen movies from the West. How long had she known that the lives depicted on-screen weren't fantasy? Did she ever question why other people ate bananas while we lived in a charcoal wasteland?

"In the video, his friends were in a kitchen. Mama, the food—"

"It's none of your business. I don't want you picking me up

anymore. You shouldn't be interacting with a foreigner. You'll be questioned by the Securitate."

Should I tell her? *It's already happened. I'm a turnător. I'm informing for them, Mama. They knew I was coming to the apartment today. Tomorrow, Agent Paddle Hands will probably be waiting for me after school. They think I'm a good comrade. But I'm going to beat their game. I'm going to get medicine that will save Bunu.*

What would she say if I told her that? How could my mother dismiss everything that was right under her nose? How could my parents accept life under the regime's heel, crushed and pushed further into the dirt each day, eating nothing but lies and fear?

"Don't you want better for your children?" I asked.

She stopped abruptly and faced me. Her chimney of patience began to smoke.

"Don't you dare tell me what I should want for my children. This is not a game, Cristian. It's dangerous. There's no use dreaming of things we can never have."

"Who says we can never have them?"

"Me! I'm telling you! We can never have them!"

Finally. She was angry. "Good, at least you're expressing some emotion."

"You know what I'm expressing, Cristi? Exhaustion. Your father and I, we're so tired. We work constantly and when we're not working, we're standing in lines. We're never home. We're never together. And there's nothing we can do about it."

"You're wrong. They steal our power by making us believe we don't have any. They're controlling us through our own fear."

Her palm cracked against my cheek. Hard. She spoke through gritted teeth.

"Don't you *ever* say things like that. Do you want to end up like your grandfather? Can you even imagine what that's done to our family?"

What? She was mad at Bunu for having leukemia? That made no sense.

Before I could reply she stormed down the slick, black pavement. Alone.

23

DOUĂZECI ȘI TREI

Thinking words. Speaking words. Writing words.

Writing things down helped the most. Seeing my thoughts on a page, it positioned them at a helpful distance, out of my head and mouth. Processing. That's the English word I found for it. Processing helped me evaluate and sort things out. So I sat in my closet and made notes.

Mama's face is permanently pinched. She's mad at Bunu for getting sick.
Dad's a ghost and poor Cici gets skinnier by the day.
If I poke her stomach I bet I'd feel her spine.
Bunu's the happiest and he has leukemia.
Isn't the Florescu family fun?!

The teachers were right. I was sarcastic.

But our family felt gloomier than most. Or maybe I was the gloomy one.

Seeing the video from Dan's friends—
so many bananas—it made me mad, sad.
Had a dream about Liliana last night.
What does she dream about?

. . .

It was Friday. I knew what was coming. If the agent was waiting for me, he'd want a report. Should I tell him that I slipped and mentioned the library to Dan? I was debating. Could it work in my favor? Make me appear honest?

I would have to wait and leave again without anyone noticing. Especially Liliana. We generally didn't interact in school. She was quiet, private, like me. So we communicated secretly in the halls: a sly smile, an accidental brush of hands. But after the exchange in her apartment, I had wanted to walk her home. I wanted to see her. Almost as much as I wanted to kiss her.

What if I skipped the meeting with the agent? I could make some odd excuse.

Speaking of odd, how did the agent circulate so close to school? Was he seen? Did he park his black Dacia out front? The secretary saw me meeting with the agent. She knew I was an informer. Did she tell anyone?

Wait.

Of course.

The crumbly old secretary. She was an informer too.

Comrade Instructor stood at the head of the room, droning on about calculus. I had found new English terms to describe the weak light in our classroom: feeble, piss yellow. Above the foggy chalkboard sat Ceauşescu, smirking down at us from his golden frame. When we were younger, the portrait was used as a disciplinary tool.

"Mind yourself. Beloved Leader is watching. He sees everything, you know."

The picture in our classroom was the old, one-eared portrait of our hero. His head was positioned in three-quarter profile, so we only saw one of his ears. In Romania, calling someone "one-eared" is an expression for crazy or insane. Whispered jokes must have traveled down Victory Avenue because in most locations, the old portraits were now replaced with a two-eared version of our leader.

An absent classmate suddenly appeared at the door—the loner kid with the ratty brown scarf. He gave our instructor a note and took his seat. He looked ill, his face the color of milk. He couldn't stop fidgeting. He was either going to throw up or pass out. I watched, waiting to find out. It was definitely more interesting than calculus. After several minutes he rocketed from his chair, waving his arms and stuttering like a madman.

"No! No! NO!"

"Comrade Nistor, sit down this instant," yelled the teacher.

He didn't sit down. He turned, wild eyed, to the class, gripping and pulling at his own hair. He began to cry. Students gasped in alarm.

"Comrade Nistor. Compose yourself!"

"I can't. I can't. Do you know?"

"Know what?" asked a girl.

His hands began to vibrate and then his entire body quaked with convulsion.

"THAT I'M AN INFORMER!!!"

The temperature in the cold classroom dropped further into frozen silence.

No one tried to console him. No one made a sound.

Comrade Instructor pointed to the door. Our classmate stumbled to it, sobbing, and left.

The lesson resumed.

And that's when it hit me:

The teacher must be an informer. He informed on the students.

The school director was an informer. He informed on the teachers.

The secretary was an informer. She informed on the school director.

Luca was an informer. He informed on me.

I was an informer. I informed on Americans.

How naive. Had I really thought that Luca and I were the only student informers? There were probably many.

And then my stomach seized.

Wait, was Liliana an informer?

24

DOUĂZECI ŞI PATRU

I lingered after school, but Comrade Director didn't approach me.

Was it because of our classmate's outburst? Did the agent retreat, fearing that students would be paying closer attention? Although I had thought about skipping the meeting with the agent, I realized that I was failing my original mission.

Medicine for Bunu.

If I didn't see the agent, I wouldn't get any medicine.

I walked home, my mind tangled with predicament and paranoia. I empathized with the student who had the outburst. It could have been me. And I did nothing to console him. I sat there, hollow-faced and hollow-hearted, relieved when Comrade Instructor ordered him from the room. What would happen to him now? And what was happening to me?

While waiting after school, I had missed the chance to walk home with Liliana. Had she heard what happened in class? As much as I wanted to, I couldn't brush the question from my mind. Were there signs that Liliana was an informer? Maybe. She was quiet. Private. She asked odd questions. And the very first day we walked home together, she was behind me, which meant she left school after I did. Which could mean—

She had been meeting with the Secu herself.

Did Liliana care about me or did she just need information? I could have smacked myself. What sort of hypocrite was I to even ponder that question?

I approached our building and saw Cici on the sidewalk. She rushed to join me. "I've been waiting for you. We can't talk inside."

I raised an eyebrow.

"Something happened. I'm not sure when or how. Someone came to see Bunu."

I thought of the old man with the spongy nose. His message about coffee. When I told Bunu, he had just shrugged and said, "I already knew that."

"Was it the friend he plays chess with?" I asked.

"I don't know. I wasn't there. But Bunu is . . . improving. *Pui,* do you think someone negotiated treatments or medicine? And if so, how?"

"Medicine?" I tried to appear deep in consideration. "Have you checked the supply of Kents?"

"Yes, they're still there. But it got me thinking. Bunu is alone all day. How would we know if anyone was coming see him?"

"Why would it matter? Bunu has friends."

"Mama wouldn't want Bunu having meetings at the apartment."

I thought of Mama's comment about Bunu. "Cici, instead of being sad, Mama seems angry that Bunu has leukemia. Isn't that strange to you?"

Before Cici could reply, a darkened silhouette appeared. Starfish.

"Cici, my lady, hope to see you at video night this weekend?"

"Sorry, I'm busy."

"Ah, that's right. You have a date with Alex."

I turned to Cici. "Alex Pavel?" Alex was Liliana's brother.

"You didn't know?" sneered Starfish. "I thought you two worked it out together. Family business."

"Shut up, Starfish. He just asked me ten minutes ago," said Cici.

"Yeah, and he's pretty excited about it. He says you asked him."

"Get lost. I'm trying to talk to my brother."

Starfish disappeared.

"That's the other reason I waited for you. I know you've been spending time with Liliana. If it's weird for me to go out with Alex, I won't."

I hesitated. "It's a little weird."

"Okay. I'll cancel."

And then I felt bad. Most guys wanted to date Cici, but she never wanted to date them. Alex was arrogant, but if she wanted to go out with him, I didn't want to stop her.

"No, don't cancel. It's fine."

"Are you sure, *Pui*? It's not a big deal."

"Yeah, I'm sure."

Is that why Alex had glanced at me in that morning line? He planned to ask my sister on a date?

"How was school today?" she asked.

The story had probably circulated. "Strange," I whispered. "A kid in class had a complete breakdown. He stood up and shouted to everyone that he's an informer."

"What?" Her face pulled with alarm. "Did you know?"

"I had no idea."

"Stay away from him, *Pui*. Far away." She wrung her hands with concern. "And surely, he's not the only student who's an informer. See, this is why Mama and I constantly tell you to stay quiet. You never know who's watching and reporting."

Guilt rose within my already sour stomach.

"You're right," I said. "You never know."

25

DOUĂZECI ȘI CINCI

Instead of lying on the couch, Bunu was standing in the kitchen, fiddling with our broken radio.

"Feeling better?" I asked.

"I'll feel better when we have the radio. I need some air. Help me out to the balcony."

I put my arm around Bunu and guided him toward the sliding glass door.

"Romania is so efficient in the winter," said Bunu. "Such a time-saver, not having to put on a coat."

I laughed. Breath fogged from my mouth. We never put on coats because we never took them off.

"Shut the door," said my grandfather. "Don't want to make it colder out here." He smirked.

"Bunu," I whispered. "In Romania, what's colder than cold water?"

"Hot water." He smiled. "I'm surprised you remember that one."

I glanced across the street to Liliana's building. Liliana mentioned she'd seen me on the balcony. How often was she watching?

Bunu cleared his throat. "Something's brewing," he said. "I can feel it. But we need the radio to hear the updates and plans."

"You mean the restructuring plan? The one they mentioned on Radio Free Europe?"

"Perestroika? Bah," Bunu scoffed. "Maybe in other countries. But not here. Ceaușescu would never allow that in Romania. That would dilute his authority." Bunu shook his head with frustration. "This five-foot-nothing man has absolute mental control over twenty-three million people. And his wife is part of that power. We have two dictators and they've insulated and trapped us."

"Some don't seem to mind." I shrugged.

"That's because we've been ruled for decades with such totality that it's impossible for most to imagine anything different. But I'm older. I've been exposed to more. I've traveled. I know what's out there. But you, my dear boy—you're young. This cult of communism, what is this life doing to you and people your age?"

"Boosting our endurance, I guess."

"Really?" Bunu's voice strained. "Is that what it's doing? Or is it corroding your judgment and vision?" The emotion behind his words caused him to cough. I put my arm around him until he steadied.

"Cristian, I have to tell you something. Someone brought me a package recently."

I waited, uncertain how to reply.

"Apparently word has traveled that I've been . . . unwell. It's attracted attention."

I was an idiot.

Did I really think that Paddle Hands would give me medicine for Bunu during our meeting? No. He'd send someone. To spy further. But if Bunu received medicine, did that mean the agent felt I was delivering?

The Van Dorns' apartment. It was definitely bugged. Maybe the agent heard me asking about the American Library. But if he was tracking my every move, why did I need to meet and report to him?

My head was spinning.

Bunu looked over the balcony and again shook his head. "Evil Secu. This regime couldn't exist without them. And this black bat who lives beneath us has the entire apartment to himself. All that space, but so much merchandise he stores some on the balcony?"

"You think he has ration limits of five eggs per month?"

"He probably craps five eggs per morning," said Bunu. "Agents. Informers. Rats. This country is full of them. We're infested. And they keep multiplying. They're in our streets, in our schools, crawling in the workplace, and now they've chewed through the walls"—Bunu looked directly at me—"into our apartment."

I gripped the balcony railing. Panic hissed throughout my body.

Bunu stared at me. "Yes," he whispered. "An informer. In *our* apartment. Right here. Can you imagine that, Cristian? And suddenly medicine appears. But at what cost?"

"Bunu—"

"Shh. Say nothing. I'm the only one who's figured it out. It's too painful to discuss. Besides, I have no idea what I swallowed. For all I know, it's the breath that blows out the candle." Bunu shuffled toward the door and I helped him inside. His grumbling voice echoed in the darkness.

"You know what, Cristian? Dante was wrong. Hell isn't hot. It's cold."

26

DOUĂZECI ȘI ȘASE

We sat, whispering in the darkened stairwell.

Liliana's arm rested on my back. Her fingers grazed the stray pieces of hair fringing beneath my hat. Her touch on my neck, it was driving me crazy. I wanted to exhale and relax into it. But as soon as I closed my eyes, the hatch of guilt turned and groaned. The conversation with Bunu felt lodged in the back of my throat.

I lifted the edge of Liliana's purple scarf. It smelled like her.

"Alex asked Cici on a date," I whispered.

"He said Cici asked him."

"Really?"

"That's what he wants me to believe," said Liliana. "You know my brother's hardly shy."

"Cici came to me about it, said she would cancel if it felt weird."

"What did you say?"

"That it felt weird."

Liliana laughed.

"But I told her not to cancel. Are you okay with that?"

"Yeah. But it is kinda weird, isn't it? Maybe we gave Alex the idea. He saw us at video night. He said we looked comfortable hanging out and asked what we were laughing about."

"Hanging out," I whispered. "Is that what we're doing?"

She laid her head on my shoulder in response and slid her hand into mine.

I smiled. "Tell Alex we were laughing about *Gumela*. And how I liked you back then but was too scared to admit it."

"You didn't have to admit it," she said quietly. "I knew."

I nodded. She probably did. There were things I wanted to know about her. "Hey, if we lived in the West and you could choose any job you wanted, what would you do?" I asked.

"That's easy," she said. "I love books. I'd work in a library."

"Yeah, you could sneak in outlawed books for me," I told her. "Speaking of librarians, did you hear? The school librarian told Luca she thinks I'm a bad influence."

"You are," she laughed. "Some are intrigued by the look of you, but they don't know what to make of you."

Could I blame them? Sometimes I didn't know what to make of me either.

"So, mister bad influence, if you lived in the West and could choose any job you wanted, what would it be?" she asked.

Could I tell her? Should I tell her? I could barely confess it to myself.

"A writer," I whispered.

She nodded. "That makes sense."

"It does?"

"Of course. Writers are dangerous. And you're a brooding, philosophical Virgo. You're not a follower. Even your hair's a revolution."

"But what if I'm an awful writer?"

"What if I'm an awful librarian?"

I smiled and tugged her hand, pulling her toward me. "I think I might like you anyway," I whispered.

I leaned in. Her face lifted to meet mine.

Footsteps.

Sounds echoed in the stairwell.

Liliana's hand whisked from mine. We waited, heads down in the dark.

The steps paused. Someone had heard us.

Was the Secu agent in our building listening?

Who was on the stairs?

27

DOUĂZECI ȘI ȘAPTE

Two more steps. They stopped. I heard breathing.

Liliana pressed into my side. I slid my arm around her.

One more step.

Closer.

Liliana shivered.

"Who's there?!" I yelled.

A scream filled the stairwell, followed by the sound of breaking glass. Muffled cries emerged from the steps, followed by a woman's voice.

"Vă rog. Vă rog."

Please. Please.

I jumped to my feet. "Mama?"

"Vă rog."

I ran down the steps. My mother lay huddled in a heap.

"Cristian?" she whispered.

"Yes, it's me. Mama, what happened?"

Liliana appeared at my side.

"I came home and the stairs were so dark. I started up and heard something. Someone hovered nearby, I could feel it. I was so frightened. And then there was a yell and I panicked."

"That was me. I was talking with Liliana and I thought someone was listening. Let me help you up." I put my arms beneath my mother's.

"*Au!* Be careful, there's broken glass."

We helped her up the stairs and into our apartment.

"Mama! What happened?" said Cici.

My mother's shoulders sagged. Her thin arms slung, trembling, at her sides. "I stood in line for three hours. They finally had rations of cooking oil. But I became frightened in the dark stairwell and fell. The bottle broke. Cici, help me with the cuts on my leg. Cristian, clean the glass and oil from the stairs."

I pretended not to notice the fear-induced urine that had soaked through the center of my mother's pants. Did Liliana see it? My sister took Mama into the small bathroom. Muffled crying leaked from behind the door.

Sometimes, when the grenade exploded, our mother would say mean things and then cry. But this time, there was no anger. She escalated straight to tears.

I felt terrible.

"The efficiency of tyranny!" announced Bunu from the kitchen. "They don't even need weapons to control us. Our own fear is more than enough. You see, Cristi, this is how it feels, being an animal in a trap."

Liliana looked at me, shocked by the comments. I quickly pulled her toward the door and out of the apartment. The episode left me feeling weird, embarrassed.

We crouched in the dark, trying to brush away the glass and soak up the oil with a rag. We needed to preserve as much as we could.

"Your poor mama. The stairwells can be so dark and scary. And now your family lost their ration of oil. That's awful."

It was awful. And I was so tired of awful.

We finished the cleanup and returned to our place in the stairwell. Any thought of a kiss was now replaced by an uncomfortable silence between us. Was she thinking of Bunu's comments?

"Hey," I whispered. "A woman screamed in the stairwell. Did you notice something?"

She nodded. "No one came running."

"Exactly."

But how could they? If they peeked out and saw something, they might be questioned. No one wanted to be questioned. But neighbors had heard. Some would try to help and share what little they had. A jar with some cooking oil was probably already outside our door.

We sat, stiff and awkward in the darkened maze of the staircase.

"Cristian," she whispered, her voice thinned with vulnerability. "Does the world know what's happening in Romania? If they did . . . would they do something?"

It was a great question. The broadcasts from Radio Free Europe came into Romania. But what information was making it out of Romania? I thought of Mr. Van Dorn's comment that Bucharest was "dark." How much did he really know and how much did he report to the embassy?

The comment in Dan's notebook floated back to me:

One U.S. ambassador resigned because Washington refused to believe reports that America has been outfoxed by Ceaușescu.

Could I communicate with Mr. Van Dorn somehow? If he happened to find my secret notebook with a request to send it to Washington . . . would he?

Liliana shifted on the stairs. The words came out before I could stop them.

"I have an idea."

28

DOUĂZECI ȘI OPT

My idea. An invitation to truth.

I shouldn't have mentioned it. But I was so comfortable with Liliana, I had actually spoken my thoughts aloud. Of course, once I mentioned it, she wanted to know more. But what was I supposed to say? *Hey, I've been keeping a secret notebook. I want to give it to the U.S. diplomat to ensure he knows the truth and shares it widely.*

No. I couldn't say that.

So instead of telling Liliana my idea, I skirted the issue. I wanted to tell her everything but knew I couldn't. The notebook itself was a huge risk. I didn't want to put her in danger. So I remained silent and hated myself for it.

Hatred. Guilt. Decisions. That night I wrote about it all in my notebook:

> DO YOU PITY ME?
> LIPS THAT KNOW NO TASTE OF FRUIT
> LONELY IN A COUNTRY OF MILLIONS
> STUMBLING TOWARD THE GALLOWS
> OF BAD DECISIONS
> WHILE THE WALLS LISTEN AND LAUGH.

. . .

The next day was Saturday. So after school I was on a bus to the Van Dorns' apartment to accompany Dan to the American Library.

I surveyed the passengers, sandwiched together.

Wrinkled faces.

Wrinkled clothing.

Wrinkled spirits.

Service was too infrequent. There was no reliable schedule and never enough room. People clutched the railings on the bus stairs, preventing the doors from closing. We hung, smashed half inside, half outside. Sometimes, the bus was so crowded that the back dragged, scraping and lapping the pavement.

We arrived at the stop. I hoped Dan hadn't forgotten his invitation.

Mr. Van Dorn greeted me at the door. He was dressed not in a suit, but in casual clothes. He eyed my coat, school uniform, and book bag.

"Always have to remind myself, school on Saturday here, right?"

It felt like bait for comment. If the light fixtures weren't listening, maybe I would reply with my usual sarcasm and engage in what Americans called "chitchat."

Yes, Mr. Van Dorn, good comrades don't take weekends, holidays, or summers off. Did you know that Ceaușescu once declared December 25th a day of labor? Speaking of holidays, Santa Claus is considered too religious here. In Romania, we replaced him with a proletarian character named Moş Gerilă, Freezer Man. We celebrate our winter season by entering the factories for work!

But I said none of that, just replied, "Yes, school on Saturday."

"Dan," called Mr. Van Dorn down the hallway. "Cristian is here."

I heard a muffled reply.

"Have a seat," said Mr. Van Dorn, gesturing to a couch in the living area. He then walked to his large desk. It held a typewriter. Was the typewriter registered?

"You have an older sister, don't you?" he asked. I nodded.

He shuffled through stacks of files, papers, and newspapers. He then took a sip from a nearby coffee cup.

Wait. Coffee.

The man with the spongy nose had warned against coffee. Should I stop Mr. Van Dorn?

Dan appeared. "Cristian and I are heading to the American Library to read the new magazines."

"Sounds good," said his father.

We had just left their apartment when Mr. Van Dorn suddenly appeared on the stairs.

"Dan, your mom wants you to wear a hat. It was snowing this morning."

When Dan returned to retrieve his hat, Mr. Van Dorn discreetly displayed what looked like an American magazine. The title appeared in block letters:

TIME

"Look for it at the library today. Make sure it's the most recent."

I said nothing. Just nodded.

Mr. Van Dorn disappeared back into the apartment. I tried to contain my smile.

My instincts were right.

I could communicate with Mr. Van Dorn. I could share the truth about Romania.

I could outwit the Securitate.

That's what I thought. What I really believed.

I didn't yet know that sometimes in outwitting others, we accidentally outwit ourselves.

|| INFORMER REPORT ||

[11 Nov. 1989]

Cristian Florescu (17), student at MF3 High School.

Observed Saturday afternoon entering and departing the
apartment of the Van Dorn family. Florescu engaged in
private exchange (undecipherable) with Mr. Van Dorn in the
hallway. Florescu then departed with Van Dorn's son and
proceeded to the American Library in Bucharest.

Appears Florescu is pursuing private communications with Mr.
Van Dorn. Advise cross-referencing with other Sources.

29

DOUĂZECI ȘI NOUĂ

I noted Dan's behavior as we walked through Rosetti Square, his general ease in all things. He swung his arms, casually looking about, speaking louder than most Romanians would.

I envied him, the courage to be himself. In public.

The American Library was housed in two elegant turn-of-the-century villas—buildings spared by the bulldozers. As we entered the library, we had to present identification in a reception area. Dan leaned across the desk.

"Hi there, Brenda. What are you doing up front?" he asked.

"Reception clerk is sick," said the older woman. "It's so chilly by the door. Sure do miss the weather in California."

"I know. I'm missing the weather in New Jersey. So that says a lot!" replied Dan.

Dan and the woman shared a laugh. He gestured to me.

"This is my friend Cristian. He's my guest today. He speaks English."

"Hello, Cristian," said the woman, smiling brightly. "Just need a peek at your ID."

A peek. What did that mean? Dan had given his ID, so I handed her mine.

She looked at the photo on my identification for an extended beat. She finally looked up and stared straight at me. A gentle smile appeared.

"My, what lovely eyes you have," she said.

"Oh, they're . . . weird," I blurted. I was uncomfortable with the exchange but comfortable with the memory of Liliana's description.

"No, not weird at all," she insisted, handing back my card. "But maybe weird that an old lady is complimenting them?" She then did something I'd seen in movies.

She winked.

An American woman winked at me, as if sharing some sort of private joke. Was this as strange as it felt? I turned to Dan for his reaction.

"Thanks, Brenda," he said, unfazed. "We're off to rot our minds with pop culture crap." He gave a salute.

"Rot away!" she said with a wave of her hand.

Was I misunderstanding their English? This was an official building. Yet they were being so casual, just like in the movies. Were Americans ever serious? No—I reframed the question. Were Romanians always serious?

Dan walked casually to a long table positioned near a shelf of newspapers. He tossed his backpack on the table and it landed with a thud.

"You can leave your bag here. Have a look around."

I wasn't going to leave my bag anywhere. It remained hanging from my shoulder as I walked through the warm building. There were shelves of fiction, nonfiction, biography, reference, and a section for children. There was also a section with books on Romanian history and language. Most of the books were in English. I wanted to read them. Every single one.

And I wanted to share them with Liliana.

I continued browsing the section. At the end of the bookshelf I noticed a wooden podium containing an official-looking album with the Romanian flag on the cover. I opened it.

The first page featured the new portrait of Ceaușescu. Two ears.

Beneath the portrait was a paragraph in Romanian:

> *Leader of the nation, Father of Romania, Nicolae Ceaușescu*
> *has established diplomatic relations all over the world and has*
> *visited over 100 countries.*

The album contained photos of our leader during his travels or hosting other countries:

> *1969—U.S. President Richard Nixon visits Bucharest. He is the*
> *first American president to visit a communist country.*
> *1975—U.S. President Gerald Ford visits Bucharest.*
> *1978—U.S. President Jimmy Carter holds a state dinner at the*
> *White House in honor of the Ceaușescus.*

The album was packed full of colorful photos featuring Beloved Leader and Heroine Mother with dignitaries and heads of state. I scanned through some of the names:

UK Prime Minister Margaret Thatcher, Queen Elizabeth II, Queen Silvia of Sweden, Indira Gandhi of India, Pope Paul VI of the Vatican, Canadian Prime Minister Brian Mulroney, Charles De Gaulle of France, King Juan Carlos of Spain, Queen Margrethe II of Denmark.

And this one:

> *President Nicolae Ceaușescu of Romania joined the long list*
> *of international celebrities who have visited Disneyland, the*
> *world-famous "Magic Kingdom" in California, to meet Mickey*
> *Mouse. Ceaușescu was accompanied by his wife and children.*

I stared at the photograph.

Mickey Mouse.

I flipped back through the pages toward the front of the album.

Ceaușescu hadn't outfoxed America.

No.

He'd outfoxed . . . everyone.

They thought he was a benevolent dictator. They'd welcomed him into their countries.

It wasn't disgust. It was despair. That's what I felt, seeing the colorful photos of our leader cuddling with kangaroos in Australia and posing with Mickey Mouse in some citrus dream called California.

And . . . Disneyland. It was a real place?

Ceaușescu and his family were free to travel to every continent and experience all the world had to offer, but he kept his people caged within the country's borders, working, full of fear, terrorized if they inquired about a passport. My parents longed to return to the Romanian seaside or to spend time in the mountains. But in recent years, Ceaușescu's work mandates and petrol rations made that difficult.

I wanted my mother to have a lighted stairwell.

I wanted my father to have a real vacation or a car.

I wanted Liliana to have the birds she missed.

I closed the album and wandered to the shelves with magazines, looking for the one Mr. Van Dorn had suggested.

TIME.

I found it. The moment is forever engraved in my memory.

The headline of the issue:

THE BIG BREAK
Moscow Lets Eastern Europe Go Its Own Way

I shot a quick glance over my shoulder. My pulse began to tick.

The magazine cover featured a large crowd with a teenager waving a flag.

A Hungarian flag.

Hungary bordered Romania.

Wait.

Hungary was no longer ruled by communism?

Hungary was free?

30

TREIZECI

I quickly scanned through the article, struggling with some of the terminology. But I recognized a few words from the Radio Free Europe broadcasts:

Democracy. Perestroika. Glasnost.

How much had we missed with a broken radio? We knew that Poland had been successful with their decade-long Solidarity movement, but now Hungary? Had they really broken free of communism? Did my parents know? I tried to memorize the details to share with Bunu.

I rejoined Dan, who was hunched over a glossy magazine. Flustered, I reminded myself of the agent. I made mental notes of the magazines Dan had pulled to read: *Rolling Stone, Sports Illustrated, Billboard*.

"Meet the love of my life," said Dan, pointing to a picture of a woman playing the guitar. "She's in a band called the Bangles." He gave an exaggerated, heartsick sigh, then laughed. "Do you have a girlfriend?" he asked.

Did I? I gave a half nod. And maybe smiled a little too.

"Yeah? What's her name?" asked Dan.

I paused. Should I tell him?

"Liliana," I finally said. "Do you have a girlfriend?"

He shook his head. "I liked a German girl who was staying in our building, but her family was only visiting. She sends me letters with cool stamps though."

He fiddled with the magazine. "Does Liliana like music?" he asked.

"Yes. Springsteen."

"Springsteen, huh?" Dan flipped the pages back to an article and photo of Bruce Springsteen. Without pausing, he tore the page from the magazine.

I took a step back. Dan Van Dorn tore the page right out of the magazine. He didn't request permission. That couldn't be legal—in any library, anywhere. That was just vandalism. He saw my eyes pop and laughed.

"I heard the U.S. Embassy really needs this information," he whispered, rolling the sheet and sliding it through a loop on his backpack. "You know, this library is open to Romanians as well. You can come on your own."

"Really?" I wondered if Bunu knew that.

"Yeah, Reagan and Bush aren't really fans, but back in the day, Nixon bartered a deal with Ceaușescu. Romania was allowed to open a cultural office in New York and the U.S. opened this library in Bucharest."

Aren't really fans. Nixon bartered. What did that mean? There weren't any photos in the album of Ceaușescu with recent U.S. presidents. Is that what Dan was referring to?

And sure, the American Library existed, but any Romanian who entered alone was probably reported to the Securitate. Would anyone take the risk?

"Thanks for bringing me. It's interesting," I said.

"Sure. I come every two weeks. Tag along. There's not much for me to do in Bucharest. Do you ever get bored?" he asked.

"No time to be bored."

"Yeah, you're always in school or standing in a line. Hey, take me to stand in line sometime. That would be interesting to write about for my college essays."

He wanted to stand in a line? Did it seem like a novelty to him? My brow narrowed.

"Sorry, what I mean is, in the States, we don't have to stand in line for things. We don't have a Kent economy either. Last week my mom had to hustle up some Kents to have our trash collected. Boy, she was griping about that. I'm still wondering what my dad did to get demoted and sent here."

Dan's comments gave me so much to think about. What did "tag along," "hustle," "griping," and "demoted" mean? But bouncing in my mind was the question of Hungary: Were the citizens of Hungary still standing in lines? Could they travel freely now?

Once we were outside, Dan thrust the rolled magazine article toward me.

"Give this to your girl. Tell her it's a present from New Jersey."

I hesitated. The article was stolen property, but I wanted it for Liliana. I took it and quickly stuffed it in my jacket. "Seems like you miss home."

"A lot. Romania doesn't have a strong international high school yet, so I'm stuck at the apartment with a tutor all day. I wanted to stay at my school in the States, but my parents insisted our family travel together. If things are quiet at the embassy next month, they've promised we'll go home for Christmas. I can't wait. I'll bring back some new stamps."

"Great."

"Hey, Cris." Dan paused. "Don't tell my parents that I ripped the page out of the magazine, okay?"

The way he said it, he was concerned. "Okay," I said. He seemed relieved. Maybe the bravado had been for show.

"And by the way," he said. "I've heard your mom call you Cristi. In the States, that's a girl's name, you know." He laughed and punched my shoulder.

My brain was full of static. I could barely process it all:

Ceaușescu had visited Disneyland. He had outfoxed everyone.

Hungary was free. They had broken away from communism.

Mr. Van Dorn wanted me to see the magazine, to know that. Why?

I had an article about Bruce Springsteen for Liliana.

What would I report to Paddle Hands?

In the United States, Cristi was a girl's name.

But shouting in refrain—

Hungary was free.

Hungary was free?

|| INFORMER REPORT ||

[11 Nov. 1989]

Cristian Florescu (17), student at MF3 High School.

Observed Saturday afternoon in the American Library with
Dan Van Dorn. Florescu scanned books in the travel section
and read through an American political magazine. He then
sat with Van Dorn at a table. Dan Van Dorn tore a page out
of a magazine and put it in his book bag. Florescu did not
object nor report him. Florescu then departed with Van Dorn.

31

TREIZECI ȘI UNU

A lie is like a snowball. It rolls, becomes bigger, heavier, and eventually, it's difficult to lift. I had thought I was strong. But how much weight could I actually carry?

I couldn't mention the American Library to Bunu. He'd ask questions and my answers would just create a bigger snowball. I decided to tell Bunu I'd heard mention of Hungary on the street and that we had to get our radio fixed to find out what was going on.

I arrived at our apartment and found a woman in the stairwell struggling with a large suitcase.

"*Bună!*" she said. "Could I trouble you to help me?"

"Sure. Would you prefer the elevator?"

She shook her head. "I don't want to risk the power going out. I can't be stuck in there."

Her shiny gold earrings were shaped like lightning bolts. I looked at her suitcase. One of the luggage tags was labeled in English. *American Airlines.*

"You're from the States?"

"I'm from Romania, but I live in Boston."

What? How did a Romanian woman get a passport to leave the country and live in Boston? People who applied to emigrate were often punished. Severely. But I could see it. Her bright green coat, fancy red boots, and the chic cut of her hair; she carried an air of elsewhere.

I took her suitcase. "Which floor?"

"Third. I'm visiting my mother. Irina Drucan."

I nodded.

Her voice lowered. "She's dying, you know."

I didn't know. I'm sure the Reporters did. Maybe Bunu and Cici too. All I knew was that Mrs. Drucan was elderly. I couldn't remember the last time I saw her.

The woman's eyes filled with tears. She took a deep breath and began pacing. "I'm sorry, just a moment."

"I'm not in a hurry."

She looked at me with gratitude. "What's your name?"

"Cristian."

"*Mersi*, Cristian."

I lugged her heavy suitcase up to the third floor. She opened the apartment door and the stale scent of illness quickly swept into the corridor. She paused, fingers clutching the doorframe while gathering herself. Her voice choked with emotion. "*Sărut mâna, Mamă.* I'm here."

I stood, waiting. Did she need help?

"*Mersi*, Cristian." She quietly closed the door.

I proceeded up the flight of steps to the fourth floor. My mother's exasperated whisper filled our small apartment.

"You infuriate me, old man! I was saving those to get medicine for you!"

I looked to Cici.

"Bunu traded the Kents to have the radio repaired," she said.

"Information is more valuable than medicine right now! Poland and Hungary. East Germany will be next!" argued Bunu. "We need the radio. We need Radio Free Europe. We need Munteanu's reports. Tell her, Cristian."

"Don't you involve him in this. You had no right," complained Mama. "Those cigarettes didn't belong to you."

"What belongs to us, truly, Mioara? Everything belongs to the Party, my dear," said Bunu at full volume. "Isn't that the truth?"

I had to agree with Bunu. I'd rather be Kentless but have the radio. Especially with what I saw at the library. We needed Radio Free Europe.

Radio Free Europe had been established by the American CIA decades prior to move information behind the Iron Curtain—the border between communist and noncommunist countries. The broadcasts were accessed only with an illegal antenna, and nearly every family had fashioned one. But no one spoke of it. It was too valuable.

Bunu had heard the news. He thought East Germany would be next?

"What about Romania?" I asked him.

"Exactly! We need the radio to find out!"

"Lower your voice!" pleaded Mama.

I turned to my sister. "Cici, did you know that Mrs. Drucan is sick?" I whispered. "Her daughter just arrived from the States."

"Oh, I'm so happy she made it. Yes, I knew. I washed and mended her nightgown last week. Poor woman weighs nothing."

"Her daughter lives in Boston?"

She nodded. "She's a researcher at Harvard. Where have you been?" whispered Cici. "School ended hours ago."

I shrugged. "Just hanging around."

She looked at me, suspicious. "Hanging around. With anyone in particular?"

"Not really."

"Liliana came by. Twice. She said to give you this."

Cici retrieved a sealed envelope from her back pocket. "Loooove notes," she teased, dancing the envelope.

"Jealous that Alex hasn't sent you one?" I snapped the envelope from her and retreated to my closet.

I used the flashlight sparingly, but a letter from Liliana was definitely worth it. Maybe I'd put the Springsteen article in the envelope and drop it off at her apartment. I tore open the sealed flap of the envelope and removed a small sheet of paper that contained just a few sentences:

> *You are a liar.*
> *You are everything I despise.*
> *You are an informer.*

32

TREIZECI ȘI DOI

I switched off the flashlight.

Invisible hands appeared in the darkness. One hand gripped my hair. The other pressed down over my nose and mouth. And then it pressed again. Harder.

You are a liar.

I couldn't breathe.

You are everything I despise.

I was suffocating.

You are an informer.

Shocks of blue flashed behind my eyes. My mouth pulled dry with panic.

I burst from the closet and bolted out of our apartment, still clutching the note.

I had no plan. No outline in my notebook. But something inside of me churned, driving me toward Liliana. Did she think I was spending time with her just to get information?

I banged on her apartment door.

Alex appeared. "Lili," he said over his shoulder, "your boyfriend's here."

Whispering hissed behind the door.

"Oh, sorry." Alex shrugged. "She's not home." He shut the door.

I knocked again. And again. And again and again until the door finally opened.

"Look, she doesn't want to see you. Keep it up and I'll take care of that hand. You won't be able to knock anymore," said Alex.

Adrenaline, molecular courage. Every nerve ending blazed within me. "Oh yeah, Alex? Step out in the hallway and we'll see whose hands survive."

"Are you threatening me, Cristi? I'd destroy you."

"Try it, *pămpălăule*."

"*La dracu!*" He grabbed me by the collar.

Liliana appeared and grabbed her brother, pulling him back. "Stop!"

"Worried I'll kill your lovebird?" he spat.

"Shut up, Alex." Liliana rushed by me and headed down the stairs. I ran to follow.

We pushed through the door and walked around the side of her building.

"What, now you want to fight my brother?"

"If that's what it takes to speak with you." I pulled the note from my pocket.

"What is this? Did you write it?"

"Yes, I wrote it."

"Why?"

"You're asking me why?" Her mouth hung open in disgust. "The Secu pulled my father out of work," she whispered. "They questioned him about bringing bones home, accused him of stealing from the Party."

"What?"

"*Yes!*" she gasped, whispering at the top of her lungs.

"Liliana, I told no one. I swear to you. Someone else must know you give bones to the dogs."

"Really? And they saw that I had a real Coke too?"

I took a step back. "Someone saw us drinking the Coke?"

"Oh, please. Stop the act, Cristian. You make me sick."

"Liliana, you're wrong. I told no one."

"I'm right. And I'm an idiot! You know why? Because I liked you." Her breath hitched. "I really liked you. *Oh, he's so smart and interesting. We understand each other.* You really had me fooled. How many other girls are you seeing for information?"

"I'm only seeing you. And *not* for information. I'm spending time with you because I like you. I've liked you for years. You know that. Lil—" I reached for her and she recoiled.

She stared at me and her eyes filled with tears. "How could you? Really, why, Cristian? I liked you so much. So much that now I hate you."

She turned and fled.

My knees went slack. I stood, swaying, still clutching the note.

What had happened?

It had taken years to get close to Liliana.

And now she hated me. Yes.

But not as much as I hated myself.

33

TREIZECI ȘI TREI

I hear them.

The clapping men.

Clapping.

The image is blurred and then I realize.

There's a plastic bag over my head, cinched at the neck.

Where did it come from?

Breathe! shout the clapping men. *Breathe!* they chant in unison.

I tug at the bag. I tug at the band squeezing my neck. I look at them.

I can't breathe. I can't obey their command with a bag over my head. I'm losing air.

A swarm of black Dacias arrives, full of agents in leather coats.

Breathe! they yell from the windows of the cars. *Breathe!*

"I can't," I croak.

The sea of clapping men parts. A small man in a rumpled suit approaches.

"Leader," I plead. "Help me."

Ceaușescu raises his right hand as if to bless me. To save me.

He then turns his back and slices his palm through the air, conducting the chorus.

Breathe! . . . Breathe! . . . Breathe!

I woke up, choking. I stumbled out of the closet, straight to the bathroom, and threw up—

Nothing.

34

TREIZECI ȘI PATRU

The crossroads of reality and nightmare. My classmate who cracked—he had been there, trying to escape the suffocation that slithered and pulled tighter.

I didn't want to be an informer.

But I didn't want Bunu to die.

Double bind. That was the English term for it.

Luca spotted me the next day. "Cristian, this standoff between us, it's stupid. Let's talk," he said. "You're not okay."

I stared at him with disgust. "Are *you* okay? You know how it is, don't you, Luca?"

He gave a small nod and looked to his feet. He walked off.

Did Luca have it as bad as I did? Somehow, I doubted it. He looked well rested, probably still recognized himself in the mirror and in his nightmares. Probably didn't spend nights on the bathroom floor. Even though I still hated Luca for getting me into this, a small part of me hoped he wasn't suffering like I was.

The next day, I tried to approach Liliana at school. She wouldn't look at me, purposely avoided me as if she knew exactly where I'd be. I tried to speak to her on the street.

"This is a misunderstanding. It's not over," I told her. "I'm not giving up."

"Give up, Cristian," she replied.

Starfish overheard and offered counsel. "Forget about her. Lots of girls talk about you. You have other options."

I didn't want other options. I wanted Liliana.

"I'm not giving up," I told Starfish.

"Did you hear that?" I shouted up to the Reporters. "I'm not giving up."

Deranged? Desperate? Who knows what people were whispering about me.

But Liliana, it had felt like she could read my mind. She had to know it wasn't true. Yes, I was an informer. But I hadn't informed on her. How could I explain?

After a few days, she no longer spent time outside, but I looked for her anyway.

My family knew something had gone awry, but they didn't know what. I couldn't tell them—or anyone—why Liliana wouldn't see me. Fortunately, she hadn't told anyone either. Was she trying to protect her family . . . or me? I clung to the possibility.

I stood on the balcony, hoping she would see me. Trying to telegraph messages to her.

One night, Cici joined me. She took a deep breath, gathered her long black hair, and tied it into a knot. "Look, I don't know what's going on, *Pui*, but I know something happened with Liliana . . . and I know you're hurting."

Sorrow crept into my throat. I couldn't speak. Just nodded.

She put her hand on my back. "Keep trying. She's worth it. And so are you."

Was it my sister's kindness? Her encouragement to persevere? Whatever it was, it broke me. And she knew it. And she had the compassion to give me privacy on that cold dark balcony, alone with my tears.

Bunu eventually shuffled out as well. He said nothing at first, just stood next to me. His presence alone was comforting.

"Your pain, it inspires me," he finally said. I looked to him. "Yes, inspires me. This regime steals so much from us. Some, like your father, are forced to go silent, dormant. But to feel so deeply, that is the very essence of being human. You give me hope."

I had to confess.

He already knew I was an informer, but I had to say it out loud.

"Bunu—"

"That's enough for tonight. It's colder than Mother Elena's heart out here." He left me on the balcony and returned to the apartment before I could say another word.

I often think back to that night and my desperation to confess. How many others across Romania were standing on their balconies at the same time, painfully picking at the adhesive, all trying so hard—

To pull the tape from our mouths.

35

TREIZECI ȘI CINCI

Comrade Director gave a discreet nod when I passed him in the hall the next day. So after school I waited in the bathroom then headed for the apartment. Did the agent meet with other informers there? If I arrived early or waited afterward, would I see them? He probably staggered his schedule. But maybe I'd see the residents of the apartment. Would I recognize them?

Each step stirred questions—and anger.

Frustration.

Bunu. Liliana. Luca. It was all such a mess.

I peered through the crack in the door. The agent didn't see me. Not at first. He sat, sucking on a cigarette.

I had a moment to evaluate the miserable creature that Paddle Hands must have been, ruining the lives of teenagers and forcing them to become spies. What motivated him to sell his soul? Was he blackmailed, like me? Perhaps he had an ill family member too? Or was it the steady supply of Kents and the shallow power of driving a black Dacia that kept him going? He didn't wear a wedding ring. No, a bottle of *țuică*, plum firewater, kept him company on cold winter nights. How did Luca deal with this guy? Luca was kind but not savvy. No wonder our classmate had a breakdown.

But I was not going to have a breakdown.

I was going to take them all down.

If I got my notebook to Mr. Van Dorn, the embassy would see me as a source of truth and report that Ceaușescu was duping everyone.

I watched as the agent fiddled with his pack of BT cigarettes. He had removed the stamp decal from the top of the package and was curling it around his little finger. The cigarette smoke, like sins rising, crept up and around his neck.

Choke him.

"Come in and close the door," he ordered, finally aware of my presence. "Take a seat."

I entered and sat. Calculus notebook in my lap.

"So, how have things been going?"

"Fine," I lied.

My thickening file sat on the desk in front of the agent. What was in it?

"Did you visit the target?"

I nodded. "I accompanied him to the American Library as instructed."

"And what did you learn?"

I took a breath and began to recite. "He reads *Rolling Stone*, *Sports Illustrated*, and *Billboard* magazines. He's bored and misses home. He has a tutor who comes to the apartment."

"What's the tutor's name?"

I shrugged. "He didn't say."

"Male or female? Does his father interact with the tutor?"

"He didn't say. He wants to go home for Christmas. He likes a girl—"

"What's her name? Is she Romanian?"

I took a breath and continued. "He likes a girl who plays guitar in an American band—"

"They're dating?"

I thought of Dan, joking about his pretend girlfriend in the magazine. I couldn't resist. "Yes, they're dating. Long-distance relationship. Serious. She's older, lives in New York."

"Do his parents know?"

"No. It's a secret. A big secret. He's going to Princeton and they're making plans to be together there."

He nodded, making notes in front of him. "The son has access to money?"

"He's never mentioned money."

"What does he think of Romanian girls?"

"He's never mentioned them. Only talks of this girl who plays guitar."

"Does his father interact with Romanian women?"

"I have no idea."

Why the questions about women? Where was this going?

"In the American Library, what did you see?"

I was happy to answer that question. "I saw an album with photographs of Beloved Leader at Disneyland in California. He and Mother Elena were playing with Mickey Mouse, having a grand time in the Magic Kingdom. I was surprised—I thought Disneyland was make believe. Comrade Major, is it a real place?"

Paddle Hands looked up at me, edgy. "Did the target remove or take anything with him from the American Library?"

The question was too specific. He knew about the magazine. How?

"Yes, he removed a page from a magazine."

"What were the contents of the page?"

"An article about American musicians." I thought of the article, still sitting in my closet.

"What was described in the article?"

"Just general sentiments of a song," I said.

"And what was the sentiment?" he asked, impatient.

One of Bunu's lectures sifted back to me, about words having power. I paused, drawing out the delivery of the phrase I had invented. "The sentiment . . . I think it was something like . . . power to the one who doesn't want it."

The agent nodded and continued to scribble. He even asked me to repeat it. I almost laughed. I was definitely losing my mind.

"Power to the one . . . who doesn't want it," I told him.

He pushed on, writing, the irony lost on him. I shifted in my seat and repositioned my notebook in the process, making certain the Steaua logo was casually visible. I had drawn it on my notebook the night after our last meeting. The agent's eyes shifted to the image. He set down the pen for a quick pull on his cigarette. I took the chance.

"Do you follow Steaua or Dinamo?"

"Steaua," said the agent quietly.

"Me too. Steaua's the most underrated team in all of Europe. Over a hundred games, undefeated."

The agent leaned back, nodding. He pulled another drag from the cigarette and resumed playing with the paper ring from the package. "And remember, the other European teams import and buy players. But our team is real—all Romanians," he said.

"Exactly. When I was little, I dreamed of being a goalkeeper for Steaua," I lied.

The agent gave a small laugh. "Didn't we all." His body suddenly stiffened, returning to tight posture, as if lashed by an invisible whip. He dropped the paper ring from the cigarette pack and picked up his pen. But the momentary, minuscule crack in his armor, I saw it. I had chiseled my way in and briefly distracted him. It was possible.

"Dan Van Dorn doesn't like soccer. He likes American football," I told him.

"Write it all down. Everything you've told me. Sign the bottom," he instructed.

The agent made notations in his ledger while I wrote. When I finished I handed him the signed paper.

"I've learned the target's father has a large desk in the apartment," he said. "I need to know what's on the desk."

"I need medicine for my *bunu*."

The agent looked up from his notes. I stared at him, unblinking.

"I told you I'd take care of that. Find out what's on his desk. We're done," he said.

I gave a nod and left the apartment. Jerk.

And then I had a thought. How did Paddle Hands learn that Mr. Van Dorn had a desk? Was there another informer assigned to the Van Dorns?

If so, who was it?

|| OFFICIAL REPORT ||

Ministry of the Interior   TOP SECRET

Department of State Security   [14 Nov. 1989]

Directorate III, Service 330

Discussion with source OSCAR at host location. OSCAR
displayed arrogance and tried to manipulate the
conversation. Signature on today's report differs from last.
OSCAR provided the following information on target VAIDA:

- -VAIDA's son has a school tutor who works with him in
  the home
- -VAIDA's son is engaged in a clandestine relationship
  with an American female musician
- -at the American Library, VAIDA's son removed an article
  from a magazine that expressed anti-communist sentiments

  For further documentation, OSCAR is now tasked with:
- -retrieving information on VAIDA's home desk

NOTE: Consideration should be given to OSCAR's family
loyalty and viability as a continued source. Recent reports
state that while at the American Library, OSCAR viewed
American political magazines. Additional reports indicate
OSCAR is distressed within his romantic relationship with
neighbor, Liliana Pavel (17).

36

TREIZECI ȘI ȘASE

I walked through the dark, so angry that even the dogs kept their distance. The cold crept in, a few degrees above nothing. The familiar smell lingered in the air, snow waiting to fall.

The agent knew about the magazine article. Had Luca followed me to the American Library? I assumed he worked for Paddle Hands too? If so, Paddle Hands had probably intimidated him, threatened him. If I asked Luca, would he tell me? Could we join together somehow?

No, that was a terrible idea. I was safer alone.

I arrived home and found the woman from Boston smoking at the bottom of our stairwell. An American visitor was an extreme oddity. How many residents had reported her and those pointy red boots?

"*Bună seara.*" She nodded to me. Her face was drawn, fatigued.

"*Bună seara.* How is your mother?"

"It won't be long," she said as she exhaled the last of her cigarette. "But she's comfortable. Your sister has been such a help. Will you ask her to stop by if she has time? I need to move a piece of furniture."

"I'll help you."

"Oh, *mersi.* That would be wonderful." I followed her up the stairs.

A bucket and mop sat outside the door. The apartment no longer smelled sour, it smelled . . . I wasn't sure what the smell was. I helped her move the couch to position it outside the bedroom.

Through the doorway, I caught sight of a figure in the bed. Small and frail. If not for the white puff of hair, I would have mistaken her for a child.

"With the sofa here, I can be closer to her at night."

I nodded. "If I can ask, how did you end up in Boston?"

"I left Bucharest in the seventies. Harvard offered me a place. Things were easier then."

"Is this your first time back?" I whispered.

"Yes. The entry was complicated, but I'm married to an American and have a U.S. passport now."

Married to an American? Oh, yes. The residents had definitely reported this woman. The throats of the Reporters were likely chattered dry. Was she aware that when she left Romania her family had probably been punished?

A whimper sounded from the bedroom.

"She wants to be moved again. Could you help me?"

I followed her into the bedroom. The stark loneliness of the small, pale room was warmed by a photo of Pope John Paul II. So Mrs. Drucan was Catholic, not Romanian Orthodox. It didn't matter. Most people prayed in secret anyway. The regime harassed religious leaders and destroyed many churches. When Ceaușescu razed the center of Bucharest, a brave engineer saved several historic churches. He put them on rolling tracks and slid them to different parts of the city. Bunu called him "the engineer of heaven."

"She likes the pillows arranged in a certain way. If you can lift her torso for a moment, I'll reposition them." She turned to address her mother. "I have some help here, Mama."

Help? I had no idea what I was doing. Mrs. Drucan looked so breakable. Tufts of her white hair were missing. The tender pink of her scalp resembled a bald baby bird. "My sister might be better—"

"Just hold her neck and head. Bring her slightly forward." I did as instructed, terrified that Mrs. Drucan might die in my arms. When I released her back against the pillows, her gaze floated to me. The look was hollow, yet still connected.

"This is Cristian Florescu, Mama. Cicilia's younger brother."

I smiled at the woman.

Her eyes slowly closed, then opened again.

"Oh, an acknowledgment. That's more than she's given me all day. Rest, Mama, I'll be here."

I followed her daughter out of the room. She rummaged through a cabinet, turned, and extended a package of Kents. I looked at her.

"Your hesitation, it tells me that you're a nice boy."

I decided to ask.

"Do people in the United States know what life is like in Romania?" I whispered.

"No. Americans don't know much at all about Romania. Ceaușescu prefers it that way. And right now, the U.S. is focused on Germany and perestroika with the Soviet Union."

I nodded, thinking of the reports from Radio Free Europe. Bunu said Ceaușescu would never allow perestroika to touch Romania.

She cleared her throat and quickly pushed the package of Kents into my hand. "Look, maybe it feels odd to accept cigarettes for helping a dying woman. But let's face it, everyone here can use them. I can't even imagine how many Kents I'm going to need to get a death certificate and a successful cremation."

I looked over to the frail woman tucked in the bed and Bunu's words floated back to me.

Please. I might be dying but I'm not deaf yet, Cristian.

Could Mrs. Drucan hear her daughter? I hoped not.

She prattled on and her eyes filled with tears. "I can't bury her. I want to take her with me. But I'm told the low gas pressure in Romania prohibits full cremations. What do families do with half-cremated remains?" She looked to me in desperate query. "Cristian, how many

Kents will I need to make sure they turn up the gas?" she whispered.

A rush of air entered my mouth that had fallen open. I shook my head. "I . . . don't know."

She exhaled her tears and moved in close. She looked at me, speaking so silently the words were mere puffs of air. "Things are moving quickly. Take care. There will be danger here." Her eyes lingered in a way that made me uncomfortable.

"I'll leave you and your mama," I told her. "Let us know if you need anything."

She nodded, wiping her eyes with the backs of her hands.

I made my way silently to the door.

And left the Kents on the table.

37

TREIZECI ȘI ȘAPTE

We sat in the kitchen, glued to Radio Free Europe and reports of revolutions in other countries.

There will be danger here.

That's what the woman said. What did that mean? Should I tell Bunu?

"Poland and then Hungary!" shouted Bunu.

"Shh . . . too loud!" said my mother.

"Now East Germany. My god, the Berlin Wall is falling!" said Bunu, his hand upon the radio. "Do you know what this means?"

"Yeah, Poles, Hungarians, and East Germans make revolutions and all we make are Bulă jokes," I said.

"Just wait. Be patient, Cristian. Trust me."

I did trust Bunu. But the woman from Boston had said America was focused on Germany and didn't know much about Romania.

"Bunu, if no one knows much about Romania, how will they know we need help?"

"Romanians who live outside of the country—the diaspora and exiles—they're on our side and will spread the word," insisted Bunu.

"Too loud! Be quiet," whispered Mama.

My father joined us late that evening. Normally quiet, he began to make comments.

Just single words here and there.

Bold. Hold. Fight.

The tone and strength of his voice sounded so foreign.

In hindsight, that makes sense.

Because at that point I didn't really know my father.

At all.

38

TREIZECI ȘI OPT

Reports continued to flow into Romania.

My often-absent father suddenly spent more time at home. In the evenings, our entire family lived in the kitchen, waiting for broadcasts. I hated that Bunu was still weak and we were Kentless, but I was grateful to him for saving our radio.

"Bunu, how do we know that these broadcasts are accurate?" asked Cici.

"Freedom of the press is democratic," replied Bunu.

"But if Radio Free Europe was created by the Americans, how can we trust it?" whispered Mama.

My father stared at her. "Mioara, what choice do we have?"

"We can turn off the radio! It's too stressful!" she insisted.

"It will be more stressful without information," said my grandfather.

"Bunu," I whispered. "Do you think the regime is listening to the reports?"

"Of course! They need the the information themselves to strategize."

The developments and reports bolstered a flutter of activity. Over the next few days, Bunu had a steady flow of visitors and colleagues who seemed very concerned about his health. News of revolutions and chats with his friends strengthened my grandfather but angered my mother. I couldn't figure out why.

"Bunu, why is Mama so angry?" I asked.

He responded with a shake of his head and just one word.

"Fear."

39

TREIZECI ȘI NOUĂ

The night air was crisp with cold. A full moon spilled light onto the street.

I stood, tucked within a shadow on our balcony. The Secu agent who lived beneath us rummaged through his boxes. I peered over the railing. The agent lifted a tarp and retrieved something from a crate. A bottle of cognac? Interesting, I had pegged him as a vodka man. Maybe he had a date. I waited, watching the street below. The agent emerged in his long dark coat and strode toward the black Dacia.

And then I saw her.

Liliana walked down the sidewalk with her brother.

I retreated into the fold of shadow, watching. She suddenly stopped and turned, glancing across the street. The ends of her purple scarf lifted in the wind. Was she looking for me—or was she looking at the agent? I had voices on both shoulders:

You don't want Liliana.

Liar. You want her more than ever.

You're angry. Be angry at her.

That's garbage. You're in love with her.

I quickly slipped back inside our apartment.

The low hum of our radio warbled with news. Bunu shivered. I put a brick in the stove to tuck under his blanket for warmth. And then I stood next to Cici, listening.

<<Satellite states formerly aligned with the Soviet Union are quickly breaking away from communism. We've yet to receive a reaction from other Eastern Bloc allies such as Cuba, China, or North Korea.>>

I shook my head. Poland, Hungary, and even East Germany, they had all marched toward freedom. "What about Romania? We'll be left behind," I lamented. "All these countries will be free, and we'll be left behind."

"No," whispered Cici, putting her arm around me. "Czechoslovakia and Bulgaria aren't free."

True. We weren't entirely alone.

Maybe it just felt like it?

40

PATRUZECI

Czechoslovakia was next.

November 17th. The beginning of the end.

The Velvet Revolution, they would call it.

Czechoslovakia had endured forty-one years of one-party rule. Nearly half a century under communism.

And now that was crumbling.

41

PATRUZECI ȘI UNU

Bulgaria.

Our neighbor on the southern border.

Their leader of thirty-five years had forced the country's Turkish minority to take Bulgarian names. He was unpopular. Even Soviet General Secretary Mikhail Gorbachev disapproved of Bulgaria's leader.

The country began . . . to oust him.

42

PATRUZECI ȘI DOI

Poland.
Hungary.
East Germany.
Czechoslovakia.
Bulgaria.

Their communist regimes had all fallen.

"Yugoslavia will be complicated," said Bunu. "They have six republics to balance. Conflicts since Tito died."

If Yugoslavia would be complicated, what did that mean? Was Romania the last ring holding the Iron Curtain? I shivered in my closet, making entries in my notebook.

	DO YOU FEEL ME?
	HEATING A BRICK
	TO WARM MY SLEEP
	DRIFTING INTO DREAMS
	IN SEARCH OF MYSELF,
	IN SEARCH OF A CONSCIENCE, A COUNTRY.

Later that week, Starfish appeared in his black boots and a brand-new suede jacket. He pulled me aside on the street.

"Nice coat. Where'd you get it?" I asked.

"Forget the coat, did you hear? Nadia Comăneci defected. She trekked through the woods, made it over the border into Hungary, and requested asylum."

"What?" Romania's star Olympic gymnast, Nadia Comăneci, had defected? "Where did you hear that?" I asked.

"Tass, the Soviet news agency. I know someone," said Starfish. "News about it has been blacked out here."

News *was* blacked out. But we soon heard it on Voice of America. Nadia Comăneci had arrived . . . in the United States.

One of Romania's biggest celebrities had no access to a passport, no privacy, and no freedom. Of course not. She had been considered property of Romania, owned by the State. Until now.

Nadia's international attention probably enraged Mother Elena. After all, there was room for only one hero in Romania.

Him.

I began the slow march to the entrance of my gray apartment block. Had Mr. Van Dorn helped Nadia? How many others were trying to run through the snow toward the Hungarian border? If Romania's superstars were suffering, would the world finally understand the terrible plight of the ordinary Romanian people?

No. Of course not.

How could we expect others to feel our pain or hear our cries for help when all we could do was whisper?

43

PATRUZECI ȘI TREI

I wanted freedom. I wanted Romania to fight back.

I filled my notebook with statements, lists, and information about our country, cries for help that I hoped Mr. Van Dorn would share with others. I created a section called *Gânduri*—Thoughts—which contained musings like these:

Paradise: *If communism is Paradise, why do we need barriers, walls, and laws to keep people from escaping?*

I raked my hands through my hair, thinking. There were probably rules. Rules preventing diplomats from knowingly accepting something controversial. I needed to get around that, make sure Mr. Van Dorn couldn't refuse the notebook. Think of ways to encourage him to share the information with others.

What if the notebook just appeared? The author, unidentified?

I took a breath and wrote the following on the cover:

SCREAMING WHISPERS
A ROMANIAN TEENAGER IN BUCHAREST

BY ANONYMOUS

Chills formed at the back of my neck. It was a netless leap. Suicide, some might say.

But I had to try. As the saying goes, better to die standing than live kneeling.

44

PATRUZECI ȘI PATRU

The next time I met Dan at his apartment to go to the library, I was ready. I would use the assignment from Paddle Hands to my advantage. I not only spied Van Dorn's desk, I decided exactly where I'd leave my notebook when I was finished.

"How are your college essays coming?" I asked Dan as we walked to the library.

"Good," he said. "My dad thinks they'll be appreciated with the recent events in Eastern Europe."

Hmm. Would my notebook be appreciated too?

"Will you go home for Christmas?" I asked.

"Mom and I will, but Dad has to stay. Punch Green is arriving. He's the new U.S. ambassador. The embassy's been without an ambassador for six months, so Dad has to be here for the transition."

A new ambassador. Interesting.

The American Library bustled with activity. Were readers gathering information from foreign media? Or gathering courage? Perhaps both.

As Dan collected his music magazines, I returned to the section of world news periodicals. The new issue of *TIME* featured young people from East and West Germany standing together atop the Berlin Wall. The title in bold type was just one word:

FREEDOM

I stood, staring at the seven letters, while a lump the size of a fist formed in my throat. Half a dozen communist regimes had fallen in succession, yet Romania remained unaffected. Why?

Had the world forgotten us? Or had Ceauşescu ingeniously built a fence of national communism that was impenetrable from the outside as well as the inside?

He had stolen us from ourselves, for himself. He had broken the soul of Romania and parched a beautiful country into an apocalyptic landscape of the lost. My notebook told the real story. But would Mr. Van Dorn do anything with it?

"You okay?" Dan asked as we left the library.

I shrugged.

"Yeah, I imagine it's hard, seeing the progress of other countries while things remain the same here. Sorry about that."

I nodded and removed the folded Springsteen article from my pocket. I handed it to him. "I should give this back. If I'm caught with it, it could cause more trouble than the dollar you gave me."

"What dollar?" asked Dan.

"The U.S. dollar you put in my stamp album," I whispered.

"What?" He looked at me, confused. "I never put a dollar in your stamp album. Just toss the article if you don't want it."

I did want it. I still held hope of giving it to Liliana. I returned it to my pocket, trying to appear calm. We said goodbye and agreed to meet the following Saturday. And then I stood, hands clenched, as Dan disappeared into the dark. The anger burned, flaring within me.

That U.S. dollar had led the Securitate to me.

It gave them leverage to recruit me as an informer and plunged me into moral misery.

It crushed my conscience.

It crushed my relationship with Liliana.

But if Dan didn't put the dollar in my stamp album—

Who did?

45

PATRUZECI ȘI CINCI

Blinks of orange.

      I saw them as I approached our building. Burning taper candles stood in pots of sand, flickering through the darkness. A six-foot wooden cross, hauled from a nearby church, leaned against the entry of our building. The tradition when someone dies.

At least Mrs. Drucan hadn't suffered long. Her daughter was probably already packed for Boston. Her comment still haunted me.

How many Kents will I need to make sure they turn up the gas?

I shook off the thought.

The Reporters were absent from their perch. I passed Mirel, standing in his familiar spot near the building. I nodded to him.

"Sorry," he said.

I shrugged. What was he sorry for?

My feet stopped.

The candles. The cross.

No.

Bunu?

I ran inside and up the stairs. My father stood outside our apartment door.

"Go inside. Now. I'm waiting for Cici."

"But—"

"I said, go inside."

His tone wasn't of someone who had just lost his father. It was terse, urgent.

Mama sat at the table, a shadowed stick figure beneath a crooked beam of light, smoking an open package of Kents. Her thin hand trembled. The tip of the cigarette glowed as she pressed it to her lips. We used Kents for bribes. We didn't smoke them.

"Mama?" I looked into the kitchen toward Bunu's narrow couch. Empty.

"Come here, Cristian."

"Mama, where's Bunu?"

"Come here, please."

A cold twist of fear seized my abdomen. I slowly approached the table.

"I came home from work," she whispered, "and found your grandfather." The illuminated cigarette in her hand began to vibrate. "We've put him . . . in the bedroom." She set the quivering cigarette on the lip of the ashtray and reached for my hand. I helped her out of the chair, then followed her to the closed door. She took a breath, turned the knob, and pushed the door open.

And then she turned her back.

Bunu lay on the bed. But it wasn't Bunu. Life had fled and left a waxy corpse—a withered leaf that had lost its water. Bunu's gray skin stretched gaunt and taut over his angular cheekbones. His open eyes stared hollow and his mouth pulled wide, as if living a silent scream, gasping for freedom.

My chest rose and fell, panting. "Bunu . . . no. He was feeling better." I stared at the husk of my grandfather and then I realized.

"Mama—"

She turned to me, shook her head, and put a finger to her lips.

I took a step closer to the bed.

Bunu's hands lay like broken birds. Their color, a purple so dark, nearly black. The bones above his palms were snapped, smashed.

Mama pulled back the blanket covering his legs. A wave of nausea rolled through me. Bunu's bare feet had been clubbed beyond recognition.

"His chest. The same. All ribs broken," she whispered in my ear. "They beat him to death."

My body was instantly cold. A rush of shock and frozen fury. I stood shaking at the side of the bed and felt myself buckling to the floor. Who did this? Who would viciously beat an elderly man? And why? My god, was leukemia not enough?

Bunu. My grandfather, my teacher, my inspiration.

My hero.

How could I ever live without him?

My mother kneeled down. She laid her hand upon my shoulder.

"This," she whispered, "is what happens to philosophers."

46

PATRUZECI ȘI ȘASE

Sorrow. Anger. An expanse of emptiness that takes form as a separate entity living inside of you. It digs, takes root, and dwells there. And somehow, you know that even if it worms its way out, there will be no relief. If it leaves, there will be nothing left but charred remains, like the inside of a house torched by fire.

What did I do wrong?

Was I somehow responsible? Could I have protected him?

I searched for answers.

For three days, Bunu lay in a stark wooden coffin atop the dining table in our living room. The traditional lighted candle was placed by his head, to help him find his way. Black cloths hung over the mirrors and shiny surfaces in our apartment to ensure that Bunu's spirit wouldn't become lost or caught in a reflection. Doors remained unlocked to allow him to exit as he pleased.

I had a small mirror in my closet. I didn't cover it, selfishly hoping to capture Bunu and keep him.

While the regime wedged and pushed us apart, death brought Romanians together. Neighbors set up chairs that lined the hallway of our block's fourth floor. They cobbled together what food and drink they could spare to share. The Reporters hovered, wrapped in traditional dark scarves and veils, hiding secrets and fallen faces.

Although I had no interest in socializing, I wanted to stay close to Bunu. I hoped proximity might bring clarity.

How many agents had come to the apartment? How many were involved in his death? Was Paddle Hands one of them? Did Bunu know they were coming?

I sat with him through the nights, mentally continuing my side of our conversations.

I became an informer to get medicine for you. What happens now, Bunu?

I'm going to give my notebook to the U.S. diplomat. How shall I describe what they did to you?

Dan didn't put the dollar in our stamp album. So who did?

And of course, I shared jokes.

Bunu, why will Romania survive the end of the world? Because it's fifty years behind everyone else!

He heard me. I felt certain of it. Was Bunu watching over the rest of our family too?

Grief had paled Cici beyond recognition. She couldn't speak. She couldn't look at Bunu. While neighbors filtered through the apartment, Cici stood detached, lingering by her sewing machine. Bunu's chess partner, the elderly gentleman from the morning line, appeared on the second afternoon.

"The message you gave me for Bunu," I asked him. "What did it mean?"

He tented his fingers, reflecting. "You know what? I'd like some fresh air. Let's step outside," he said.

I followed him down the stairs. We passed the large cross at the door and headed to the sidewalk. He pulled a stub of a cigarette from his pocket and lit it as we walked.

"Your grandfather was a wonderful man. Intelligent, energetic, with such a sense of justice. But his thoughts and ideas—they labeled him a dissident. You know that, of course."

Dissident. A protester. An objector. Someone who disputes established policy.

"Bunu kept his thoughts within the family. He said there was no such thing as a confidant."

"No. His thoughts were not as private as you were led to believe," he said, exhaling a mouthful of smoke. "And now I must warn you. Your family's hardship will extend beyond your grandfather's death. The monitoring and meetings may continue."

"Meetings?"

"Your grandfather had been called to Securitate headquarters several times."

I stopped and looked at the man. No. How was I unaware of this?

"Yes. And during those interviews with the agents . . ." He looked squarely at me. "He drank a lot of coffee. Don't make the same mistake. Do you understand?"

I didn't understand.

Bunu had told me everything. Shared his opinions and refused to whisper. Why didn't he tell me that he'd been summoned to Secu headquarters? And if the Securitate had pegged Bunu as a dissident, why would they recruit me as an informer?

"The coffee," whispered the gentleman, so low I could barely hear. "I suspect it contained radioactive poison."

I turned to him on the sidewalk, my mind racing.

They poisoned Bunu. The poison caused symptoms that mirrored leukemia. It was a quiet way to get rid of someone. Mama wasn't angry at Bunu for being ill, but for being a dissident.

"You're telling me they poisoned him. Eventually it would have killed him. So why did they have to beat him?" I asked the man standing in front of me.

"To stall progress, set an example, make a statement. Don't you see? If they'll do that to an elderly man, what will they do to hopeful young students who want to ride the tide of revolution?"

What would they do to a young student? The possibility didn't scare me.

I was more inspired than ever.

And now? I had nothing to lose.

47

PATRUZECI ŞI ŞAPTE

lex Pavel arrived at the apartment carrying two chrysan-themums. The funeral ritual of an even number of flowers puzzled me. In flower shops, they only sold bouquets with odd numbers, saying even numbers were reserved for funerals. But wouldn't an odd number be more appropriate for a funeral? To signify that one is "missing?"

Luca and his mother brought *coliva*, spiced pudding made of boiled wheat that's molded into the shape of a cake. Theirs was deco-rated with a cross.

Alex stepped toward Cici with the flowers. When he moved, I saw her.

Liliana.

Standing in my apartment, hair hiding her eyes.

Instead of being happy to see her, I was angry. My reaction made no sense. At that point, nothing made sense. I looked away, suddenly nervous. Why was she here? She couldn't stand the sight of me but wanted to be seen as polite? Was that it? Or did her mother force her to come and cling to a wall?

But she didn't cling to a wall. She greeted my parents and Cici. And then, out of the corner of my eye, I saw her coming my way.

I felt her slide in near me. The painful house fire raged within. I took a breath and turned to her. "Why are you here?" I whispered.

She looked at me and lifted a shoulder. "I . . . don't know," she whispered. "But I wanted to come."

Her reply was so genuine—and genuinely confusing. I didn't know how to respond.

We stood together, looking at Bunu. I didn't want her there, but suddenly I didn't want her to leave. Did she notice his gloved hands? Generally, coins are placed in the hands of the deceased so they can pay tolls along the way. Cici was so distressed by the look of Bunu's hands that she made pale, thin gloves for him to wear.

"I'm so sorry, Cristian," whispered Liliana. She stepped in close. So close that our arms were touching. So close that it was distracting.

She was sorry. Did that mean she was sorry for Bunu? Or sorry that she accused me of informing on her? Or sorry that we were no longer together?

I nodded but said nothing.

Liliana was so close to me in that crowded room. I took a breath, trying to manage the sensation of heat flooding throughout my body. I swallowed and stood, desperately hoping she'd reach for my hand. If she reached for my hand, I'd wrap my arms around her. I wanted to wrap my arms around her.

"Lili, let's go," said Alex. He wedged in beside us.

I stared at him, remembering our last exchange. I wasn't sorry, and clearly, he wasn't either. He still looked like he wanted to punch me. A part of me hoped he would.

A soft touch swept across my hand. "Goodbye, Cristian," said Liliana.

And then she was gone.

Luca stepped forward a few minutes later. "*Hei*, can I talk to you?"

"No."

"C'mon, Cristian. Please?"

We exited the small space into the darkened hallway. Luca grabbed two wooden chairs. "Too crowded here." He carried the chairs down to the third floor and tried to make small talk.

"I'm not in the mood for a chat, Luca."

"You've been in a mood for weeks. I tried to give you space. But we need to resolve this. Should I let you sucker punch me again? If that's what it'll take, I'll do it."

"I didn't sucker punch you."

"Yeah, you did. You know I'm not a fighter. And you also know that I'm fair. But you're so tight-lipped." His voice dropped to a whisper. "I had no idea that you liked Liliana. If you would have told me, I never would have tried."

I turned to Luca. "You never would have tried what?"

"To spend time with her."

"You've been spending time with Liliana?"

"Not recently," said Luca. "But she's smart and I liked her. She lives in my building, so I was trying to get to know her."

I looked at Luca, running a mental timeframe. "You were trying to get close to Liliana?"

"Yeah, and you're mad about it."

Was this a sick joke? My best friend turns me in to the Securitate *and* tries to steal my girlfriend?

"Listen, Cristian, you have nothing to worry about. The last time I saw her, she said she only wanted to see you. I was disappointed, but you're my friend. Just wish you would have told me."

"You were disappointed? So disappointed that you ran to your Secu agent and informed on her? She thinks it was me, asshole."

Luca's gentle face pinched into anger. *"Du-te dracu."* He stood up, kicking his chair back in the process. "You know what, Cristi? Go to hell," he muttered, and walked down the stairs.

My fists tightened. The agent, Luca, Liliana, and now Bunu. Go to hell? I was already there. And there was no way out. I'd be chained at the ankles for the rest of my life. I grabbed Luca's wooden chair and heaved it against the wall, smashing it to pieces.

An apartment door flew open. The woman from Boston ran to me and grabbed my arms.

"Stop," she ordered. "Breathe."

I hadn't been able to breathe for weeks.

"Breathe, Cristian," she whispered.

"You don't understand. I can't." My voice caught in my throat. The words "I can't, I can't, I can't" came sputtering from my mouth as tears appeared and streamed down my face. "I can't!"

I slid down the cold cement wall of the hallway, crying.

"I can't."

She kneeled down and gripped me by the shoulders. "Yes, you can." She leaned in close to whisper. "Listen to me. You are fine. You . . . are fine. The regime is sick, not you, okay? Don't ever forget that."

I didn't forget.

Ever.

And I hope no one else does.

|| INFORMER REPORT ||

[5 Dec. 1989]

Liliana Pavel (17), resident in Salajan sector 3. Observed
Tuesday evening in the stairwell. Pavel exited Florescu
family apartment with her brother, Alex Pavel (21).
Liliana began to cry and argue with her brother. Crying
and argument escalated. Liliana insisted to her brother
that Cristian (Florescu) was different, that no one could
understand, and to leave her. Alex Pavel then departed.

Shortly thereafter, Cristian Florescu (17) exited the
apartment and began a private conversation with Luca Oprea
(17) pertaining to discovery of mutual relationship with
Liliana Pavel. Unbeknownst to both boys, Liliana Pavel
remained hiding in the stairwell, listening. Conversation
escalated into an argument in which Florescu accused Oprea
of informing on Pavel.

Liliana fled from the stairwell just prior to Oprea
departing. In a fit of anger, Florescu proceeded to damage
Party property.

As Florescu broke a chair, target BARBARA appeared in the
hallway and spoke (undecipherable) to Florescu in an attempt
to calm him.

48

PATRUZECI ȘI OPT

A human pendulum.

That's what I felt like. Swinging between fear, sadness, confusion, and rage.

After three nights of funeral visitations, the atmosphere in the apartment felt darker than the stairwells. The light between the walls shifted to an anemic blue gray. My parents spoke only behind the closed door of their bedroom. Black crescents appeared under Cici's eyes.

"I'm frightened," she whispered. "It's going to be awful, *Pui*. Bunu must have been involved in something dangerous."

"Like what?" I asked. "Supporting a revolution?"

"Shh . . . I don't know, but whatever it was, they wanted him to stop. And now they'll start hauling us to Secu headquarters to be interrogated. We need a plan. They may come to my work. What if they come to your school?"

I looked at her fear-filled face. If she only knew. "We'll just tell them the truth, Cici. That we don't know anything."

"But it could be endless. Mama is declining by the day. She's a shell of herself."

Cici was right. Our mother was becoming more withdrawn. The lines on her forehead etched deeper. She paced the apartment muttering, kneading her hands, and checking the window frames for listening devices.

That night I sat on the rugs in my closet, leaning against the wall. I had kept my end of the bargain. I gave Paddle Hands what he asked for. How had I miscalculated? I would finish my notebook and give it to Mr. Van Dorn as soon as possible. The strategy had worked before.

The year prior, a Romanian professor and writer named Doina Cornea saw a car with a foreign license plate. She gave the driver a doll, requesting he take it when he left Romania. Hidden inside the head of the doll was an open letter to Ceaușescu, written in tiny type on cigarette paper. The letter was delivered to Munich and broadcast on Radio Free Europe. Her sentiments echoed those of many Romanians who couldn't speak them aloud. I wanted to do something similar—give our country a voice.

"She's crazy, taking a risk like that," Mama had insisted.

"Not crazy. She's brilliant," said Bunu. "We're punished for our sanity."

I snapped on my flashlight to add "we're punished for our sanity" to my notebook. As I positioned the flashlight, something fluttered in its beam. A small piece of paper was pinned to the inside of the doorframe. How long had it been there?

I grabbed the note and opened it. Lines of Bunu's shaky handwriting filled the small piece of paper.

> *I know you're confused.*
> *Remain quiet, unseen.*
> *Things will soon become clearer. Listen to Radio Free Europe.*
> *Remember—*
> *Be patient. Be wise. Search within yourself always.*
> *As Socrates told us, an unexamined life is not worth living.*
> *I'm proud of you.*
>
> *~ Bunu*

I stared at the note in my trembling hand.

Despite everything, he understood. He didn't judge me. He was proud of me. Tears welled within my eyes. I didn't try to stop them. *An unexamined life is not worth living.* The notebook was my way of searching within, examining life and asking questions that I couldn't speak aloud. I drew a breath and read the note again.

Listen to Radio Free Europe. That's what it said.

Not, *"We'll* listen to Radio Free Europe."

Me. Alone. It was a directive.

I had my answer.

Bunu knew they were coming for him.

49

PATRUZECI ȘI NOUĂ

The puzzling weight of absence. When one potato is removed from a basket, the weight is lighter, easier to carry. But Bunu's absence created the opposite effect. The atmosphere in the apartment hung heavier, more crowded. Cici was irritable, smearing lipstick on and continually altering her clothes as if that might alter the situation.

"Are you okay, *Pui*?" she asked constantly.

None of us were okay.

Mama orbited in a perpetual state of agitation, whispering to herself and putting a hand to her hair, making sure it was still there. My father shifted about like an iron ghost. He mourned quiet and dormant, like Bunu had said. When he came home, he often went right to sleep. But one night, he joined me on the balcony.

We stood next to each other, watching the snow fall. Several minutes passed. He cleared his throat.

"An old woman is fast asleep when she hears a knock at the door. *Who is it?* she whispers, terrified.

It is death, the voice answers.

Oh, good. I thought it might be the Securitate."

I turned to my father, impressed. "Not bad."

"Your *bunu* didn't make them up on his own, you know." My father smiled.

"Really?"

"C'mon, we used to joke around all the time when you were younger."

"Yeah. I guess I had forgotten about that."

What else had I forgotten?

I hadn't forgotten the notebook for Mr. Van Dorn. It was a welcome distraction. I had started a letter and worked through several drafts. When I felt it was complete, I tore out the drafts and rewrote the letter on the very last page.

If I left the notebook on his desk, would Mr. Van Dorn think someone had accidentally forgotten it there? I decided to wrap it, like a gift, and put his name on it. I didn't have any wrapping paper, so I used pages from *Cutezătorii*, the Romanian teen almanac. I flipped through my almanac, deciding which pages to use. The front section was always about Ceaușescu, so Luca and I read the almanac from back to front, starting with the comics and crossword puzzles.

I chose two pieces for wrapping:

The cover, because the title of the teen almanac, *Cutezătorii*, meant "Brave Ones."

I also chose an interior page that featured Ceaușescu alongside an article titled "Romania—the Country of Creative Work."

Yes, Ceaușescu's plan was creative. But so was mine.

I opened Cici's sewing basket, looking for a piece of string to tie the package. I rummaged through buttons, pins, Neckermann catalogs, and at the very bottom, a couple of coins, a piece of ribbon, and a ring of keys. I took the ribbon and secured the pages around the notebook. It definitely looked like a gift and, this being the middle of December, would probably be mistaken as one.

A gift of truth. That's what Bunu would have called it.

And then I was finally ready.

Or so I thought.

Everything changed the moment I tucked that wrapped book in my bag. My heart took off from some invisible starting block. I began to sweat. Profusely.

I had never taken the notebook out of my closet. It lived beneath my mattress of rugs in the secret pocket under the vinyl flooring. But that Saturday, it would sit in my bag through the entire school day until I met Dan to go to the library. I hadn't been summoned for Paddle Hands recently. What if the agent chose today for a visit? I had been so confident, a great pretender. But it now felt like the notebook had its own heartbeat in my bag. If the agent didn't notice that, he'd surely notice the vein pulsing wildly at my temple.

But I had come this far. It was too late to change my mind. And I didn't intend to.

I adjusted the strap on my bag.

And left the apartment.

50

CINCIZECI

I made it to school.

On my way to class I spotted Liliana down the corridor, walking with a group of navy-pinafored girls. The girls were huddled together talking, but suddenly Liliana's face turned.

Toward me.

Her hair was grasped by the uniform's white headband, but her bangs obscured her eyes. I couldn't tell where her gaze landed. Was she looking at me?

Or at my book bag.

The bag carrying the bomb.

I turned away and headed to class.

I sat through calculus, empathizing with my classmate who had cracked. I imagined it was me, jumping out of my chair and shouting.

I'm an informer! There's a bomb in my bag!

My grandfather's dead! He was a dissident and my hero!

My heart is destroyed. I'm in love with Liliana Pavel!

Looking back, I should have said it all. Just let it fly.

But instead, I said nothing.

When class was over, I stood, leaving sweat prints of my hands on my blue trousers.

Comrade Director wasn't in the hall. Now that Bunu was gone, was the agent finished with me?

I wasn't finished with him. He was prominently featured in my notebook.

Luca lingered outside of the school building. I dodged him and rushed away.

As I made my way to Dan's apartment, I thought through my plan. Dan usually left the living room to retrieve his coat. That's when I would leave the notebook. But I needed an alternate plan. What if his parents were around? My last resort was to use the bathroom and drop the package in the TV room when no one was looking.

My conscience issued unwanted reminders:

Writing negative things about Romania was illegal.

Exchanging items with a foreigner was illegal.

Defying the Securitate was illegal.

At that moment, everything about me—

Was illegal.

Was I scared? Absolutely.

But I stepped off the bus.

I took a deep breath.

And walked straight to Dan's apartment.

Sweating.

51

CINCIZECI ȘI UNU

I'm very sorry about your grandfather."

That's what Mrs. Van Dorn said upon opening the door. "Please tell your mother it's perfectly fine if she needs additional days off."

"*Mersi*. I mean, thank you."

She looked at me, full of pity and sympathy. "Dan's with his father at the commissary, but I expect them any minute. Do you mind waiting?"

"That's fine."

What was "the commissary"?

The phone rang and Mrs. Van Dorn excused herself to answer it. I grabbed the notebook from my bag and ran to Mr. Van Dorn's desk. Just as I slid it beneath a stack of newspapers, the door of the apartment opened.

Dan entered, carrying a crate—a crate full of food and American products. My stomach groaned. Clearly, the commissary was the U.S. Embassy store.

"Hey, Cris, have you been waiting long?" he asked.

"No. I just got here."

"Hello, Cristian." Mr. Van Dorn nodded, carefully eyeing my proximity to his desk.

I quickly pointed to a nearby painting on the wall. "I was looking at this painting. Is the artist Romanian?"

"Nah," said Dan. "One of my mom's paintings from Spain. Just let me grab my backpack and we can go."

I stood, acutely aware of Mr. Van Dorn's gaze upon me. He moved toward his desk, still wearing his coat. My heart thumped. It was all crumbling. If he discovered the notebook now, he'd ask me about it. What would I say?

"So, whatcha been up to, Cristian?" he asked, taking a step closer.

I stood, frozen. "Whatcha been up to." What did that mean? I felt a trickle of sweat slide down the channel of my back.

"Sorry. I'll rephrase. What's new? What have you been doing lately?"

"Nick? Is that you?" his wife's voice called from the kitchen. "Ana's on the phone to discuss plans."

"Excuse me." Mr. Van Dorn headed for the other room, and Dan appeared with his backpack.

"Ready to go?"

"Yes." I nodded quickly.

Dan put a finger to his lips. He quietly lifted two cellophane-wrapped items from the crate of food. He held up the packages, smiling. The blue and red label said *Twinkies*. He dropped one into my coat pocket. What did the word "Twinkie" mean?

We exited the building onto the street. The frozen, snowy air refreshed my sweat-soaked neck. "When do you go home for the holiday?" I asked.

"The day after tomorrow," he replied. "And I have some news."

"News?"

"I'm not coming back."

I turned to look at him. "What do you mean?"

"I struck a deal with my parents. They're letting me spend next semester in Dallas. I'll go to school there and live with my godparents."

Dan was leaving Romania and he wasn't coming back. I felt an odd twinge. "And what about Princeton?"

"I've finished my essay. Hey, when we get to the library, would you read it? Of course, it's just my point of view, but I'd like your opinion."

"Yeah, sure."

As always, the American Library sweltered like an oven. But I was already drenched in sweat.

Dan chose a table and dug into his backpack. "Hey, since I won't be around for the holidays, I have something I want to give you."

He produced a small envelope and tossed it on the table.

I stared at it. I looked around.

"Take it. It's for you." He laughed. He pushed it toward me.

I had just gone through this. Accepting something from a foreigner had to be reported. He must know that. Besides, how many people were watching us? But I was curious.

I pulled the envelope across the table and lifted the unsealed flap. Inside was a pane of four mint U.S. stamps. Each stamp displayed a different illustration, along with "USA" and the value of 22 cents in the lower corner.

"They were issued a few years back," said Dan. "I thought they were kinda special."

They were special.

So special that I didn't care if I got in trouble for having them.

Along the top of each stamp were the words STAMP COLLECTING.

They were stamps specifically created to commemorate collectors. Bunu would have loved them. A knot formed in my throat.

"Thank you, Dan," I whispered.

"Aw, it's no big deal, just something to remind you of your pal from New Jersey."

"Pal?" I said.

"Sorry, 'pal' means friend. Just something to remind you of your friend from New Jersey."

My friend from New Jersey.

A friend I spent time with because the Secu had blackmailed me to. A friend who was referred to as my "target." A friend whose father I was exploiting to get information out of Romania. How easily Americans made "friends."

Emotion swelled within my chest.

"Here's the essay. It's only a couple pages," said Dan, sliding it across the table.

I stared at the papers.

The sheets in front of me held information that the Securitate was desperate for. Information I could use to my advantage. An American's thoughts on Romania—officially presented to a U.S. college admissions board.

Read it. Come on, turnător. *This was the deal you made, wasn't it?*

What sort of friend was I? Could I really blame Luca for informing on me when I myself was informing on a friend? A pal? Liliana's words echoed in my head:

> *You are a liar.*
> *You are everything I despise.*
> *You are an informer.*

"You okay, Cristian? You don't look so good."

If I didn't read the essay, I wouldn't be able to inform on my friend. "I'm, um, not feeling well." I told him.

Dan reached across the table and snatched the essay. "It's my only copy. If you puke, I'm out of luck."

Luck. *Noroc.* That was the only word I understood—and I understood that I didn't have any.

"I think I better go. Thanks again, Dan. The stamps, they're great."

"You might like the Twinkies more than the stamps." He laughed. "Hey, give me your address. We can keep in touch about stamps and stuff." He tore a page from a spiral-bound notebook. I wrote my address on it, knowing it was forbidden to communicate with a foreigner, but knowing it was the last time I'd ever see Dan Van Dorn.

"Have a good Christmas," said Dan, his face full of sincerity.

Was anyone thinking about Christmas? I wasn't. I gave a wave and headed toward the door. I exited the building and pulled several deep breaths.

My notebook was on Mr. Van Dorn's desk.

Dan was leaving Romania for good.

Bunu was dead.

What would the Securitate do with me now that I was no use to them?

Friendship. It was something valuable. Something I wanted with Luca. Something I wanted with Dan Van Dorn. And Dan wanted it too. If he didn't, he wouldn't have given me the stamps and the Twinkies.

Would he?

|| INFORMER REPORT ||

[9 Dec. 1989]

Cristian Florescu (17), student at MF3 High School, resident in Salajan sector 3. Observed Saturday at the American Library in Bucharest with American Dan Van Dorn. Florescu and Van Dorn engaged in a brief discussion and exchanged an envelope and a piece of paper. Florescu left with the envelope after just five minutes. After Florescu departed, Van Dorn was approached by an American adult male (identity unknown) and proceeded to take part in a hushed conversation that lasted nearly ten minutes. Van Dorn gave the sheet of paper from Florescu to the American male. Following conversation, Van Dorn quickly left the library without reading any books or magazines.

52

CINCIZECI ŞI DOI

A week felt like a year, wading through waist-high mud.

I didn't eat the Twinkies. I wanted to save them for Cici's birthday.

But there was little to celebrate. Starving dogs, dark streets, Reporters, the cold getting colder. And all around us, other countries were preparing for their first Christmas in freedom.

Had Mr. Van Dorn found my notebook?

I stood on the freezing balcony, hoping the cold air would dull my emotions. Cici appeared with a bundle in her arms. "Here, try this on."

"What is it?"

"Something I made for you, so you don't have to sleep in your coat."

Cici had found an oversized work shirt and stitched thick, quilted layers of padding on the inside.

"I love it. It's super soft."

"And it'll be warm." She began fastening the buttons and evaluating the fit. "Did you hear about Bunu's chess partner?" she whispered. "He's been placed under house arrest."

I wasn't surprised. Each night when we listened to Voice of America and Radio Free Europe we learned of writers, poets, and journalists who fought against the regime.

"Apparently Bunu's friend was affiliated with a literary magazine that . . ."

My sister's words faded from importance as something emerged in my line of sight. I squinted down at the street, trying to make out the figures.

Cici tugged gently at my arm. "Come inside, *Pui*."

I shook my head. The moon shifted beneath a cloud, illuminating the scene.

Cici meant well. She was trying to protect me. But I couldn't pull my eyes from what I saw below.

Standing on the dark sidewalk was Liliana.

With Luca.

"Don't do this to yourself," whispered my sister. "I've told you. You can't trust Luca."

But what did that mean for Liliana? She couldn't trust me. She couldn't trust Luca. Who would protect her?

My sister's hand remained on my arm. "After Bunu, we need to be smart, *Pui*. Mama is not herself. She's terrified the Secu will summon her. We need to be careful," whispered Cici.

I nodded. She was right. Our parents were definitely not themselves. Our mother had gone silent like our father.

"What are you thinking?" asked my sister.

I so desperately wanted to tell her, to confess everything, but I couldn't bear her disappointment. I had lost Bunu, Liliana, and Luca. I couldn't lose Cici.

"What am I thinking? Nothing. And everything." I shrugged. "Thanks for the sleeping coat."

I left the balcony and shut myself in my closet. I no longer had my notebook to confess to. So instead, I wrote one of the entries from memory on the wall:

12 DECEMBER, 1989

WILL YOU REMEMBER ME?
A BOY WITH WINGS OF HOPE
STRAPPED TO HIS BACK
THAT NEVER HAD A CHANCE TO OPEN,
DENIED FOREVER KNOWING
WHAT HE COULD HAVE BECOME.

WHAT WE ALL COULD HAVE BECOME.

53

CINCIZECI ŞI TREI

Paddle Hands was finished with me, I was certain.

But I was wrong. I was wrong about so many things.

That Saturday, Comrade Director gave a discreet nod, so after my usual waiting, I made my way to the host apartment. What approach would I take this time to burrow beneath his skin? Would I try to be friendly, talk about soccer, and worm my way in? Or would I be honest?

"My *bunu*'s dead."

The words came out of my mouth faster and louder than they appeared in my head. Honest.

The agent looked up from the table.

"Close the door," he instructed.

I entered the box of a room and closed the door. I did not sit. I was not told to.

The agent began fiddling with the paper stamp from his BT cigarette package, making a ring and slipping it on his pinky finger. Was that a nervous tic?

"I'm sorry about your grandfather."

Sure he was. According to rumor, some of the Secu agents were orphans trained by the regime to fight for Ceauşescu or serve as his bodyguards. Were they the ones who beat Bunu? This guy couldn't care about someone's grandfather.

"Have a seat."

I sat.

"How are you?"

I stared into my lap, thinking of everything that would bring tears. When my eyes moistened, I looked up at the agent. "I'm not . . . well."

"That's understandable." He nodded. "Medicine was given to your grandfather. But I was told he was quite far gone and suffering severe mental disorders."

Mental disorders? No. Bunu was mentally sharp until the very end.

Parasitism. That's what they called it. People who opposed the regime were parasites and mentally ill. This idiot was calling Bunu a parasite. The irony.

"It's not just my *bunu*. I can't believe Nadia Comăneci fled the country. Will our soccer stars leave too?" I gave him my best innocent look.

"What? No. Have you visited the target?"

"He's gone. Dan and his mother returned to New Jersey. He gave me a Christmas card."

"What was in it?"

"A Christmas greeting." I sighed and stared into my lap.

"Nothing inside the card? No gifts? No articles about Bruce Springsteen to cheer you up?"

Şahmat. Checkmate.

Yes, I had thought I was so smart. But suddenly, I was backed into a corner.

I didn't raise my face. I didn't raise my eyes. Just shook my head.

I had told the agent that the article Dan ripped out of the magazine was about American music. I never mentioned Springsteen.

Someone else must have.

If he realized his slip, he didn't show it. Or maybe he wanted to emphasize he had the upper hand and knew everything. Even the contents of my closet.

My notebook. Did he know about my notebook? I fought to keep up the ruse, to act calm.

"The father's desk. Were you able to note anything on it?" he asked.

"American newspapers and magazines with reports about freedom in other countries. Some file folders. The contents weren't visible."

"Did the target speak of his father's work?"

"He said his father is staying in Romania for Christmas because a new ambassador just arrived."

"Did he give his opinion on the new American ambassador?"

"Oh, yes," I lied. "Said he's not your average diplomat. He's more aggressive. Plans to make changes."

"What kind of changes?"

I shrugged.

"So . . . the target's father will now be alone for several weeks?"

A menacing feeling rose from beneath the desk. Were they planning to harm Mr. Van Dorn? I pretended not to understand the question.

"The target and his mother are gone," said Paddle Hands slowly. He smiled. "That means Van Dorn will be alone in the apartment for several weeks."

"I'm . . . I'm not sure," I said.

"Oh right, he won't be alone." The agent stared right through me. "Your mama will be there with him." He let the dig sit for a beat. "Just to clean, of course," he added.

With a flick of his large hand, he shed the paper ring from his pinky and flung it across the desk at me. He grinned, pleased with himself.

"We're done," he said.

|| OFFICIAL REPORT ||

Ministry of the Interior

Department of State Security

Directorate III, Service 330

TOP SECRET

[15 Dec. 1989]

Discussion with source OSCAR at host location.

OSCAR displayed arrogance and pretended to be upset about his grandfather's death in an attempt to manipulate the conversation.

OSCAR provided the following information on target VAIDA:

-VAIDA's son has left Romania with his mother for the holidays. Prior to departing, he gave OSCAR a holiday card. OSCAR accepted the card.

-the new American ambassador is rumored to have "aggressive" attitudes toward Romania and plans to make "changes"

-for the next several weeks, "VAIDA" will be alone in his apartment

Recommendations:

• OSCAR is no longer of use. Take necessary measures.
• VAIDA is alone. Accelerate plan.

54

CINCIZECI ŞI PATRU

I thought I was a great pretender. But at that moment, I wasn't so sure. Paddle Hands was smug, too smug. I'd assumed an agent dealing with teenagers had to be mediocre. Had I assumed wrong?

Starfish intercepted me in front of the apartment block. "I might have something for you."

"Yeah? What?"

"A British guest at the Intercontinental threw some papers in the trash. They're in English. A contact is holding them for me."

"How much?

"Got any Western currency?" he asked.

I thought of the dollar I gave to Cici. "I might. You have the papers?"

"No, but I can get them."

"Well, get them and we'll talk."

I left Starfish and turned toward my building.

Orange flickers.

The candles had returned along with the large wooden cross outside of our apartment block. Death was paying another house call. Tiny snowflakes swirled in the glow like specks of winter dust. Mirel lingered in his usual spot.

"Mrs. Drucan," he said. "A couple hours ago."

I nodded.

I made my way up the stairs to the third floor. Cici was moving chairs into the hallway.

"Mrs. Drucan," she said.

"Mirel told me."

"Can you ask her daughter if she needs any help?"

The woman from Boston rushed around, organizing things in her mother's apartment.

"*Salut*, Cristian."

"I'm sorry about your mother. Do you need any help?"

"*Mersi*, but I think I'm all set. She was very peaceful. We had a final exchange. I know she heard me. She took a breath and was gone."

I thought of Bunu. A smile. A relieved exhale. That was the way he should have died. Deserved to die. I nodded, just standing there. Hands stuffed in my pockets.

"When are you leaving for Boston?" I asked.

"In a few days. My cousins will remain in the apartment. You've been so helpful and—unlike others—you've refused to accept or ask for anything. Could I treat you to a cup of coffee? I brought some Nescafé from the States."

Coffee.

"Don't drink the coffee," I blurted.

She looked at me, confused. "Why not?"

"It's . . . unhealthy."

"Well, it *is* instant coffee, but I thought most people here liked Nescafé."

"Yeah, sorry, they probably do. Have a safe trip home." I turned to leave and felt her hand upon my arm.

"Oh, and Cristian," she whispered.

I looked over to her.

"Three cartons."

"Excuse me?"

"That's the answer. It takes three cartons to turn up the gas."

She smiled, relieved, peaceful.

Mrs. Drucan's daughter. The woman from Boston. Red boots and lighting bolt earrings. I realized only later.

I never knew her name.

Cici continued to arrange chairs in the hallway. "Mama is home. Dad is out standing in line." I nodded and headed up the stairs.

Like our parents, our apartment was silent. The door to the bedroom was closed. I headed to my closet to confirm my suspicion. I lifted the stack of books in the corner.

Just as I thought.

The Springsteen article was gone.

The Secu was still coming and going from our apartment.

But the next time they came? They'd be in for a surprise.

Because I would be there.

55

CINCIZECI ŞI CINCI

Sad emptiness has a presence that seeps into everything. Each time I inhaled, it entered me—a spirit-crushing loneliness and the strange, shameful feeling that accompanied it.

I missed Bunu.

It was Sunday evening and for a rare moment, our family was together. We ate our quiet dinner of soup with a wedge of bread that Mama had soldiered hours in the cold for. I then settled in on Bunu's couch to wait until 10:00 p.m. for the headline recap on Voice of America. Cici joined me. The signal wasn't clear, so I adjusted the illegal wire that ran from the radio to the kitchen window. As I finessed the dial, a few words emerged from the static.

<<Protest in Maria Square>>

"Where's Maria Square?" asked Cici.

Our mother appeared. "In Timișoara, the western part of Romania. Why?"

"Shh . . . I'm trying to tune in," I told them.

I landed on the frequency. The radio knob pulsed beneath my fingers as the announcer's voice warbled into our kitchen.

<<In Timișoara, what began as a vigil over the forced eviction of

church pastor László Tőkés has escalated into an antigovernment protest. Romanian security forces opened fire, and there are reports that civilians have been killed. This story is still developing and we'll come back with details.>>

Cici jumped off the couch.

Mama turned and ran to the bedroom. She returned with our father in tow.

"A protest?" whispered Mama, gripping the doorframe. "No, no. They must stop. There will be consequences."

I wasn't thinking of consequences. I was thinking of Bunu. My brave *bunu* who refused to whisper, who was beaten to death for what he believed in.

"Bunu, are you hearing this?" I said. "It's happening!"

"Shhh . . ." said Cici. "The announcer's coming back on."

<<The vigil began on Saturday with parish members holding candles and requesting that persecution of Pastor Tőkés be stopped. But hour by hour, residents joined together and the brave people of Timișoara united and took to the streets. The crowd grew overnight and today the swarm of protestors was so large that it blocked traffic in the square and overflowed onto the surrounding streets. As the protest continued, the crowd began to oppose not just the pastor's persecution, but the regime itself.>>

"YES!" I cried.

"Oh my god."

"Shh . . ."

<<Today, as the crowds swelled, the mayor called for the protestors to disperse. But the mayor's voice was soon

overpowered by the repeated call of the masses. Together, the citizens of Timișoara joined as one voice, continuously chanting: *Li-ber-ta-te.*>>

The word pierced through the radio. My skin chilled and a knot formed in my throat.

Libertate.

Liberty.

It was happening.

It was really happening!

Romanians were joining in hand and heart. And together they were finally calling—

For freedom.

56

CINCIZECI ŞI ŞASE

I stayed awake all night on Bunu's couch, searching for radio updates. State radio and television reported nothing. Of course not. Radio Free Europe and Voice of America were the only sources of information. The regime knew that. Would they jam the signal? No, that was too expensive. They hadn't jammed signals in years and probably lacked the equipment to do so.

The announcer said civilian deaths had been reported.

Timişoara. The heart. The courage. We had to help them. I pulled the faded map from the cabinet drawer. It was 550 kilometers from Bucharest to Timişoara, a seven-hour drive, longer with our precarious roads. Could groups or buses be arranged? Perhaps we could build a chain of protests across the country. Together, we could close in on Ceauşescu. Trap him. Overthrow him.

Right here in Bucharest.

"It's happening, Bunu," I whispered.

Poland.

Hungary.

East Germany.

Czechoslovakia.

Bulgaria.

Their communist regimes had all fallen in nonviolent, bloodless transfers of power. But Romania remained, the last flap of the Iron

Curtain. For decades, Ceaușescu had tied a strangling noose of national communism around our necks. If we wanted our freedom, we'd have to fight for it. And our ruthless dictator, he would fight back. He'd mobilize his death squads of blue-eyed boys from beneath the belly of the capital to kill his own people.

And he'd do it without a second thought.

57

CINCIZECI ŞI ŞAPTE

I hadn't slept but by morning felt invincible. I ran to school, passing a banner proclaiming LONG LIVE CEAUŞESCU! What if I tore it down? No, we needed a group. We had to join together. In Romania it was against the law to gather in groups larger than a few people. But no one would pay attention to that now, would they?

I couldn't wait to get to school. There would be chatter, discussions, plans. Cici and my parents were full of fear rather than fortitude. I missed Bunu. He would know what to do and how to do it.

But school that day was a morgue. Cold silence. Blank faces.

Comrade Instructor spoke the same waste of time, wooden tongue nonsense. I couldn't understand it. Had no one heard the radio reports? Did they care nothing for the brave people of Timişoara? Were they too scared, or just programmed to believe that they were owned by the State and could do nothing about it?

Winter break began the next day. This was our last opportunity to be together and make plans. Between classes, I whispered to a fellow student.

"Hey, did you hear about Timişoara?"

He nodded. "My parents are terrified we'll all be mowed down. They've ordered me to stay inside."

I looked at my classmate. Stay inside? I thought about Bunu, about his comment that an unexamined life wasn't worth living, his reminders that sometimes to go inside, we needed to go outside.

I left school and walked home in the dark. A tall figure fell into step beside me.

Luca.

"Did you hear the reports last night?" he whispered.

"Yes! You?"

"Yeah. Couldn't sleep. Can't stop thinking of the people in Timișoara."

Finally. Someone who understood. And of course, it was Luca. Luca with his eager heart. With everything that was happening, it was impossible to stay mad at him.

"I looked on the map," I told him.

"Me too. Over five hundred kilometers to Timișoara."

"Finally, Romanians have taken a stand."

"And not just Romanians," said Luca. "The report said that local Hungarians and Serbs took part. Real solidarity. We have to support them."

I threw a glance over my shoulder. "In school, no one mentioned it."

"Of course not," said Luca. "They're terrified. Can you blame them? What do you think your *bunu* would say?"

"I wish he was here to help."

"If he was, what would he tell us?"

I thought for a moment, trying to think like my philosophical grandfather. "He'd say . . . this is bigger than the 'I' or the 'me.' This must be 'we.'"

"Exactly!" said Luca, his feet slowing. "Wait, the university students are probably mobilizing."

Of course. Why hadn't I thought of that? "I bet you're right."

"I'll ask around," said Luca. "You too."

I nodded.

We arrived on our street. Luca paused before heading to his building. "If you have an update, call my house and let it ring once. That'll be our signal. I'll meet you in the street," he said.

"Okay. You do the same."

Luca nodded, and we went our separate ways. And then I heard his voice.

"Hey, Cristian," he called.

I looked across the street. Luca smiled at me. He raised his hand and flashed a signal.

The peace sign.

Before I could signal back, Starfish appeared, our block dogs beside him. "The English papers I mentioned. I'll have them tomorrow."

"Okay. You have any updates?"

"Waiting for tonight's radio reports like everyone else," he said. "I heard they blocked the borders. But things must be quieting down. They say Ceaușescu left for meetings in Iran."

If Ceaușescu left for Iran, did that mean he didn't take the protests seriously? What had happened to the people in Timișoara?

"Find me tomorrow for the papers. Bring your money," said Starfish.

That night, all of Romania sat by their radios. Was Mr. Van Dorn listening? Had he found my notebook?

My father stood with his hand on the radio, as if to protect it.

"Gabriel, step away. What if the regime sends an electric shock of some sort?"

"You think they'll blow up the radio?" I said.

"Well, the transmitter for Radio Free Europe must be powerful if it can broadcast all the way from Munich," whispered Mama.

The transmitter was powerful. Over a thousand kilowatts. I

thought of Bunu, trading the Kents to repair our radio. It was our main source of information, but only if the electricity was on. When would it snap off?

At 10:00 p.m. the announcer's voice appeared through the static. I jumped from the couch.

<<Tensions escalated yesterday in Timişoara. It's been reported that thousands have been killed. The recording you're about to hear was smuggled out of Romania by a German tourist and delivered to us at Radio Free Europe.>>

I stepped closer to the radio. Audible static—and then the sounds came through.

Chaos. Screaming. Crowd noise.

A woman's pleading voice. "Stop! Shame on you, they're Romanians, just like you!"

A man's voice, "Shoot, you bastards. Shoot!"

A breath of silence.

A wave of gunfire.

Children screaming.

"They're shooting them," I gasped.

"The sound could be misleading," said Cici. "Please, let's hope it's wrong."

"I don't care if it's three people or three thousand. Our country is murdering its citizens!" I exclaimed. "We can't just stand here and do nothing!"

"You're right."

The voice, it startled me.

"You're right," repeated my father. "They've blocked the borders. They're trapping us." He quickly began gathering things in the kitchen. Knives, broom and mop handles.

"Gabriel, what are on earth are you doing?" asked Mama.

"Preparing," said my father. "When it's time, we have to be ready."

"For what?" asked Cici.

"To fight," he replied.

58

CINCIZECI ŞI OPT

The next morning I sat alone in our apartment, alone with my thoughts.

Would the protests continue? Had Mr. Van Dorn read my notebook? Was Dan back in America? What time did the Secu generally come to our apartment?

The phone rang. One ring. The code from Luca.

I ran downstairs to meet him. Oddly, the weather had warmed. Nature was joining our crusade, inviting Romanians to take to the street.

I passed the Reporters, dutifully stationed on their balconied perches.

"University dorms are under surveillance," Luca whispered.

"Where'd you hear that?"

"Overheard it in the stairwell. The Reporters heard rumors that Beloved Leader will give a TV address tonight."

"Luca, he's not beloved."

"Sorry, habit."

Luca's eyes drifted over my shoulder. I turned to look.

Liliana stood on the sidewalk, staring at us.

"Hey, there's Starfish," said Luca, pointing in the opposite direction. "See if he knows anything. I'll be around. Call me and use the signal if you hear something."

I nodded, half listening. My eyes were on Liliana, following her as she walked alone down the sidewalk, away from our buildings. Where was she going?

The dogs, Turbatu and Fetița, clipped behind Starfish. "Got the papers I mentioned. You got the money? I'm only taking Western currency," he said.

"How many papers and what are they? How do I know they're worth it?"

"Oh, they're worth it. Two sheets of paper, covered in coffee but still legible," said Starfish. "Lots of big English words."

"And why would you sell them to me?"

He shrugged. "Don't have to."

It felt like a trap. "Fine, then don't," I said. Another English word I had learned that described Starfish: hustler.

Starfish nodded slowly, staring at me. "Your *bunu*. He was rare, one of the few good ones. He was my friend. He'd want these papers, so I figured you would too."

Starfish was friends with Bunu? I looked at him, skeptical.

"You don't believe me? Your *bunu* told me that I was special. That with one eye I had a unique view of the world. He gave me a book of poetry by some guy named Homer. Said the guy was blind and if he could write beautiful things with no eyes, imagine what I could do."

That definitely sounded like Bunu. "Did you read the book?"

"Nah, I sold it," said Starfish. "You want the papers or not?"

"Yes, I want them. You hear anything new this morning?"

"Yeah. A new American ambassador arrived recently. Lots of activity at the U.S. Embassy. Bring the money down. I'll be around for another fifteen minutes."

A new American ambassador. Dan had told me.

And I had told Paddle Hands.

I nodded to Starfish and started for my building.

Our apartment was empty. I needed the dollar from Cici's locked box. I also wanted the pocketknife she kept hidden for me. I retrieved the box from beneath her bed. Could I pick the lock? And then I remembered—the ring of keys in her sewing basket. She wouldn't mind.

It was easy to determine which key fit the lock. It was smaller than the rest. I opened the box and found my dollar beneath the white tubes she called "tampons." I also grabbed my small pocketknife. What else did she have? I quickly poked through.

A small bottle of perfume, a wrapped square called "Trojan," rose-scented soap, a thick envelope, two packs of Kents, and—lightning bolt earrings. Wait, those belonged to the woman from Boston. Why did Cici have her earrings?

And then I saw them.

My fingers went cold.

Loop rings made from the package of BT cigarettes.

The loop rings that Agent Paddle Hands constantly fiddled with during our meetings.

A wave of nausea rolled through me.

No.

I opened the thick envelope. Inside was foreign currency. *A lot* of foreign currency.

American dollars. British pounds. German marks. And something else—

My Bruce Springsteen article.

The one I'd kept hidden in my closet. The one that disappeared. The one that Paddle Hands mentioned.

My hands trembled.

No. How was this possible? The walls slowly began to fold in on me.

Cici.

My beloved sister.

My devoted friend.

She was working with the Securitate.

59

CINCIZECI ŞI NOUĂ

I carefully returned everything to the box as I had found it, including my dollar. But I kept the knife and pinched some other bills from the thick envelope. I slid the locked box back under the sofa and returned the keys to her sewing basket.

I left the apartment.

My hands shook. I felt frozen straight through.

And then I heard their voices. Below me. Cici was talking to the woman from Boston. I stopped on the third-floor landing, listening.

"*Mersi*. You've been such a help, Cici. I don't know how I would have done this without you," said the woman.

She's not helping you. She's betraying you. She's betraying everyone.

My head was spinning.

I exited the building, giving a wave to Starfish. He nodded for me to follow him.

We walked, saying nothing. He handed me his pack of cigarettes. Against the pack was a thick square of folded paper. I slid the money inside the cigarette pack and handed it back to him. I kept the square of paper in my closed palm and transferred it casually to my pocket.

"How's your pretty sister?" he asked.

Starfish knew most everything and everyone.

I raised my eyebrows and gave him my best knowing look. "C'mon, Starfish, is she pretty, or pretty sneaky?"

"Both!" He laughed and disappeared between two buildings.

I walked down the rutted sidewalk and joined a line outside the *Alimentara*, killing time, pretending to wait for a stump of bread, so I could think. My mind was full of maybes.

Maybe Cici was blackmailed into being an informer, like me.

The thick envelope of foreign currency—maybe Cici was an agent?

Or maybe Cici was dating Paddle Hands?

Every option disgusted me. Cici told me I couldn't trust Luca. She told me I couldn't trust Starfish. Her cautious nature, always suspicious—was that an act? I thought of my conversation with Bunu on the balcony.

Agents. Informers. Rats. This country is full of them. We're infested. And they keep multiplying. They're in our streets, in our schools, crawling in the workplace, and now they've chewed through the walls . . . into our apartment.

I had thought Bunu was referring to me. Was he actually talking about Cici? Did Bunu know? Cici took the article from my closet. Had she discovered my hiding spot and my notebook? The questions pushed at me:

Did Cici really work at a textile factory?

Did she care about our family?

Did she care about our country?

I felt sick. I felt scared. I felt lost.

I left the line and started walking. If I kept going, could I eventually make it to Timișoara?

60

ŞAIZECI

I arrived. Not in Timişoara. At Luca's. I knocked on the door.

Luca took one look and pulled me in. "You okay?" he asked.

I shrugged.

"My parents are at work. It's just me and my sisters," he said.

Luca had four younger sisters. "Hello, Cristian!" They shrieked and giggled when I walked in.

"Your hair," laughed Dana, the oldest. "Do you use a comb?"

"Nah, I use a hatchet," I told her.

"Are you shy? My sister says you're shy," chimed another.

"She didn't say he's shy—she said he's cute!" said the youngest. The girls erupted with swats and laughter.

"Is it worth the stupid medal?" whispered Luca.

With five kids, Luca's mom had received a maternity medal from the State. But five wasn't enough. Ceauşescu wanted women to birth ten kids. If they did, they received the title of Heroine Mother.

"Want to head outside?" he asked.

I shook my head. I motioned as if I was writing.

He nodded. "We'll be doing homework," said Luca to the girls.

"Liar," sneered Dana. "It's winter break."

The electricity was on. Luca's family didn't have a sofa in their kitchen. They had three narrow wooden chairs and a small table with a red-and-black embroidered tablecloth. Luca pulled a pad and pen from a drawer. He set it down in front of me at the table. He turned on the radio, and then the faucet. Noise decoys.

We sat, saying nothing, me staring at the pad of paper. Could I do this? Should I do this?

I picked up the pen, hesitating. Then I began to write.

First, everything I thought I knew—it's all a lie.

Secu came to school. They knew about the dollar in my stamp album.

You were the only one I had told. I was mad. I thought you informed on me.

I pushed the pad toward him.

He read my writing, eyes expanding. He shook his head.

"No," he whispered.

"I know that now," I told him. I grabbed the pad and took a breath. I wrote the word.

Cici.

"No way," said Luca. He grabbed the pad. I watched him write.

You're paranoid. Everything that's happening, it's making us all crazy.

"Bunu knew. He tried to tell me," I whispered.

Luca sat back in his chair, eyebrows raised.

I nodded.

My friend shook his head slowly. "There's gotta be an explanation."

Luca. Kind, patient Luca. I wrote the words and passed the pad to him.

I'm sorry.

He stared at the pad. He gave me a small nod and took the pen.

I knew something was wrong.

Liliana's brother. Could it be Alex, not Cici? I've seen them together.

I shook my head. I didn't think so.

We sat, serenaded by State propaganda warbling from the radio.

How can I help? wrote Luca.

I took the pad. *Maybe forgive me for being an ass.*

"You're always an ass." He pulled the pad toward him.

The suffering here—it's beyond physical. It's mental stuff. They're messing with you. They do it to a lot of people.

I shrugged.

Luca tore the page from the pad. He turned on the gas burner, lit the paper, and tossed it into an empty pot on the stove. "Stand up," said Luca. "I can't punch a guy who's sitting down."

He was going to punch me? I couldn't blame him. I stood up. He raised his fists then quickly wrenched his arm around my neck and rubbed his knuckles through my hair. We laughed and wrestled around the kitchen, like we did when we were young.

I had told Luca that I thought he was an informer.

I had told Luca that I thought Cici was an informer.

But I hadn't told Luca that I *was* an informer.

But the way he said it: *They're messing with you. They do it to a lot of people.* I somehow thought he knew.

I left Luca's apartment and trudged down the stairs. When I got to the front door of the building, someone opened it.

Liliana.

We stopped and stood, staring at each other. And suddenly this crazy feeling emerged, like birds were flapping around in my chest.

"*Bună*," she said.

"*Bună.*" I nodded.

We lingered, suspended in silence. She casually brushed her bangs from her eyes and I saw the outline of something drawn on her hand.

"You were wondering something," she said.

"Oh, was I?" The birds in my chest, they flapped faster. She was so pretty.

"Yeah. I'm a Pisces."

How did she know I had wondered?

She smiled.

And then we went our separate ways.

61

ŞAIZECE ŞI UNU

I sat in my dark closet, avoiding family. Could there be an explanation, like Luca said?

    Cici sewed for people. Maybe they paid her in foreign currency. Maybe she took the Springsteen article to keep me safe. Maybe she made the loop rings from the cigarette packages herself.

Maybe?

I snapped on the flashlight to read the English pages I had bought from Starfish. They were crumpled, clearly retrieved from a trash bin. And they weren't original. They were multigeneration, poor copies, stapled together.

The words at the top said:

Romania,
Human Rights Violations in the Eighties

First published July 1987,
Amnesty International Publications, London

Amnesty International's Concerns
*This report documents the persistent pattern of human
rights abuse in Romania in the 1980s, a period in which the
authorities have imprisoned their critics and jailed hundreds*

of other men and women for wanting to exercise their rights to leave the country. Some prisoners of conscience have been tortured, beaten, and jailed for years after unfair trials. Other critics of the government have been put under house arrest, have lost their jobs, or have been attacked in the street by security thugs.

"Prisoner of conscience." I made a mental note to research that term.

Torture and Ill Treatment
. . . It has been reported that political prisoners have been tortured by being beaten on the soles of the feet or being kicked and beaten with rubber truncheons. Two prisoners are reported to have died after torture.

Bunu. That's exactly what happened to Bunu. The descriptions were detailed, listing several names of specific victims. The papers were so lethal, they nearly burned my hands.

"*Pui?*" Cici's voice appeared at my door. I jumped, clutching the papers. "*Pui* . . . Ceaușescu's going to be on TV."

I couldn't leave my closet. Cici would take one look at me and know I was hiding something. I needed more information first.

"I'm tired. And sick of it," I told her. "He'll just say the same old thing."

I was right. Partially. I put my ear to the door and heard our leader's ranting voice. According to Ceaușescu, hooligans and foreign agents were creating turmoil and unrest.

Was I a hooligan?

Maybe.

Was there unrest?

Definitely.

The papers from Starfish were dangerous. So dangerous that I couldn't leave them in my closet. I had to carry them with me at all times.

So I stuffed them into my jacket pocket and finished devising my plan.

I was going to confront Cici.

At the time it seemed straightforward. She was either working with Paddle Hands or she wasn't. I hadn't yet absorbed one of life's universal truths:

Things that seem straightforward?

Often aren't.

62

ȘAIZECE ȘI DOI

5:00 a.m.

Layers.

Two pair of socks. Three shirts. Hat. Gloves. Jacket. Ration card.

I left the apartment as if to stand in line but hid across the street. And then I waited.

Cici left the apartment wrapped in a yellow scarf. I followed at a distance.

The textile factory she worked at was supposedly across town and that's why she had to leave so early. After a fifteen-minute walk, she turned down a street. I rushed to keep up.

When I got to the street, she was gone.

I looked up at the buildings. It wasn't a commercial district, it was a residential district. And then I saw the pop of her yellow scarf. Behind the window—

Of a black Dacia.

Each step I took toward the car felt like a kilometer.

Should I do this?

Yes, I had to know.

I approached the passenger-side door. A package of BT cigarettes sat on the dash, next to my sister's elevated foot.

Through the window, I saw the shape of two figures amidst a

swirl of hostaged cigarette smoke. I pressed my face against the glass.

Cici jumped. So did the driver. It was quick, but I saw.

The thinning hair, one eyebrow, his huge mitts foraging my sister's lap.

Paddle Hands.

I pointed my finger at the glass. I slowly shook my head.

And then I ran.

Her voice rang out behind me. "*Pui*, wait. Wait!" The Dacia's engine roared to life. I continued to run, cutting and dodging quickly across the sidewalks. My lungs burned, my pulse raged.

My state-made sneakers were ragged, with barely any tread. I slipped, almost fell, and lost time. Those who were out early looked at me. There's a difference between someone who's running, and someone who's running *from* something. I looked more than suspicious.

The black Dacia sped to my side, squeezing closer and closer, trapping me.

My sister jumped out of the car, and Paddle Hands drove off.

Cici's face burned plum. Her lipstick was smeared. "*Pui*, let me explain."

"There's nothing to explain. You became an informer, a traitor, for perfume and tampons."

"No, you don't understand. They were poisoning Bunu. They were serving him irradiated coffee! I had to help him. They promised me medicine and a passport if I would cooperate."

"Cooperate how?"

"They were badgering Mama for information on the Americans, but she wouldn't give them anything. They came to me, said if I seduced Van Dorn, they would treat Bunu. But Van Dorn wouldn't have me. He immediately knew what I was up to. The Secu pressured me. They suggested you might have better luck getting information from the son."

I stood on the sidewalk, staring at my sister.

"So you framed me. You put the American dollar in my stamp album so they could blackmail me."

"No, I mean, not exactly. You didn't let me finish. I felt so guilty, *Pui*. The day you came home and I was crying, it wasn't because of an exam at the factory; it was because I knew that the Secu had gotten to you. Bunu was so sick. I knew how much he meant to you, and I—"

"Bunu's DEAD! He's gone, but we're still enslaved to the Secu. And you know what? Bunu knew exactly what you were doing."

Cici took a step back.

"Yes, Bunu tried to tell me. He knew, Cici, and you know what he said? That it was so painful. That we had a rat in our very own apartment. You got us into this and now Bunu's dead anyway. Did your agent boyfriend kill him? Or was it the agent who lives in our building? Are you seeing him too?"

And then the realization hit me.

"You asked Alex out. You informed on his family, told them that his father brings bones home from work. It was you. Everything, it's all been you. You killed Bunu. You killed my relationship with Liliana."

"No. Please," she whispered.

"You've killed all my plans. You've killed—me."

I turned.

And left her on the sidewalk.

|| OFFICIAL REPORT ||

Ministry of the Interior

Department of State Security

Directorate III, Service 330

Meeting with source FRITZI was compromised this morning
by the appearance of her brother, OSCAR. As previously
reported, OSCAR is now a liability and must be dealt with.
Circulate name and photo immediately.

63

ŞAIZECE ŞI TREI

I made excuses and stayed at Luca's. Anything to avoid Cici.

During the day, I walked around the city, trying to calm myself. The snow was melting in the warmer temperatures and now resembled lumps of sooty porridge along the roadside. I passed hobbling old people with knees full of rheumatism and faces corroded by fear, people who should have been resting, not prowling for rations. I joined a line for potatoes and got an onion the size of an olive instead.

Betrayal. It's undigestible. It instantly changes the frequency of things. Every Romanian carried a world inside them, and mine had quickly gone from dark to black.

I took the long route home. Young people loitered, filling the pavement in front of the apartment blocks. Luca's head towered over a group that had gathered. He spotted me and ran my way.

"Where have you been? I've been looking for you," he whispered.

"Why?"

"Ceauşescu's back from Iran. He's going to speak in the square. A group of university students will be there. C'mon, let's go."

By the time we arrived at Palace Square, a sea of thousands had gathered. The *Aplaudacii* were stacked rows deep below the balcony of the Central Committee Building where our leader would appear. Some hoisted red signs declaring LONG LIVE CEAUŞESCU and other phrases extolling the glory of communism. The warmer weather had inspired a massive crowd.

"Forget it," I told Luca. "It's just another rally of applauding men."

Communist adulation rallies were commonplace in Romania. Over the years, we had all been dragged from school or work to hold signs and salute the leader. On our own, we weren't allowed to gather in a group of five, but Ceaușescu could demand fifty thousand gather for him.

The mayor of Bucharest began his introduction over the sound system.

"Our much beloved and esteemed leader of the Party, the eminent patriot . . . has given us prosperity and provided full independence of socialist Romania . . ."

Eminent patriot? After Timișoara? Our leader had gunned down innocent human beings—students my age. Prosperity and independence? I couldn't stomach it.

Ceaușescu and Mother Elena appeared on the balcony to rounds of applause. Ceaușescu stepped to the microphone, waving, wearing an expensive black coat with a fur collar and matching hat. He began speaking his usual nonsense.

"I'm not staying for this," I told Luca. I turned to leave.

BOOM!

A blast thundered nearby. Screams shot through the crowd. What was happening? Had someone set off an explosive? Luca looked at me, eyes wide.

A mass of people pressed in behind us. The new crowd suddenly began swaying, yelling.

"Boo!"

"Murderer!"

"Down with Ceaușescu!"

My heart began to pound. Everyone knew that plainclothes

Securitate were always among us. But people continued to jeer anyway.

Groups of university students appeared, booing and shouting. They carried flags.

"Murderer!"

"Down with Ceaușescu!"

Others joined in. They were heckling the leader of our country. Ceaușescu stopped speaking, confused, and looked out into the crowd. He stuttered into the microphone.

"Hallo! Calm! What? Hallo!"

Mother Elena pushed toward the microphone. "Silence!" she screeched.

And then the chanting began near the back of the swarm, quiet at first, then louder, pulsing:

Ti-mi-șoa-ra.

Timișoara!

TIMIȘOARA!

Chills erupted over my entire body. The volume grew, a freight train of sound. A feeling of solidarity rose, growing within the crowd. Romania had found its voice. And we were using it, together. And our despicable leader was rattled, shaken, trying to calm the people, trying to remain in command. In a quarter of a century, this had never happened in Bucharest. The feeling was palpable, a breaking and cracking, the dam of oppression bursting.

Emotion leapt within me. My hands began to vibrate. For Bunu.

"Timișoara!" I yelled.

I couldn't stop. The screams came from deep within me, tearing at my vocal cords. "You're thieves and murderers! Betrayers! TIMIȘOARA!"

"Down with Ceaușescu!" yelled Luca.

The university students encouraged others to join in. The response was spontaneous, full-throated. Thousands of people were protesting!

Ceaușescu attempted to regain control. He couldn't. Random noise echoed from the sound system. He was rattled, confused. And the crowd—we felt it.

The sensation of speaking up, speaking aloud instead of in whispers, it was euphoric. And you could sense that others felt it too. Ceaușescu blabbered something about raising wages but the jeering continued.

"Empty promises! We want food. We want freedom!" I yelled.

Ceaușescu left the balcony and scurried into the Party building. But the crowd didn't disperse. We looked to one another and made eye contact.

We *saw* one other.

It was December 21st.

Romanians in Bucharest were united and ready.

For revolution.

64

ŞAIZECE ŞI PATRU

The crowd lingered. People stood, shocked, waiting.

Luca's mouth hung open and he began to laugh, nervously swatting my shoulder.

A woman in a babushka shuffled up to us. "Go home, boys. Now!" she said. "It was probably televised. There were cameras. There will be consequences. Be quick. Go home and hide, they'll kill all of you."

"We're not cowards!" I told the woman.

"We're already dead!" replied a university student in a green cap. "Their system has killed us."

"We have to fight for the future!" said a man.

"We have to fight for Romania!" I yelled.

The crowd cheered. The terrified old woman tottered away.

A university student stood on a lamppost, holding a flag. "Remember, this is peaceful. We're asking for food and electricity. We're asking for freedom of opinion, freedom of religion. For those of you who are undecided—please, join us! Workers, come join us! Students, come join us! The world is watching Eastern Europe. Show them that Romanians aren't cowards. Together we'll stand up against tyranny. We're going to march for freedom. Join us!"

An elderly man took off his hat and clutched it in his hands. With quivering voice, he began to sing.

Deşteaptă-te, române, din somnul cel de moarte.

Awaken thee, Romanian—wake up from your deadly sleep.

The old song of patriotism. It had been outlawed when the communists destroyed the monarchy. Those who knew the words joined him.

Better to die in battle, in full glory

Than to once again be slaves upon our ancient ground.

The student in the green cap turned to me. "I'm Adrian," he said. "What's your name?"

"I'm Cristian; this is Luca."

"How old are you guys?"

"Seventeen." I removed the knife from my pocket. "Hey, give me that flag."

I grabbed the flag and cut the communist coat of arms from the center, leaving a hole amidst the vertical stripes of blue, yellow, and red. I held it up to the crowd.

Without the emblem in the center, the flag resembled our national flag of the 1800s:

Blue for liberty.

Yellow for justice.

Red for blood.

"Cristian and Luca, you carry the flag," said Adrian. He gently steered the elderly gentleman in front of us. "And you, sir, will lead us for as long as you feel able."

We walked together, chanting and singing. The crowds grew as we marched.

As people left work for the day, I encouraged them to join the swell of protestors. Our column expanded and became one massive surge of thousands of people. Demonstrators brought flags with holes, they carried signs. Our voices were ragged from shouting and singing, hoarse with happiness.

My body had felt uninhabitable for so long. But now the emptiness was replaced by a closeness. A true camaraderie. We all felt it. We saw it in one another's eyes. It was freedom—and it was glorious.

We continued for hours.

Darkness fell. The crowds increased. Information circulated.

TV and radio stations over the border in Hungary—they're reporting the protest.

Ceauşescu deployed the army. They're setting up stations.

Plainclothes agents, they're everywhere. Be careful!

A group of wet demonstrators ran by us.

"Stay alert," shouted Adrian. "They're hosing people!"

We arrived at University Square.

"Oh my god," said Luca.

People—as far as the eye could see. Thousands and thousands of people—pregnant women, adults with children on their shoulders, countless students. The sound of the crowd roared.

Olé, olé, olé, olé, Ceauşescu nu mai e!

My heart beat in rhythm to the chants.

Li-ber-ta-te, Li-ber-ta-te!

Ceauşescu no more. Liberty!

Near the Intercontinental Hotel, I helped demonstrators build a barricade using a tumble of chairs and tables. Kids ran near our blockade, using their fingers as guns, crouching in poses like the renegades they saw in American movies. I tried to shoo them away.

"Adrian," shouted Luca. "Should we tell people to take kids home? It's probably not safe for little ones."

"It's fine. They won't shoot kids. It's important for all ages to demonstrate. The world must see that everyone wants change."

Luca looked at me. Our thoughts were in sync.

Adrian said they wouldn't shoot kids.

After what happened in Timişoara, how could he say that?

They could shoot any of us. Or worse.

All of us.

65

ŞAIZECE ŞI CINCI

Soldiers, tanks, armored vehicles. Army and militia units moved in.

A young man ran toward us. "Ceauşescu's called in more military. Securitate and snipers, they're in tunnels under the city. They're coming. Soon!"

"It's just to scare us," said Adrian.

Luca tried to negotiate with a young soldier. "Hey, put down your weapon. You're Romanian. Your obligation is to defend our nation and its citizens."

"He's right," I said. "You're in service to the country, not the criminals. No one wants violence."

"Do you have a cigarette?" asked the young soldier. "I smoke when I'm nervous."

Adrian lit a cigarette and gave it to the soldier. "C'mon, put the gun down. You're Romanian, man, just like me."

The soldier's eyes flitted briefly beneath his helmet. "You guys should leave. Hurry."

"Leave? We're not leaving. This is our country! Are you Romanian? Are you with us?" I yelled in his face.

Luca pulled me away.

The armored vehicles rolled closer. Some protesters fled. Others scattered and hid.

"Follow me!" yelled Adrian. We ran behind him, closer to the hotel. As we stepped onto the sidewalk, a stutter of tracer fire blazed above our heads.

"Watch out! They're marking our position."

We ducked behind a car. A little boy crouched by the tire, eyes pinched closed, hands over his ears. An ungodly pitch of screaming shrieked through the streets.

"We need to get to the barricade," yelled Adrian. "Strength in numbers."

"Wait, stay down," I shouted. "Get the kid under the car."

"PAPA!!!" screamed the boy.

Red lines of tracer fire flew through the square. I looked above. If snipers were positioned in windows, it didn't matter where we were. They had an open shot. And then I heard my name.

"Florescu!"

As I turned toward the sidewalk, Adrian took off running for the barricade. A bullet pierced his chest. He took a step, tripped, and crumpled face-first onto the pavement.

"That's Florescu!" Hands seized me from behind.

Luca jumped up to protect me, and the world dropped into slow motion.

"Criiiistian!" yelled Luca.

A bullet tore through Luca's right shoulder, another ripped through his arm. Blood burst like fireworks in front of me. Multiple rounds flew nearby. I felt my heartbeat in my ears. Luca swayed, staggered, and buckled to the ground.

"LUCA!"

I fought, kicking, trying to escape the hands. A thud to my head. My vision blurred, warping the view of my best friend lying in a pool of blood on the street.

"Luca," I whispered.

And then the world went black.

66

ŞAIZECE ŞI ŞASE

C'mon, wake up. You gotta wake up."

Someone was slapping me.

I blinked, trying to make out the scene. Over a dozen people, crammed together in a moving vehicle.

"You've had a nasty blow to the head. You passed out, but you gotta wake up," said a man.

"Where are we?"

"In a police van. They're taking us to Station 14."

I slowly sat up and looked around. There were adults in the van and also children.

"Luca," I whispered. My head was so heavy.

"They dragged him away," said a small voice. Peering through the darkness was the little boy who had been crouching near the tire.

"Who dragged him away?" I asked.

"I don't know," said the boy. "That's when they took me. They got my dad and sister too." He pointed to shadowed figures in the vehicle.

The van jerked to a halt. The back door flew open.

"Get out!"

They herded us from the van toward what looked like a garage. I stumbled, my head pounding.

"Put your hands up!"

We put our hands on the building and they began to search us. *Let them*, I thought. And then I remembered. The papers from Amnesty International. They were in my coat pocket.

And they were a death sentence.

Was it the left pocket, or the right pocket? My *head*, I couldn't remember which pocket I had put them in. I had to check. Had to shove the papers down my pants.

There was a tart, oily smell and moisture beneath my fingers. I squinted: wet green paint.

Our hands in paint, they were marking us. If I touched my jacket or my pants, they'd notice. And then I heard it.

Screaming.

Torturous screaming from inside the garage. Male voices. Female voices. Screaming and begging for mercy. They made us wait, listening, anticipating our turn. The children began to cry. I closed my eyes and thought of Luca.

Hang on, Luca. Please.

When the guard got to me, he didn't search me, he merely frisked me. I was both relieved and terrified. The papers were still on me.

After several minutes, the sound of screaming dissipated. Guards lined us up and marched us inside. Yellow, caged lights buzzed and sizzled, illuminating the square space. Green handprints of all sizes lined the walls. Water dripped from a pipe in the center of the room, plunking into a pool of blood. A patch of hair, still attached to a piece of scalp, lay discarded.

A guard tossed water from a bucket, rinsing torture from the cement.

"Next round. Face the wall!" barked the guard. "Hands up!"

"Please," a man pleaded. "Leave my children. Take me, but let my children go."

They grabbed him and pulled him to the center of the room. While they beat the man, they slashed at our backs with canes.

"Why didn't you leave your children at home?" they yelled. "You brought them to an illegal demonstration. You will pay for that."

"Papa, no!" cried a girl.

They took us in turns, dragging each person to the center of the garage, kicking, punching, and clubbing each one of us. When it was finally his turn to step forward, the little boy fainted and slid down the wall.

To gather courage, I focused on Luca. *Hold on, Luca.*

Yes. I would think of what they did to Luca. What they did to Bunu. Resolve rose within me. Three men dragged me to the center of the room and pushed me down on the concrete. Each time I tried to stand, they slammed me down. I tried nonetheless.

"He's the one," commented a guard from the corner of the room.

The torturer circled me, thumping a rubber club against his thigh.

"He's one of the special ones, huh? And young. Good evening, traitor."

The first blow was to the top of my spine, between my shoulder blades.

Bunu.

Then they sat me up and clubbed my ribs.

Luca.

They took turns punching my face.

Romania.

Then they kicked me below the waist. I lost breath and all track of what was happening.

My cheek pressed against the cold, wet concrete. The room distorted. A garbled voice appeared at my ear. "We've been told you're on a special list, so we have something special for you."

My eyes fluttered. I heard the ring and clank of a metal chain. A growling. Feral.

"He's very hungry. And very devoted to Beloved Leader."

The other prisoners gasped. A child whimpered.

They corralled the other captives and pushed them out of the room and into a hallway.

I lay, splashed on the floor. Blood, wet and metallic-tasting, leaked from my mouth. I blinked. Two bloody teeth came into focus on the ground. Were they mine?

The dog pulled, bucking against the chain, ready to attack. Would he eat my face first? My groin? The guards made a semicircle and lit cigarettes to watch the show.

I looked to the dog. Once a sweet face, now twisted into madness. He was a prisoner too—denied food, shelter, and security. Beaten and driven to a state of desperation and savagery. I felt a tear slide from the corner of my eye and stream down my cheek. The dog watched me and calmed.

They let go of the chain and the animal leapt toward me. He stopped. His face cocked, evaluating. One of the officers kicked him, prodding him on. The dog stiffened, turned from me, and lunged at his attacker. While the guards scrambled to protect themselves, I dragged myself up off the floor. I wouldn't give them the satisfaction of knowing they'd hurt me. No.

Better to die in battle, in full glory

I limped to join the others in the hallway.

We stood, lining both sides of the corridor. They tied our hands in front of us. Some with wire, others with rope.

"You will all make official statements!" yelled a guard.

They slapped us, over and over, prodding us to confess guilt. No one did. Not even the children.

"I am living history. I am freedom," said a man. "That is my statement."

"You've taken everything. I have nothing to lose," whispered a woman.

They made their way to me, demanding confession.

I licked the wash of blood from my lips and nodded. My voice was hoarse with revolution, but I was ready. I would turn the tables. "He smokes BT cigarettes. Likes Steaua. Has hands the size of tennis rackets. He meets a pretty girl on the side of the road in the early mornings," I said. "He has big plans. He's the one you want."

The guard's brow narrowed with confusion, but he wrote down my words. They believed I was confessing. They looked at my identity card.

"Wait, I thought you said that this one . . . He's only seventeen," said the guard.

The torturer shrugged.

They began herding us outside, toward a line of waiting vans.

"Where are you taking us?" said a man.

"Where do you think?" sneered the guard. "To Jilava."

Jilava.

No.

Jilava was where they sent maximum-security prisoners. Prisoners serving over ten years. Prisoners who would be tortured. They were sending teenagers and children to Jilava?

The vans were packed with injured captives. Some were crying.

No, I would not get in the van.

I stood at the back of the line, planning to escape at the last minute. I would kick the guard in the crotch. I'd try something, anything. I approached the open back of the vehicle. Smoky heat from the exhaust pipe swirled around my ankles. I needed to stay. I needed to fight. I needed to find Luca. I was not getting in the van. I was not going to Jilava.

"Hey, you," whispered a man in the van. I looked to him.

He motioned with his head to a person sitting near him. "Someone's trying to get your attention."

I peered through the darkness. Beneath the interior light of the van I saw a familiar face, streaked with blood and tears. She raised her roped wrists and gestured with a green palm.

I jumped in the van.

67

ŞAIZECE ŞI ŞAPTE

The doors of the police van slammed and the vehicle began moving. A man lit a cigarette lighter to inspect his children's wounds. The light filtered briefly across her face.

Liliana.

I jostled over huddled bodies and wedged in next to her.

"Are you okay?" I whispered.

"Cristian, your face. The blood."

Exclamations of blood covered my shirt and coat. I couldn't draw a full breath. A rib was probably broken. My nose felt out of place.

I reached up with my tied hands and pulled at my nose. I felt a grinding beneath my fingers and heard a loud crunchy sound. I wrenched my nose back into place and an explosion of pain rocketed across my cheeks, down the back of my throat, and into my stomach. Blood gushed over my mouth and chin, but I could breathe easier. A man handed me a flask. I took a swig and cleaned my nose and mouth.

Liliana began to cry.

I set my wire-bound hands on hers, trying to hold her fingers. "I'm okay," I assured her. "Are you okay?"

"They beat us with canes, kicked us, punched us," she said through tears. "A man was on a special list . . . They scalped him."

I knew about the special list. "How long have you been here?" I asked.

"I'm not sure, over an hour," she whispered. "They grabbed me in University Square."

"Me too."

"Were you with Luca?" she asked.

I nodded and without warning, my face distorted with tears. "Luca," I whispered. "They shot him."

"What?!"

"At least twice," I croaked. "I saw him fall to the ground and then everything went black. I couldn't save him. I don't know where he is." I raised my hands to wipe away the tears.

"Oh my god." Liliana leaned against me and whispered into my ear. "We'll find him, Cristian. We will."

"We have to."

She nodded. Her forehead touched the side of my face. I pressed against her, ignoring the pounding in my head. We stayed that way for a long time, faces together. Silent.

"Are you kissing?" asked the little boy.

"No," said Liliana, sniffing back tears. "I'm telling him a secret."

"A secret? The regime is beating, shooting, and killing kids," said a man with a thick mustache. "That can't remain a secret. All of us, we had empty hands and empty bellies. They turned a peaceful protest into a bloodbath. And these torturers at the fourteenth precinct, they're inhuman!"

"Shh . . . they'll beat us again," someone whispered.

"Yes, they'll beat us again. Didn't you hear?" replied the man with the mustache. "They're taking us to Jilava. This is just the beginning."

"What about the other demonstrators?" I asked.

"They'll continue protesting," he said. "The demonstrations are beyond Bucharest now. They're happening in Arad, Satu Mare, Sibiu, Cluj, Iași, and other cities. But we need to turn the army. There are rumors that the Romanian military might side with the people."

I thought of the young soldier who warned Luca and me to leave. He was trying to help us. "How can we turn the military?" I asked.

"We can't. The generals have to make that decision for themselves."

We sat in the dark van, exhausted and frightened. Would the military turn on the regime?

Liliana's voice pierced the darkness. "I'm Liliana Pavel and this is Cristian Florescu. We're seventeen years old, students at MF3 High School, and live in Salajan sector three. I don't know what will happen when we arrive at Jilava. If any of you are set free, will you please contact our families? Liliana Pavel and Cristian Florescu. Tell our families you saw us together and tell them . . . we were alive."

68

ŞAIZECE ŞI OPT

Jilava.

A sprawling monster the color of dry bones that lived south of Bucharest.

Brick archways. Thick metal gates. Grisly history.

I had said nothing in the van, but I was worried. Bunu had told me of Jilava.

"It's the worst of the worst, reserved for political prisoners and people incarcerated for their faith. The inmates are tortured, mutilated, burned, and locked in frozen boxes."

We were considered political prisoners. And we had been marching with a group of what looked like a hundred thousand.

The van came to a stop.

"Cristian," whispered Liliana. "What's going to happen to us?"

The fear in her voice pained me. "I don't know. Stay close."

The father of the two children issued warnings. "Stay alert and stay together! No matter what, stay together. Promise me." The children nodded and whimpered.

Our van sat alongside many others parked at the prison; arrests had been plentiful. Guards appeared and marched us in a line down the drive. A decayed sign above the archway was illuminated by a red bulb. It was frightening in its simplicity.

FORTUL N°13

JILAVA

We exited the van and guards jabbed at our backs with batons, corralling us into a tunnel lined with militia. A swarm of canes rained down upon us, smacking, as we tried to make our way through the corridor. We were herded into a large, damp cell, already packed with people. Questions flew.

"Where did you come from? Do you have any news?"

"Have you seen my daughter?"

"My god, they've arrested children. They're covered in blood."

"SILENCE!" boomed a guard.

People began whispering.

Another prisoner untied our hands. "Children and minors sent to Jilava? The regime must be desperate."

"What are you hearing?" I asked.

"Rumors that Ceaușescu is arguing with the military. The soldiers don't want to fire on citizens."

"My friend, he was shot from above, from a window, not by a soldier."

"Maybe a Secu sniper. You're shaking. Are you okay?"

Was I okay? Was anyone okay? "I'm worried about my friend," I told the man.

He nodded. "We'll try to get you kids out of here."

Liliana pulled me under a light. "Cristian, your nose is broken. You need a doctor."

"Take a look around. We all need a doctor. What I need is to find Luca. Besides, it's not my nose that hurts, it's my head. And my ribs. It's painful to breathe."

Liliana pulled the purple scarf from her neck. "Take off your jacket."

I removed my coat and she wrapped her scarf around my rib cage. "Ow."

"Sorry. It needs to be tight," she said, tying a knot. It helped.

I rifled through my jacket pockets to find the papers. I quickly shoved them down the front of my pants. Liliana squinted, watching.

"Don't ask."

Men filtered through the crowd, collecting cigarettes. "We're going to negotiate with the guards, give them cigarettes to let the kids out."

Trading Kents for the lives of children. And he said it without hesitation, without the pain and shameful truth it carried—that the guards cared more about nicotine than humans.

Liliana and I moved toward the corner. The plaster on the cell wall had peeled away in patches, like dead skin, revealing raw bricks. Messages from former prisoners remained etched for us to see:

Straw under clothes softens beatings.

Remember Richard Wurmbrand.

Tell the world—We're innocent.

Liliana moved in close. "I'm scared, Cristian. I'm scared they'll torture us, but I'm even more frightened the uprising will fail."

"You heard the man in the van. There's too much momentum. It's only going to grow. But it was dangerous for you to be out so late. Were you alone?"

She shook her head.

"I was with Alex," she said, then paused. "And Cici."

"Cici?"

"She came to our apartment, looking for you. She was frantic, said you hadn't been home all day and was terrified something had happened. She was going to search for you and asked Alex to help. I wanted to come along, and then we got separated in the crowd."

Cici had betrayed me. How could she claim to care about me? I looked at Liliana's tear-streaked face.

"Tell Alex to stay away from Cici. She's . . ."

Liliana reached up and put a finger to my lips. "I know. I figured it out the day of the funeral. She was informing on me. She saw us drinking the Coke."

"She framed me," I whispered. "She sent the Secu to blackmail her own brother. What about Alex? Can we trust him?" I asked.

"Honestly, I don't know. But he and Cici, they seemed to have a plan. Before we got separated, Cici told me something. She said that if I found you, I should give you a message."

I looked at her, waiting.

"The message is, 'Mr. Van Dorn sends his thanks.' Does that make sense?"

Tears of relief pushed at my eyes. It did make sense. Van Dorn was acknowledging that he got my notebook. But how did Cici have that information?

"What does it mean?" asked Liliana.

There was no reason to hold back. Not now.

"Remember that night in the stairwell, when I told you I had an idea?" I whispered. "Mr. Van Dorn is a diplomat at the U.S. Embassy. My idea was to give him a notebook full of information I compiled, a cry for help to share with other diplomats."

"Oh my god, Cristian, no wonder they beat you like this."

"Honestly, I don't think they know about it yet."

"What was in the notebook?" she whispered.

"The truth. Pages of information on what the regime is doing to Romanians. A bunch of Bulă jokes. Notes from Bunu. I wrote a letter at the end. I titled the notebook *Screaming Whispers: A Romanian Teenager in Bucharest*. My name wasn't anywhere on it."

"And you just gave it to an American diplomat?"

"No, I hid it on his desk."

Liliana's jaw dropped. "What if the Secu found it?"

"You just gave me a message from Van Dorn. Well, a message supposedly from him, confirming *he* received it." I looked toward the front of the cell. "We need to get out of here. I need to find Luca and get you home."

"If they see we want to be together, they'll split us apart," said Liliana.

I looked at her battered, defiant face. She wanted to be together.

"You told me you weren't giving up, Cristian."

"I'm not giving up."

But what if this was my end? I'd never even kissed her.

"Get the young people to the front of the cell!" a guard's voice barked.

"Hurry," said a man. "This may be your only chance."

"I'm Liliana Pavel," she shouted as they jostled us to the front of the group. "My friend Cristian Florescu and I are classmates at MF3 High School and we live in Salajan sector three. If any of you are set free, please contact our families. Tell them that you saw us together and we were alive."

"My friend Luca Oprea was shot in University Square," I yelled. "He's also a student at MF3 High School. If any of you are released, please try to help him!"

A guard grabbed the young brother and sister by their collars.

"Papa!" cried the little boy, reaching for his father. "Where are they taking us? We want to stay with you!"

"I'll see you very soon," said the father, swallowing his tears. "Remember, stay with your sister. You must stay together."

"Where are they taking us?" whispered Liliana. "What if it's worse? Should we stay here?"

A man grabbed my shoulder, stopping me. "I knew your grandfather," he whispered quickly.

He knew Bunu?

The man nodded. "He would be very proud of you."

69

ŞAIZECE ŞI NOUĂ

They pushed us into a room with long tables and benches. The guard ordered us to sit, locked the door, and left. Facing me, next to the door, were two framed portraits. One featured Mother Elena and the other, a one-eared Ceauşescu. I stared at their faces.

We had no food or freedom.

Because of them.

We were surrounded by spies and torturers.

Because of them.

We had no trust.

Because of them.

I couldn't look at the portraits. I grabbed them from the wall and tossed them in the corner.

"What are you doing?" gasped Liliana. "You're putting us all in danger."

"If I have to look at them for one more minute, we'll all be in danger anyway."

Liliana turned to the kids. "Keep your heads down. If the guard asks, tell him the pictures were like that when we came in."

The guard returned carrying buckets and a clipboard. He yawned. "Because of you criminals, we haven't had rest since Timişoara. Do you know what that does? It makes us angry."

We said nothing. He set down the buckets and noticed the heap of portraits in the corner.

"Who did that?"

Silence.

"I said, who did that?!"

I shrugged. "They were like that when we came in."

"No, they weren't."

"Yes, they were!" we all insisted.

The guard blinked, fatigued, not used to dealing with a chorus of kids. He eyed us and waited, uncertain.

"Well, you will pledge your obedience to our hero and Heroine Mother. Each one of you will get down on your hands and knees and kiss their portraits or you'll be taken back to the cell. And my superior must witness you doing it." He turned on his heel and locked the door once again.

"Do we have to?" asked the little boy.

"Yes, we probably do. I'm sorry." I sighed. Why did I have to mess with the portraits? Why couldn't I have just ignored them?

"Kiss me."

She said it so softly, I thought maybe I had imagined it.

But then she said it again.

"Kiss me. Please, Cristian. Before our lips are forced to touch . . . them," she whispered.

I turned and looked at Liliana, despair filling her face. I pulled her into my arms and paused, holding her close, my forehead against hers. Her breathing fluttered against my mouth.

I kissed her. And kissed her again. And again. More gently each time. I kissed her nose, her jaw, her neck. I swept the hair from her brow and kissed each one of her eyes.

A single tear dropped onto her cheek.

I held her against me, not wanting to let go.

The children sat, mouths open, staring.

Footsteps echoed beyond the door. We quickly separated. The guard returned with another uniformed officer in tow. He surveyed the room.

"No," snapped the officer. "The portraits were not on the floor. And that one," he pointed to me. "He's the only one tall enough to reach them." He retrieved the portraits and set them on the tile floor. "Come along, comrade. Time to give thanks."

He was going to hit me. I knew it. I couldn't reveal that my ribs were in pain. If I did, he'd go there first. I stood quickly, trying not to wince. He walked toward me.

"Oh, too bad about your nose, comrade. Does it hurt?" A quick punch sent me to the floor.

He smacked my back and legs with his club. "Ungrateful young people. The Party gave you a beautiful home and this is how you thank them? Crawl to Beloved Leader and Heroine Mother. They're waiting for your apology."

I inched forward on my hands and knees toward the portraits. Liliana's kiss lingered more strongly than the punch. It might be the first and last time I ever kissed Liliana and I didn't want to surrender the feeling.

"Stop stalling! Hurry up."

I hovered over the portrait of Ceaușescu. I wanted to chew it up, swallow, and then vomit it on Mother Elena. But the quiet in the room, the kids, Liliana, they were scared. I couldn't do that. I quickly touched the side of my mouth to Ceaușescu and then to Elena. The dust on the pictures coated my lips. Diseased them. Thank god Liliana was so smart.

They made the others perform the same ritual. Liliana kneeled down, her face a mixture of disgust and defiance. Her nose touched the portrait, but I swear her lips didn't.

The officer kicked the metal pails. "Buckets? No, no, no. These comrades don't get buckets. After they kiss the portraits, they'll do the job with their hands."

They took us to a tiled, windowless room. The air spit with flies.

"System's been plugged for a while. Bag is in the corner. Clean this up, Comrades. Better hurry or you might miss the van."

A bag *was* in the corner. But it sat beneath a huge mountain of feces.

One of the children began to cry. The guard loomed, poking and taunting the child's belly with his baton.

"No, no, little brat. There's no crying. If you're big enough to protest and take part in illegal acts, you're certainly old enough to clean a bathroom. Look at this steaming pile. This is where you belong." He left the room.

We stood, arms hanging by our sides. *What is the cost of self-worth?*

Bunu's question. It lingered in my mind.

We were the pile on the floor.

That's what they were telling us.

That's what they thought.

What did the outside world think? Did they know of our decades of struggle? Did they blame the Romanian citizens? Did they know the regime kept us insulated, or did they believe the unfair stereotypes?

I turned to the kids.

"Dracula is a fictional character created by some Irish author. Dracula has no connection to our history," I said.

"We know that," replied the sister.

"And Romanians are brilliant people. Some are Nobel Prize winners!" I yelled.

"Why are you saying this?"

"Because we're not shit. Do you hear me? We're more Romanian than those guards are!"

The room fell still. A pulse of emotion pushed at my hoarse throat. "No matter what they do or say, we're better than this."

Why was Romania such a dark corner of the map? Was it the distance? Was there a point when a country became too remote to care about?

Amnesty International was trying to share the truth. But if the guards discovered the documents on me, I'd be killed. I couldn't risk harming the others. I pulled the pages from my pants and used them as a shovel.

"What are those papers?" whispered Liliana.

"A nail in the coffin," I told her.

70

ŞAPTEZECI

Three more children were brought to the tiled room. Five children plus me and Liliana. I tried to do most of the work, using the papers and my shoes.

I thought of the portraits in the other room. "Those portraits, they would make a good shovel," I whispered to Liliana.

"Don't you dare."

Finally we finished. We reeked.

"Move!" yelled the guards. They pushed at our backs with guns and clubs, shuffling us back down the cement corridor where we'd entered.

"Are we going home now?" asked the sister.

"You're going to a new home," said the guard.

"I want Papa," cried the brother. "Papa!"

"The older ones, make sure they're restrained."

A guard pushed me against the wall and jammed his club beneath my throat. They tied my hands in front of me with rope. The pain from my ribs, I nearly passed out.

The sun was up. As they loaded us back into a van, a truck arrived carrying a dozen new prisoners. They looked at us, faces full of shock.

"What time is it?" I asked. "What do you know?"

"It's around eight a.m. Fighting continues. Stay strong, we're close!"

The guards pushed us into a van. The children began to cry and the newly arrived prisoners tried to intervene. "Bastards! Let the kids go!"

"Freedom!" yelled a man. They clubbed him before he could say another word.

I sat in the van, trying to breathe. I extended my wrists to Liliana. "Can you loosen the rope?" I whispered.

"It smells. Where are we going?" said a small voice.

"Ask the big boy."

The big boy. Really?

I suddenly felt so small, so tired. So frightened. They said fighting continued, but what if the revolution failed? How much worse would things get? Where were we going? Were our families looking for us? Was the Secu looking for me? Was Cici telling the truth about the message from Van Dorn? What would they do to the prisoners who helped get us out of the cell?

Liliana leaned against my shoulder. My head touched hers and at some point, my exhausted thoughts surrendered to shallow sleep.

We arrived midmorning. I recognized the location the moment they opened the van doors. Strada Aaron Florian. We were near the U.S. Embassy and the Van Dorns' apartment.

In front of us stood a white, ornate building. Decorative plaster garlands draped over each door and window. But the Belle Époque beauty and smooth white plaster exterior fooled no one. Darkness and cruelty lived inside the building, belted tight by bars over each window.

We waited in the van, hands still bound, while the tired guard trudged to the tall front door. The sister and brother clung together as their father had instructed. Explosions and the sound of gunfire hovered in the distance.

I lifted my wrists toward Liliana. "Try the rope again."

My voice wasn't my own. It was hoarse and weary with injury. I put my mouth to her ear. "Starfish once told me about this place. It's a juvenile jail. They sent his cousin here. They shaved his head, beat him, and all sorts of awful things. I say we make a run for it."

"You're in no condition to run, and we can't leave these kids."

She was right.

"You go," she suddenly said, pulling the rope from my hands. "Hurry, sneak behind the van, then hide behind a building. Go! Send someone for us. We'll tell them you escaped the van at Jilava."

I hesitated. "No, I'm not gonna leave you."

"Go! Now!" she whispered, pushing at me. "Find my parents and Alex. They'll have something to bribe with. They'll get us all out of here. Save us!"

Could I save them?

Liliana thought I could. She believed in me.

Bunu believed in me.

I couldn't let them down.

71

ŞAPTEZECI ŞI UNU

I crept to the open van doors and watched the guard approach the beastly building. The driver of the van leaned against the vehicle. He closed his eyes.

Quietly, painfully, I stepped down from the back of the van, and hid by the tire. I made it across the street and crouched in a pool of shadow by a building. I crawled until I was beyond the line of sight.

And then I tried to run.

Pain jolted through my torso. I clutched my ribs, stumbling, but kept going, looking over my shoulder. I darted between buildings and saw a thick crowd in front of the U.S. Embassy. I waded into the swarm. I picked up a filthy knitted hat from the ground and put it on, tucking my wild hair beneath it. I zipped up my coat so the scarf around my torso wasn't visible. The tired guards wouldn't be able to distinguish one protester from another. One positive about bland communist clothing—many of us looked alike.

My conscience pecked at me. Should I have left Liliana and the kids? Would they punish them when they realized I was gone? I pushed my way up to the gate, armed by an American soldier.

"Please, I need to see Mr. Van Dorn. Is he here?"

"Do you have a U.S. passport?"

I shook my head.

"I'm sorry, we're only allowing entrance to Americans."

"But I really need to see Mr. Van Dorn. I need his help."

"You need a doctor. You're badly injured," said the U.S. soldier.

A man next to me tugged at my arm. "Here, drink some water."

I took a sip then poured the water on my hands to try to clean them.

The man eyed me. "Where have you been?" he asked.

"Jilava," I whispered. "I need to go home."

"My son has a bicycle. Radu, help this boy."

"Salajan sector three," I told the guy on the bike.

"Get on. I can take you."

He pedaled as fast as he could, taking side streets, trying to avoid crowds. The morning chill was balmy and the smoke-smothered streets frothed with war. Bloodstained pavement, buildings pocked with bullet holes, burned portraits of Ceauşescu. A child's bloody shoe lay orphaned beneath a spray-painted wall that said *Jos Tiranul*, down with tyranny.

As we passed wide avenues, street cleaning machines chugged along, hosing blood from the pavement. Removing evidence of our murderous regime.

A black Dacia appeared at the end of the road. The rider swerved the bike off the street and bounced up onto the sidewalk.

"Ow!" My ribs screamed.

"Can't help it, man. You want to get home or what?"

"Where are they taking the wounded?" I asked the cyclist. "My friend was shot last night in University Square."

"If he survived, they probably took him to Colţea Hospital. If not, the morgue."

If he survived.

"Have many died?"

"Too many to count. Vehicles plowed over crowds."

It hurt too much to inquire further.

"You smell. Where have you been?" asked the driver.

"Jilava. There were lots of us. Including little kids."

"People are looking for their children. They're going to morgues and hospitals."

"Spread the word they're holding children on Aaron Florian. Tell them to check there," I told him.

"Will do. Don't give up. We just need the military on our side."

We approached my street. Would Paddle Hands or the Secu be waiting for me? "I'm on a list," I told him. "I don't want to put you in danger. You can let me off here."

The cyclist rolled to a stop and I climbed off the bike, wincing in pain.

"You don't want to put me in danger?" He laughed. "In case you haven't noticed, we're all in danger."

He pedaled off, disappearing into the smoke.

72

ŞAPTEZECI ŞI DOI

I walked, head down, toward Liliana's building. The street milled with people. I turned to leave. I couldn't be seen.

"Psst."

A figure motioned to me from between two buildings. Starfish. I joined him in what appeared to be a makeshift command center.

"People are looking for you," he said.

"They should've checked Jilava."

Starfish whistled below his breath. "You okay?"

"Do I look okay?"

"Not really."

"Liliana was there too. They're holding her and a bunch of kids at the detention place your cousin was at. I have to let her family know. And I have to find Luca."

"Was Luca with you? His family is looking for him."

Could I trust Starfish? I had no choice. "Luca was shot," I whispered. "They arrested me, and I don't know what happened to him. I have to check the hospitals."

Starfish shook his head, taking a breath. "Your sister's looking for you too."

"I can't go home. My mother will make me stay there. Help me, Starfish. Please."

"Reporters are on watch. Don't let them see you. I can get you into Liliana's building through the back. Follow me."

Starfish gave a whistle and a young man appeared from nowhere to take over his post. He worked his magic and got me into the building without being seen.

The electricity was off.

"Thanks, man. I don't have anything to give you. But to get to Luca and Liliana, I'm gonna need Kents," I told him.

"I'm out. I'll see if Mirel has some. I'll meet you in the stairwell."

I slowly climbed the steps and knocked on Luca's door. No one answered, but I heard noise inside.

"It's Cristian," I said, knocking louder. I took off my filthy shoes.

The door opened a crack. A sliver of a face appeared. Her eyes expanded.

"Your face is broken."

"C'mon, Dana, let me in."

She opened the door and quickly shut it.

"We're here alone," announced one of the younger girls. "But we're not supposed to tell anyone and we're not supposed to open the door. Our parents are out looking for Luca. Have you seen him?"

"I saw him last night around eleven o'clock."

"Was he okay?" asked Dana.

I paused. "I'm not sure. Is the water on?"

"It's poisoned." She shrugged. "That's what people are saying."

"I just need to wash up." I grabbed a candle from their kitchen, a pair of Luca's pants, and went to the bathroom to change. I had to hurry. If someone was following me—or if Starfish was informing on me—I was putting Luca's sisters in danger.

"Luca's tall. His clothes won't fit you," said his sister outside the bathroom door.

Luca was tall. When he jumped up to save me, he was an easy target. Scenes from the street rolled back at me: tracer fire, pops of gunfire, Adrian falling, Luca's shoulder and arm moving in that unnatural way. So much blood. I grasped the cold sink and shook my head to clear the thoughts.

A stranger stared at me from the mirror. My face was covered in crusty badges of dried blood. My nose was a swollen knot. I washed as best I could and rolled the hems of Luca's pants to fit. I went into the kitchen, pinched a small piece of bread, and retrieved the pad of paper from the drawer. I wrote a note and put it in my pocket. I'd slide it under the door of Liliana's apartment if no one was there.

Dana cornered me in the hall. "Just tell me," she said.

"If your parents come back, tell them I was here and that I'm looking for Luca. Tell them I'm checking the hospitals."

"The hospitals?" Her eyes filled with tears. "Is he okay?"

"I'm not sure," I whispered.

Because I wasn't.

73

ŞAPTEZECI ŞI TREI

A bowlegged silhouette lingered on the stairs. Starfish. Was he alone? The thick darkness of the stairwell made it impossible to tell.

I followed him outside to the back of the building.

"Mirel came through, but you're gonna owe him." He thrust several packages of Kents at me. I thanked him and shoved them in between the layers of scarf that Liliana had wrapped around my rib cage.

"It looks like you're strapped with ammunition," said Starfish.

Was that a positive or a negative?

"Listen, I slid a note under the door of Liliana's apartment, letting her family know where she is. If you see them first, send them to the detention facility on Aaron Florian. Maybe they can bribe her out. I'll be heading to the hospitals to look for Luca. In thirty minutes, shout up to the Reporters that you saw me. I'll call home when I can."

He nodded. "Hey, maybe you should be at the hospital yourself. Your color's awful. I almost didn't recognize you."

"That's probably a good thing. Just tell me, what am I facing out there?"

"Mixed patrols. Militia men, Secu snipers, patriotic guards, security teams in civilian clothes. It's been a hell of a night. You'll see people hiding in yards, trees, garbage cans. The regime broke through the blockade at the Intercontinental and they've cut power to specific parts of the capital. Give me info on Jilava. How many protestors were brought there?"

"Hundreds, maybe close to a thousand. They let me out early this morning with a bunch of kids. But there are plenty of young people still there and more were arriving when I left."

"I heard that students are recruiting people in the Titan and Berceni neighborhoods. Join a group," said Starfish. "It's too easy to be picked up if you're alone."

A car sped up to the corner. A man scrambled out and began looking around. Starfish gave a whistle. The passenger door of his car opened and another man appeared. They ran to us.

"I've got a hot one, Starfish. I need to hide him."

"Okay. Take this guy to Colțea Hospital. He'll give you a pack of Kents."

"Colțea's full."

"I don't need a doctor," I told him. "My friend was shot last night in University Square. I think he may be at Colțea."

He flapped a hand toward his car. The back was riddled with bullet holes. I jumped in. The driver sped down side streets, avoiding the city center.

"What's been happening?" I asked him.

"The Securitate are working in small groups, bands of assassins," said the driver. "They've shot hundreds of civilians. I'm told they're taking identity papers and getting rid of the bodies."

"They shot my friend from a window."

"Yeah, there are rumors they're using infrared scopes. No one knows what to believe. Don't stand out in the open. Find cover."

We turned a corner and saw a young man stumbling on the side-walk, holding his face. We swerved to a stop.

"My eye. They attacked me with a water cannon," he cried. "It's bad." He moved his hand and his glassy eyeball was dangling from the socket.

"No! Keep pressure on it." The driver jumped out of the car and sent the boy into the back seat. He screamed in pain.

"Just hang on," I told him. "We're heading to the hospital. We're almost there."

"As soon as they bandage me up, I need to get back. We set up a new barricade. I have to help my friends. Will you wait for me?" he asked.

I had no time to respond.

The driver pulled up to the hospital. I tossed a package of Kents on the dash. *"Mersi."* Trails of people snaked around the perimeter of the building:

Lines of injured.

Lines of Romanians giving blood to help the injured.

Lines of student volunteers from the university.

I steered the young man into the line for the wounded.

"Wait for me," he repeated. "Once they bandage my eye, I have to get back."

People ran by us shouting and carrying bloodied bodies. Had someone helped Luca?

"I'm sorry. I can't wait for you," I told the boy. "I'm looking for my friend."

An orderly walked the line, inspecting wounds. He took one look at the dangling eyeball and pulled us from the group. "Can you help him inside?" the orderly asked me.

We banged through the doors, pushing across tile floors patterned in a mosaic of bloody footprints. The orderly took our names and returned with a nurse.

"Your eye, come with me," said the nurse. She whisked him out of line.

"I just came for a bandage!" protested the boy. "I need to get back to the barricade."

"My friend was shot. Can you tell me if he's here?" I asked the orderly.

"I'm too busy. Ask at reception."

"Show me where that is," I begged. "Please."

He pointed in a random direction and disappeared into the crowd.

I made my way through a crush of people to a desk. A woman at the front began to shake. "No. NO! Please, not my boy," she pleaded. She slid down in a heap and someone carried her to a chair.

"Please, help me," I pleaded to the desk clerk. "My friend Luca Oprea was shot last night. He's seventeen years old and I think he was brought here."

The clerk sifted through papers. "What's the name?"

"Oprea, Luca."

His finger stopped on the page.

"I'm very sorry—"

No.

Luca.

No.

"I'm very sorry, but you can't see him. He's in the critical care unit."

"What?" I croaked.

"You can't see him."

"But he's here? He's alive?"

"I don't have details. If you need dressing for your own wounds, there's a volunteer triage down the back hallway. Next, please . . ."

He waved me aside, and I was propelled down the hall with a crowd.

Luca was here. In critical condition. What should I do? Should I wait for him?

I made my way to the triage area. University students were set up with makeshift supplies. A young guy inspected my nose. "Can't really do anything for that, a doctor might have to re-break it."

I unzipped my coat. "My ribs, can you wrap me up in something tighter?"

"Don't think we should. You need to breathe deeply or you'll get pneumonia. I can give you some pain meds."

"I'll take them." And I did. "How long have you been here?" I asked.

"Since nine last night. Hospital staff is totally overwhelmed. Many have never seen gunshot wounds, let alone treated them."

"HELP ME, NOW!" A Securitate agent in a long black coat burst through a nearby door. One of his arms hung limp, wounded.

"You need to help me!" he yelled.

No one moved.

And then I saw it. He reached into his coat. And pulled out a gun.

74

ŞAPTEZECI ŞI PATRU

People screamed and ran.

"The army, the army. Who cares about the army!" raged the Secu agent, waving his weapon. "You're outnumbered. We're going to kill *all* of you!" He pointed his gun at the forehead of an injured young woman sitting on a chair. He pulled the trigger.

The gun didn't fire.

Orderlies, patients, and volunteers—they jumped the agent, pummeling him to the ground. He fought and thrashed. We formed a circle around him until he was restrained. Chattering ensued.

"He mentioned the army."

"Have they turned?"

"Someone said Milea committed suicide."

Milea killed himself? Was that true? General Vasile Milea was the Minister of Defense.

"Let's go!" yelled a man.

I exited the hospital with a crowd and stumbled out into the street.

A growing swell of people moved down the road. I joined them and together we walked to Republic Square. I arrived and immediately lost my breath. Shoulder to shoulder, a sea of citizens as far as the eye could see. I had never seen so many people. Probably a hundred thousand. And I immediately noticed something. Romanians were standing, side by side, with the men in green.

It had happened.

The army had turned against the regime. They had joined the Romanian people! Choruses of chanting climbed through the air in front of the Central Committee Building:

Jos Ceaușescu!

Down with tyranny!

The army is with us!

Protected by the army, we sang, chanted, and called for freedom and justice for Timișoara.

Students climbed on top of tanks and thrust their hands in the air with the peace sign. They stood together with the military, waving Romanian flags. A woman ran by me with a bouquet of carnations and began giving them to the soldiers.

The crowd pulsed, agitated. Demonstrators suddenly rushed the building, pushing their way inside. Hearts defiant, we erupted in cheers and the chanting began:

Li-ber-ta-te.

Li-ber-ta-te.

I joined in, calling for liberty.

Then we heard it. A loud whir.

People pointed to a helicopter on top of the building. "It's them! The Ceaușescus!" The crowd jeered, booed, catcalled, and whistled.

A throng of protestors appeared on the balcony of the Committee Building.

Voices echoed through loudspeakers in the square. The propeller on the helicopter began to turn faster, whisking the air with loud chugging sounds.

"He's fleeing!"

"We've done it!"

The helicopter lifted, then sagged, struggling to get airborne. It finally elevated and we watched as it floated across the city.

The sound system crackled and a man's voice filled the square.

"We've done it! Victory is ours! Please, do not be afraid. Have courage. Nothing can stop us now. Nothing can stop us!" He repeated his words over and over until the crowd began to sing.

Ole, Ole, Ole, Ole, Ceauşescu nu mai e.

Ceauşescu no more? Could it be true?

I felt a brief wave of joy until I realized.

Bunu. Luca. Liliana. They'd sacrificed so much.

And they had all missed it.

I left the square and began to limp.

I had to find a pay phone—I had to save Liliana.

75

ŞAPTEZECI ŞI CINCI

Elation. Exhaustion. Determination.

Looting began. Fighting and violence surged in the streets. Ceasescu had fled, but his henchmen weren't backing down. "Teams of terrorists are assisting the Secu assassins!" someone yelled.

But it was all in the background. I had to help Liliana.

The inside of the phone booth was streaked with blood.

I wiped the drops of perspiration from my face, deposited the coins, and dialed.

"*Alo?*"

I paused. My mother's voice cracked a whip of reality.

"*Alo?* Who is this?"

"Mama, it's me," I finally croaked.

"Cristi! Where are you? Are you okay?"

"I'm okay. Mama, listen. Luca is at Colţea Hospital. Please find his parents and tell them. Liliana is being held in a detention facility on Aaron Florian. She's in terrible danger. Have Cici find Alex and bribe the—"

"Cici? Isn't Cici with you?"

"No, Mama. If Cici's not home, please, go across the street to Luca's and Liliana's. Go quickly!"

An explosion detonated, shaking the phone booth.

Mama's voice went tight, shrill. She spoke each word slowly. "Where . . . is . . . Cici?"

"I don't know. Did you hear me, Mama? Luca's at Colţea Hospital and Liliana's in danger at a facility on Aaron Florian. Please, Mama. You have to send help to Liliana. Did you hear me?"

"Yes. And now you hear me. Come home this instant. Is that clear? Your father has been out all night, risking his life to find you both. This is not a movie. They're killing people. And the protesters, they'll all be punished. How can you do this to me? How can you do this to our family?"

"No! The military has turned. Ceauşescu's gone! We've won, Mama."

"No, Cristian. You're wrong. There is no 'winning.' Come home. Immediately."

And then she hung up.

I stood in the blood-spattered phone box, looking at the corded handset. What did Mama mean? Did she know something I didn't?

Fists pounded on the glass of the phone booth. "If you're done, leave!"

I stepped out, suddenly feeling warm and woozy. Was it the pain meds?

A helicopter buzzed overhead and small blue particles began descending from the sky.

"What are those?" shrieked a girl in line for the phone. "Are they explosives?"

Pieces of paper floated and fluttered down like snow, magically settling on the pavement.

I grabbed one of the blue squares. "It's a message." I looked at the words and could barely breathe.

Români, nu vă fie frică. Veţi fi liberi!

I stared at the sentences, trying to swallow through the emotion.

"What does it say?" she asked.

"It says, 'Romanians: Do not be afraid. You will be free.'"

Free.

We would be . . . free.

76

ŞAPTEZECI ŞI ŞASE

The street battles raged on. If victory and freedom were ours, why did the violence continue? Was Mama right? Would we all be punished?

Mama had ordered me to come home. Instead, I made my way back to Colţea Hospital.

The hospital pulsed with rumors and desperation. Kents—they were my only hope to find Luca. I pushed my way up to an orderly. His uniform was painted with blood.

"Please. A young man, Luca Oprea, was shot last night. He was in the critical care unit earlier. Two packs of Kents if you can tell me where he is now."

The orderly looked over his shoulder. "What's the name?" he whispered.

"Luca Oprea."

"You're family?"

I nodded.

"Wait over there."

Children. Teens. Adults. Old people. They walked, ran, crawled, or were carried into the hive of chaos at the hospital. Now that Ceauşescu was gone, who were we really fighting?

The orderly finally reappeared. "Second floor ward. Stairs are at the end of the hall."

We exchanged the Kents in plain view and I headed for the staircase. Each step sucked breath and energy from my diminishing reserve.

Colțea Hospital was the size of a small city. What if I couldn't find Luca? What if they threw me out? A nurse yelled down the stairwell to no one I could see, "Catch the truck before it leaves for the morgue!"

I exited the stairs on the second floor, deciding which way to go.

She saw me before I saw her. Her long legs cycled toward me, hair swinging behind her like a silky, black horse tail.

"*Pui!*"

Cici.

Alarm bells and caution flags flickered through my brain. My sister was waiting for me. My own sister was going to turn me in.

"Oh, thank god, *Pui*. I knew if I found Luca I would find you."

"Get out of my way."

"No, listen, *Pui*. You have to listen."

"I don't have to do anything."

"I'm sorry! I never meant for this to happen. I can help."

"You want to help? Then help me rescue Liliana. They've got her locked up at a detention center on Aaron Florian. Find Alex or go there yourself. Hurry!"

"It's probably safer here. And we need to talk."

"There's nothing to say. If you want to help me, go save Liliana, now! Do you hear me? It's going to take a huge bribe to get her out. Use some of your dirty money."

Cici began to cry, "*Pui*, please wait. Please . . . it's safer here."

"Go!"

I left my sister standing in the hallway, crying and begging. The image and sounds still live like ghosts in my mind.

I reached the ward. Dozens of beds rowed tightly together, side by side. I saw Luca's father. And then I saw him.

Luca.

Eyes closed, head against the pillow, connected to all sorts of bags and tubes. I couldn't get there fast enough.

"Cristian, you're alive!" said his mother.

So was Luca. The enormity of it all surged through me and a rush of tears began to flow. Brave Luca, who jumped up to grab me, who risked his life to save mine.

I swiped at my tears. "Will he be okay?" I asked.

"He lost a lot of blood. The doctor says the next twenty-four hours will be critical."

I moved toward Luca and my eyes pulled to the pad of bandages on his left shoulder. Layers of gauze created a bulky knob. And then I realized that the branch—his arm—it was missing. I stepped closer and his father pulled me aside.

"He doesn't know yet. He's sedated. At this point, we just want him to pull through."

I nodded slowly.

It was my fault. Luca jumped up to reach for me, to save me. Because of that, he'd lost his arm. He'd lost his path to medicine. And now he could lose his life. Families and so much destroyed. What was the cost of freedom?

"Cristian, the girls are alone. Could you go to the apartment and stay with them until one of us comes home?"

I looked at them. I couldn't. No. I needed to help Liliana. "My sister was here. Maybe she could—"

"No," said his mother quickly. "We'd prefer if it was you. The girls know you. Please, just until we get home."

"But . . . my friends . . ."

"Please, Cristian. This will help us. This will help Luca."

I nodded blankly. We were amidst a revolution, my friends

needed help. The Secu was probably looking for me. And suddenly I felt so sleepy and woozy. Would Cici help Liliana? But if Cici went to Aaron Florian, would that create a trail of breadcrumbs—straight back to me?

77

ŞAPTEZECI ŞI ŞAPTE

The electricity was on. Revolutionaries had taken over the radio and television. I lay on the floor of Luca's apartment, my head on a pillow, my ear to the TV. My body quickly sank, heavier and heavier. Exhaustion reached through the seam of revolution and finally pulled me into sleep.

"Cristian. Cristian, would you like to lie on the sofa?"

I opened my eyes. Luca's mother was at my side.

"How long have I been sleeping?"

"A couple hours. But you need proper rest."

"How is Luca?" I asked.

"He's awake. He asked about you and I told him that you're here."

"I want to see him." I shifted to sit up, but pain pinned me to the floor. Wrecked from adrenaline and injury, I could barely move.

"You need to go home and rest."

I rolled over onto all fours and pushed myself off the floor. My head spun and everything hurt. I didn't want to go home. I had to help Liliana.

"What's happening? What are they reporting?" I asked.

"Ceauşescu hasn't been seen. Ion Iliescu has taken over. There are rumors that terrorists have moved in to fight the citizens and the military. It's very dangerous."

I pulled myself up to a standing position.

"Are you okay to walk home?" she asked.

I nodded, lying. My legs were liquid.

I shuffled down the hallway, hugging the wall, and limped down one flight of stairs, making my way to Liliana's apartment. I slumped against the doorframe and knocked.

The door opened a crack, and Alex's face appeared.

"Liliana," I whispered.

"We brought her home an hour ago."

My shoulders sank with relief. "Is she okay?"

A beat of silence. "She's sleeping."

"But is she okay?"

"Are you okay? You look terrible."

"I feel terrible. Even worse than I look."

"I figured. I'll help you home."

Alex propped me up and walked with me. "Thanks for leaving us the note," he said. "I heard about Luca."

"It's all my fault. He was trying to save me."

"No. We're all trying to save our country," said Alex. "Every one of us. And if you haven't noticed, the young people have been the bravest. No regrets in bravery."

We exited his building onto the sidewalk. The Reporters whispered at their post, watching Alex help me across the street.

Electricity sizzled in the stairwell. "Elevator," I muttered.

He walked me over. The doors rattled open and he turned to leave.

"Alex," I said. "Have you been working with my sister?"

He gave a low chuckle. "Cici's not the kind of girl you work *with*. She's the kind of girl you work *for*. But for the record, she did help rescue my sister."

"That's all I care about. Tell Liliana I came by to see her."

The elevator doors rattled shut.

Mama exploded the moment I walked through the door. She

stalked around me in a rattling fit, alternating between fury, fear, and relief.

"You selfish boy! Do you know what you've done to our family? To my nerves? There's hot water. You must bathe. It will ease the pain. Do you think you're indestructible? Do you only care about yourself? Where do you hurt?"

"I just want to lie down."

She fluttered around me, poking and prodding. If I showered, at least I could have some privacy. I headed toward the bathroom.

"I'll make cabbage soup," she said. "Your father's out looking for Cici. The radio and television say the streets are very dangerous."

My sister was more dangerous than the streets.

"I saw Cici."

"Where?" demanded my mother.

"At the hospital. She was visiting Luca. But she left. Don't worry about Cici, Mama," I told her over my shoulder. "She'll take care of herself."

That's what I told my mother.

And shame on me, I believed it.

78

ŞAPTEZECI ŞI OPT

I slept in my parents' bed. Fever sucked me in and out of mangled dreams. I was fighting at the barricade, dodging bullets, lying in a pool of green paint at Station 14, running through the corridors of Jilava, and reaching for Luca. He reached back with his remaining arm and gently touched my forehead.

My eyes fluttered. The room was dark. My father leaned over the bed, touching my forehead.

"How are you feeling?" he asked.

"Tired."

He nodded. "You've been sleeping for several hours."

I closed my eyes, wanting to sleep for several more.

"Liliana's here to see you. Do you feel up to it?"

"Yeah, of course." I summoned some nonexistent energy and boosted myself up in bed.

A few moments after my father exited, the door opened, and the shadow of Liliana appeared. She moved toward me and sat on the edge of the bed. She set her hand upon mine.

"*Bună.*"

"*Bună.*"

I wanted to see her face, sweep her hair from her eyes, and tell her she was safe. I reached beside me and turned on the lamp.

We stared at each other, mouths open.

"Cristian," she gasped, looking at me. She gently touched the wreckage of my body and the ruin of my face.

I said nothing. I couldn't. Liliana's face was badly bruised and swollen. Her necklace was gone and in its place was a slicing red rope burn circling her neck. "Are you all right?" I asked.

She reached up and slowly pulled the winter hat from her head. Her beautiful, mysterious brown hair—it was hacked off, uneven, and partially shaved. Small scabs patched her scalp.

"Oh my god, Lili. Are you okay?"

She nodded. "I was lucky. But the brother and sister. They're still there." Her eyes welled.

"This will all be over soon," I said, not knowing if it was true. We sat in silence, hands clasped.

"You liked my bangs," she whispered.

"I like your eyes," I told her. "And now I can finally see them. Your hair, it kinda looks like mine now."

She laughed and placed a hand on my chest. "You're still wearing my scarf."

"It smells like you."

Liliana smiled. She moved her hand to my face. "Are you okay?"

"I'm fine," I lied.

I was a mess.

It was all a mess.

"Luca," I said.

"I heard."

She held up a hand, clean, but shadowed in green paint. "Cristian, how could anyone understand this?" she whispered. A tear fell onto her cheek. "Will they believe us?"

I shrugged, then shook my head.

They wouldn't. They couldn't. But we were there, together. We understood. And Liliana, she understood *me*. And she knew it. She leaned in to make the point and kissed me. I scooted over on the bed, making room. I wrapped my arms around her and we lay there, sharing the pillow.

An hour passed.

Her breathing slowed to sleep.

Gunfire sounded in the distance.

"I love you," I whispered.

79

ŞAPTEZECI ŞI NOUĂ

December 24th.

Two days passed and the revolution continued.

Liliana and I sat on Bunu's couch in the kitchen. We alternated listening to reports from Radio Free Europe and watching the newly formed station, Free Romania Television. My father began to speak. He asked us about our experience. He asked us how we felt. He asked if there was anything he could do for us. He said more in two days than he had said in two years. Poor Mama fell silent, frightened, muttering into her ashtray.

"I saw Starfish on the way over," said Liliana. "He says there are rumors about a discovery at the Ceaușescu's villa. Incredible wealth."

It was true. And they eventually broadcast it on TV. "Wealth" didn't accurately describe it. Excess, extravagance, greed, and gluttony, those words were more accurate. Countless estates across the country, hundreds of millions salted away in foreign bank accounts. They broadcast a video tour of the homes, including their daughter's, which had a solid gold meat scale and packages of imported veal for her dog.

"I can't bear it," said Liliana. "We've been suffering for years, existing off scrawny chicken feet, with just one forty-watt light bulb per home. And they've been living like kings. Gourmet food, foreign goods, antiques, jewelry, fur coats, hundreds of pairs of shoes?"

I didn't care about that. Where was Ceauşescu and what was he planning?

Just before 5:00 p.m. the news was announced.

The Ceauşescus had been captured.

Messages of support poured in and were read on the air. A special message from Romania's long-exiled king was broadcast. With heartfelt emotion, King Michael expressed his admiration and congratulated Romanians on our fight for freedom.

French Foreign Minister Roland Dumas pledged humanitarian aid and said he would urge the United States and other countries to do the same.

"The U.S. worked with Ceauşescu for years," said my father. "What will happen when they learn the truth about him?"

Following mention of the U.S., the radio host cleared his throat.

<<Speaking of the United States, an American diplomat sent something to us here at Radio Free Europe. It's a very poignant account from Romania, given to him as a Christmas gift. It's entitled *Screaming Whispers*: *An American Teenager in Bucharest*, authored by Anonymous.>>

Liliana and I sat—frozen on the couch.

We didn't move. We didn't look at each other. We didn't utter a sound.

<<The pages of *Screaming Whispers* are full of heart, painful truths, and also humor. But above all, we note its courage, to speak such truths plainly and openly.>>

"Courage?" snapped Mama. "Foolishness. That's so dangerous."

I swallowed what felt like a throatful of bullets.

<<We'd like to share a piece called "A Letter from Romania" that was included in the very end of the notebook. Although this teenage author is anonymous, the sentiments might feel familiar to many listeners.>>

A LETTER FROM ROMANIA

Do you see me?

Squinting beneath the half-light,
Searching for a key to
The locked door of the world,
Lost within my own shadow
Amidst an empire of fear.

Do you feel me?

Heating a brick
To warm my sleep.
Drifting into dreams,
In search of myself,
In search of a conscience, a country.

Do you hear me?

Reciting jokes
Laughing to hide tears of truth
That we are denied the present
With empty promises
Of an emptier future.

Do you pity me?

Lips that know no taste of fruit,
Lonely in a country of millions,
Stumbling toward the gallows
Of bad decisions
While the walls listen and laugh.

Will you remember me?

A boy with wings of hope
Strapped to his back
That never had a chance to open,
Denied forever knowing
What he could have become.

What we all could have become.

Empty static buzzed from the radio.

I sat, unable to move or breathe. A warming presence suddenly pressed in close, surrounding me. Enveloping me. I closed my eyes.

The announcer's voice returned.

<<In this notebook, the young author also asks: *If communism is Paradise, why do we need barriers, walls, and laws to keep people from escaping?* A great question indeed. In the days ahead, let us not forget these sentiments as we reflect upon communism's aim to create a man without a memory.>>

The broadcast continued.

Liliana turned to me, trembling, tears streaming down her face.

My father cleared emotion from his throat. "That letter was very moving. Something your grandfather would have loved."

Bunu.

I sat on his couch fighting a rush of tears. My stubbornness, my defiance, my letter, it was all inspired by Bunu. And he had heard it. I felt him.

"Actually, it was accurate," admitted my mother. "The mention of no taste of fruit—we haven't had any for years."

"I loved it. I really loved it," said Liliana, squeezing my hand.

I wondered what Cici would have said about my letter. I assumed she hadn't been home since I saw her at the hospital.

But that night, I found her locked box and key in my closet. Inside was a note:

Take care of yourself. And please—be careful, Cristian. A revolution eats its heroes.

80

OPTZECI

December 25th.

Christmas Day. 1989.

The Ceauşescus' trial lasted less than two hours. The chief military judge delivered the verdict in minutes. Crimes against the people. Genocide—guilty. Sentenced to death.

4:00 p.m. Executed.

Beloved Leader and Mother Elena, shot by firing squad near a military toilet block. Their death was televised. I stood, staring at their crumpled bodies on the gritty screen. After decades of prolonged suffering, the hasty finality felt confusing somehow. Was that how it was supposed to end? So quickly? I suddenly had an odd, lingering sensation, unsure of what I was feeling. Did we have the full truth? What exactly had happened—and how?

And then, a smell. I couldn't quite place it. And the noise, a pounding at first, filtered into my ears. Was it my own breath and heartbeat? And then I realized. No, it was the desperate scent of long-trapped prayers beating against the walls and windows, tripping over photographs of dead relatives, trying to find a way out.

I ran across the room and threw open a window.

To finally set them free.

1

UNU

Merry Christmas," smiled Liliana.

"Merry Christmas."

My breath smoked on the air. Sure, the apartment might have been warmer, especially now, with fewer heat restrictions. But we had more privacy in the hallway. So we sat, huddled next to each other against the wall.

She passed me a narrow box.

"A new rib?" I grinned.

"Sorry, couldn't find one quick enough. Open it."

I removed the lid. Inside was a pen. A sleek, black ballpoint pen from Germany. It was so special, much nicer than anything I owned. I looked to her.

"Keep writing, Cristian. You have a lot to say."

"*Mersi*. I love it. I have something for you too." I lifted the small bag next to me. "First, this." I reached inside the bag and handed her the colorful square. She unfolded it carefully.

"Springsteen! And it's in English! *Uau*, where did you get it?"

"A pal gave it to me."

"What's a pal?" she asked.

I paused, thinking of Dan Van Dorn. "It's an American term. It means 'friend.'"

"It's great. I love it."

"I have something else." I dipped my hand into the bag, held it there for suspense, then revealed the shiny plastic package with grand ceremony.

"What are those?" She laughed.

"They're called Twinkies. They're American too."

"Should we eat one?"

"Of course we should." I pulled off the cellophane wrapper. Liliana took one of the yellow cakes and I took the other.

"*Unu . . . doi . . .*"

On "*trei*" we both took a big bite. We watched each other, chewing and laughing.

"Oh! There's whipped cream inside," she said.

A dot of vanilla fluff lingered on the side of Liliana's mouth. I leaned in and kissed it away, hovering close to her. "Merry Christmas," I whispered.

"Merry Christmas, Cristian."

For years, life had felt frozen thick, obscured, like looking through a window blinded with ice. I slowly exhaled a chestful of emptiness and inhaled a breath of possibility. We each took another bite. The Twinkies weren't spectacular, but in that moment, sitting in the hallway next to Liliana on Christmas Day, they tasted like something we had never experienced:

Spectacular hope.

EPILOGUE

EPILOG

How long does it take to uncover the truth? For me it took more than twenty years. I was teaching English and Liliana was managing a bookstore. Luca had emigrated to England with his parents.

The Securitate Archives, CNSAS, contained over twenty-six kilometers of files—sixteen miles. And those were just the surviving files. After Ceaușescu's execution, many of the Secu files disappeared. So did some of the agents. But communism didn't disappear, not for many years. A group of second-tier communists took over. The Van Dorns never returned to Romania, but I'm still in occasional touch with Dan. And guess what? Disneyland is a real place. I've been there. But I've never developed a taste for coffee.

When the Securitate Archives were finally opened, Liliana and I agreed that I needed to see my family's files. There were still so many unanswered questions. My parents were no longer alive. I needed the truth.

They had found Cici's body the day after Christmas. Dumped between two buildings; beaten, bent, and buckled with bullets. The revolution had taken my sister. But until I saw the files, I never knew what had really happened.

I was contacted by CNSAS when the Securitate files were "ready" for me.

I arrived in the reading room to find five massive stacks of decaying papers. Each stack held hundreds of pages wedged between a flimsy cardboard cover and a string binding. Our family wasn't famous or infamous like some, but regardless, I estimated our files to be about three thousand pages. That's the equivalent of ten three-hundred-page novels.

It took me many visits to get through them. The files, they were poisonous, disrupting my life and my conscience. Photos from hidden cameras, transcripts from the listening devices in our apartment. Countless reports on Bunu. Over fifty different people had informed on our family. The extent of the surveillance was shocking.

And haunting.

As was my unknown role in it.

When we don't know the full story, sometimes we create one of our own. That's what I had done.

And that can be dangerous.

But I didn't realize my error—until I saw the reports from a source called MARIA.

|| OFFICIAL REPORT ||

Ministry of the Interior

Department of State Security

Directorate III, Service 330

TOP SECRET

[3 November, 1988]

Meeting with source "MARIA" revealed the following:

• MARIA confirms that her father-in-law is a dissident and her husband harbors anti-communist sentiments. She will continue to provide information and advises that she has found ways to cause the radio to malfunction.

• MARIA also agrees to provide information about the U.S. Embassy in exchange for merchandise and the safeguarding of her children—whom she fears are being negatively impacted by their grandfather

• today MARIA requested a carton of Kents

I thought I knew my family.

It turns out, I didn't.

Mama was an informer. She very willingly informed on Bunu, and she informed on her own husband. And my father knew. That's why he retreated into silence. Did Bunu know? Was Mama the rat in our apartment that he referred to? Her reports contained many statements that informing about dissent was not only her patriotic duty, but her maternal duty.

The stress took its toll. The Secu took the upper hand.

To me, Bunu was a hero. To Mama, he was a threat.

And Cici, she understood both perspectives.

In early 1989, Cici was recruited as an informer.

She was my sister. She was my friend. She was also a double agent for the Americans, trying to secure a better life for our family.

The files indicated that Cici repeatedly rejected the idea of enlisting my help to inform on the Van Dorns. She had tried to protect me. What finally changed her mind? The promise of two passports. She planned that we'd emigrate to Canada or the U.S.

Just the two of us.

The Secu used her, blackmailed her, and repeatedly criticized her in the files. Her code name was FRITZI and the reports from Paddle Hands about her were denigrating and demeaning. The reports suggested ways to exploit Cici's body to gain information on a multitude of targets. The files said she helped the woman from Boston get to the U.S. Embassy so she could leave the country just prior to the uprising. And that's when the regime discovered she had been working with the Americans.

Cici had tried to help others but couldn't save herself.

She had begged to stay at the hospital that night. She told me it was "safer."

I didn't realize Cici was in danger. I left her, believing she was working against me when in reality, she was trying to help me. But what exactly had happened when she left the hospital?

Those details weren't in the files.

Nor was the fact that I had misunderstood and failed my sister.

In addition to his reports on Cici, Paddle Hands's reports on me were sobering and, at times, chilling:

OSCAR *is no longer of use. Take necessary measures.*

"Take necessary measures" was also the phrase they applied to Bunu before his death.

There were so many disturbing details of the surveillance. Things I felt sure were private were not private. Not my first kiss at fourteen, not my trades with Starfish, not even the Twinkies. Reading the files was indescribably violating and needled trust issues I had hoped were long buried. Seeing the reports opened a door I couldn't close. I constantly wondered: Was it better to know, or better not to?

Me personally, I needed to know. But I still had unanswered questions about my sister.

A year later, at my high school reunion, I lingered near the bar with a classmate.

"So, what are you doing these days?" he asked.

"Teaching English. You?"

"Accounting. We were in the same class," he said. "Do you remember? I'm the guy who had the breakdown and screamed about being an informer. That's how most people remember me."

"You know what I remember?" I said. "That none of us did anything to comfort you. I'm sorry. I was in the same position. I should have helped you."

"Same agent?" he asked.

"Big hands and BT cigarettes?"

"Yeah, that's him. I thought he was so evil, but now I sometimes wonder—maybe he was a pawn of the regime, just like the rest of us. But you know what's weird?" he whispered. "His daughter goes to the school right next to my apartment building."

A cold clench gripped my abdomen. "Wait, you see Paddle Hands?"

"Yeah, he lives right near me, in building F2."

Paddle Hands, the guards at Station 14, most of the torturers were never charged. They lived among us. Maybe the events of 1989 are a distant memory to them. But they're not a distant memory to me. Like I said, too many unanswered questions.

"He lives near you?" I asked again. "Do you know his real name?"

He gave me the name.

I repeated it in my head.

Memorized it.

Vowed never to forget it.

And that's how I eventually ended up at the cemetery, standing at our family gravesite with a manuscript. I've spent years panning for truth, interrogating my memories, correcting false narratives, and pondering the fact that when betraying others, we often betray ourselves.

My students sometimes ask about the revolution and I share stories. I change the names, just in case. They love hearing about Liliana, Bunu, and Starfish. When I speak of Cici, their sadness is palpable.

Sometimes we think we know. We're sure we know. But we know nothing. Years pass and eventually, time becomes the unveiler of truth. And that painful shift in comprehension, I tell my students, is called "a rite of passage"—that's the English term for it.

"Mr. Florescu, you should write a book about it," they constantly tell me.

So I have.

The story ends well: Liliana. Me. Spectacular hope.

I've left it for Bunu to read. Maybe one day others will read it too.

But now I've arrived at Paddle Hands's apartment, and I'm ready for answers. I'm ready to put the past behind me.

I've knocked.

I've heard his footsteps, and I can smell the cigarette smoke.

It's happening.

This is it.

He's going to open the door.

"All changes, even the most longed for, have their melancholy;
for what we leave behind us is a part of ourselves;
we must die to one life before we can enter another."

—ANATOLE FRANCE

December 1989. The Romanian Revolution in Bucharest.

Elena and Nicolae Ceaușescu

*"The communist regime under Ceaușescu had become totalitarian.
It was one of the most repressive regimes in the Eastern Bloc at that time.
It was so bad that even Soviet leader Mikhail Gorbachev described it as,
'a horse being whipped and driven by a cruel rider.'"*

—COLONEL BRANKO MARINOVICH,
Foreign Area Officer, U.S. Embassy in Bucharest, 1989

*"I believe that Ceaușescu had gotten away with one of the greatest
Cold War ploys, which was appearing one way to the West and yet maintaining
in his own country probably the worst cult of personality dictatorship and
abusive human rights that had existed since Stalin . . . It was just
so out of control that it even out-Stalined Stalin."*

—SAMUEL FRY,
Deputy Chief of Mission, U.S. Embassy in Bucharest, 1981–1983

*"Evil is unspectacular and always human
and shares our bed and eats at our own table."*

—W. H. AUDEN

Gerald R. Ford, Richard M. Nixon, and Nicolae Ceaușescu

The Ceaușescus visit with Queen Elizabeth and Prince Philip, 1978

Official portraits of the Ceaușescus

Magazines Cristian sees at the American Library, November 1989

Vintage BT and Kent cigarettes in Romania

Ceaușescu's Palace of Parliament

Apartment blocks of the Romanian people

Bucharest citizens stand in line for cooking oil, 1986

Dacias and a propaganda poster
on the streets of Bucharest, 1986

Entrance of Jilava prison

Interior of Jilava prison

Romanian students in Timișoara get updates during the Revolution

Romanian students in Timișoara during an
exchange with the Romanian military, 1989

A Dacia draped with a revolutionary flag, 1989

AUTHOR'S NOTE

"When justice cannot shape memory,
remembering the past can be a form of justice."
—Ana Blandiana

I Must Betray You is a work of historical fiction. The Ceaușescu dicta-torship and the extended suffering of over twenty million Romanians, however, is not fiction. It was hauntingly real yet remains unfamiliar to many.

I am indebted to the many incredible writers, poets, historians, scholars, photographers, and journalists who have chronicled the dic-tatorship and communist period in Romania. I am also indebted to the many people listed in the "Research and Sources" section who shared their stories and knowledge with me. If historical novels stir your interest, I encourage you to pursue the facts, nonfiction, mem-oirs, and personal testimony available. Those are the real stories—the shoulders—that historical fiction sits upon.

As a child in a Lithuanian American family, I watched Romanian athletes compete in the Olympics. Unlike Lithuania, whose name was removed from maps during the Soviet period, Romania walked under their own flag in the opening ceremony. Their uniforms featured the word ROMANIA, along with their own national colors. I remember marveling at what I thought was their good fortune. Of course, at the time, I knew nothing of their suffering. I knew nothing of their history. How many others were unfamiliar with the plight of Romania?

I first explored Romania while on tour for my debut novel. At each turn, the Romanians showed incredible generosity and hospitality. They not only welcomed me warmly, they showed tremendous empathy for the hidden history described in my work as well as those who had experienced it. They focused on others rather than themselves. It was only after repeated requests that stories of their own recent history began to flow and my bald ignorance became fully apparent.

Following World War II, Romania became an allied nation of the Soviet Union. Under Soviet influence, communism took hold and Romania's King Michael was forced to abdicate and leave the country. Nicolae Ceaușescu came to power in the 1960s and ruled until he and his wife, Elena, were executed by firing squad on December 25, 1989.

Though Ceaușescu had only an elementary school education, some have called him a mastermind. Building and maintaining his dynasty was a family affair. It's estimated that at one time over thirty of his family members served in key positions for the regime.

Ceaușescu's criticism of the Kremlin convinced leaders of many countries that he was a maverick, when, in reality, his reign revealed him to be a monster. Ceaușescu understood that in order to rule through tyranny, his first step was isolation. He isolated Romania from the rest of the world and then proceeded to further isolate individual citizens by separating and positioning them against one another.

The Securitate, Ceaușescu's brutal secret police force, served as a repressive tool for the regime. My research interviews revealed episodes of cruelty, punishment, and human rights abuses to Romanians that were indescribably barbaric. In addition to arrests, torture, and murder, the Securitate recruited, intimidated, and commanded an enormous network of civilian informers. Some recruits were pressured and told that informing was a patriotic duty to their homeland. Others were promised favors or food for their family. The desperation for survival ran so deep that many had no choice. It's estimated that one in every ten citizens provided information.

Although Securitate agents were often identifiable, informers were not. They bridged all ages and demographics—even children. The result was a national atmosphere of fear and suspicion. Romanians were unable to speak freely, and the inability to trust created obstacles for friendships and even family relationships. As the years progressed, the Securitate controlled the population through their own fear.

Fear, suspicion, and the constant threat of listening devices forced Romanians to divide themselves into public and private personalities. Spaces often considered personal, such as a home or even a bathroom, were not private. Under the ever-present threat of observation, behaviors were modified and thoughts were rarely voiced aloud. Instead, they were imprisoned within an internal mental landscape, repressing the psyche and soul of a population.

When I began researching *I Must Betray You*, my thoughts immediately turned to the Romanian children and students living under the Ceaușescu regime—innocent young people who felt deeply and passionately as they were coming of age but were powerless to direct the course of their life. Radio Free Europe and Voice of America provided crucial links to the free world. Books, films, magazines, and music were windows to democracy. Some scholars have stated that VCRs and movies from the West exposed teens to concepts of freedom and loaded the guns that eventually killed Ceaușescu. As with my other novels, it was the desperate plight of the young people that I chose to focus on.

Although most communist regimes in Eastern Europe transitioned without violence, when revolution arrived in Romania, brave citizens faced a hail of bullets and bloodshed. Students took to the streets in Timișoara, Bucharest, and many other cities, armed with nothing but courage. Hearts defiant and desperate to free their country, young people willingly put themselves in the path of destruction and in some cases, attacked Ceaușescu's weaponry with their bare hands. Their bravery, their heart—it was astounding. They gave their lives for freedom and will forever remain heroes of the revolution.

Communism in Romania did not end with the death of the Ceaușescus. After the execution, a replacement set of communists took over, and for many years, some of the preexisting networks remained supported. Some began to question the legitimacy of the revolution. As such, there was no clear or satisfying "ending" to the period. Things were confusing, questions remained—and still remain. I've tried to reflect that in the epilogue. As a reader, unanswered questions and sadness may feel frustrating, but it's difficult to grasp how frustrating it must feel for those who actually experienced the events.

Unlike other countries who opened their secret police files for review and a path to atonement, Romania's Securitate files remained closed for over fifteen years. It's alleged that during that time, some files were altered or destroyed. Historical lustration—the process of clarifying—is ongoing in Romania.

To further complicate matters, while innocent Romanian citizens grappled with the consequences of the revolution, they unfairly inherited responsibility for the dysfunction caused by the communist leaders. In the early '90s, reports of orphanages and poverty distilled a partial narrative about the country and the time period. But without the context of Ceaușescu's fertility tyranny and the ongoing battle with communism, the outside world wasn't privy to the full story.

Also underrepresented is the experience of Romania's Jewish population. At one time Romania had nearly seven hundred thousand Jewish residents. In 1989 only twenty-three thousand remained. Ceaușescu demanded a per-head payment for Jewish inhabitants to be relocated to Germany, Israel, or other countries. In a nation of nearly twenty million people, Romania's Jewish population today is approximated at only three thousand.

Ceauşescu betrayed his own country and countless other countries. His particular brand of national communism and his use of the Securitate caused trauma and plural identity, at times forcing Romanians to betray even themselves. In addition, by isolating the country and its people, Ceauşescu robbed the world of access to Romanian culture and history. Recent studies have shown that some believe Transylvania to be a fictional place and are unaware that it's a beautiful, historic region in Romania.

I hope that through reading *I Must Betray You*, readers might be inspired to research the histories of the captive nations, the fall of communism in Europe, and, most relevant to this story, the incredible fortitude and endurance of the Romanian people. Romania joined the European Union in 2007 and continues to make progress. How can we assist that progress?

We can share their story.

History is the gateway to our collective story and the story of humanity. Historical fiction allows us to explore underrepresented stories and illuminate countries on the map. But as an author, I have nothing without readers. Thank you for reading this novel. Please share the history with someone. As I acknowledge in the "Research and Sources" section, there were true witnesses who greatly informed my research but for various reasons requested to remain anonymous. With an adequate buffer of time, perhaps one day we can look upon events with a wide lens of reflection and create a compassionate environment for people to take ownership of their own story.

And finally, to the students and young readers: You are the stewards of history who will carry our fading stories into the future. I am so honored to work with you and I am so honored to write for you. Please remember that when adversity is drawn out of the shadows and recognized, we ensure that human beings living under oppression—past and present—know they are not forgotten.

Together, we can shine a light in dark corners of the past.

Together, we can give history a voice.

Ruta Sepetys

RESEARCH AND SOURCES

The research process for this novel was a global, collaborative effort that spanned many years. That said, any errors found herein are my own.

My Romanian publisher, Epica Publishing House, connected me with people, places, and experiences to bring this story to life. I am forever grateful to Anca Eftime Penescu, Dan Penescu, and Dana Popescu. Anca and Dan spent years working with me on this project. Together with my interpreter, Dana Popescu, they accompanied me throughout many regions of Romania during my research and endured many long days of travel. They all read drafts and answered endless questions. This novel would be impossible without the three of them!

I am extremely indebted to Stejarel N. Olaru. Stejarel is a Romanian historian, political scientist, and bestselling author based in Bucharest. Stejarel is also an expert on the history of intelligence services. He generously informed my research on the Securitate as well as Ceaușescu's particular brand of communism. Stejarel helped guide my research, arranged many interviews, and introduced me to historian Claudiu Secașiu, former president of National Council for the Study of Securitate Archives (CNSAS). Stejarel answered my many historical questions about the structure and function of the Securitate and its effects on the population, and also acquainted me with the current Securitate archives.

Nicoleta Giurcanu was fourteen at the time of the revolution.

On December 21st, she was arrested with her father and little brother and endured the horrors at Station 14, Jilava, and the juvenile facility on Aaron Florian. Nicoleta bravely and generously shared her history with me and spared no detail. She is an ambassador for the unsung heroes of December 21st. Her story, her humanity, and her continued quest for truth and freedom inspire me beyond description and helped shape the scenes of the revolution and the spirit of the young people in the novel.

Maggie Chitoran served as the interpreter for my meeting with Nicoleta and facilitated the interview while patiently navigating my bouts of tears.

Ionel Boyeru was a military captain within a special unit of Romanian paratroopers when he volunteered for a mysterious Christmas Day mission. Unbeknownst to him, he would become one of the three soldiers on the firing squad assigned to execute the Ceauşescus. Ionel traveled a long distance to meet with me and described the complex situation of the military in 1980s Romania, the intensity around the execution, as well as the evolving perceptions during and after the revolution. Ionel's personal testimony was incredibly informative, honest, and an important reminder that often history is nuanced, complicated, and doesn't easily fit into defined categories. I am indebted to Ionel for his generosity and perspective.

Paulina Huzau-Hill was an incredible resource and supporter. She went above and beyond to share her family's very moving story as well as items from her personal family archives. Her perspective made the history very human.

Irina Margareta Nistor is a Romanian translator and film critic. She is also an iconic voice of freedom. During the communist period, Irina secretly dubbed over three thousand movies from the West into Romanian. Through movies, Irina brought the outside world inside of Romania and shared concepts of democracy with Romanian citizens.

Irina answered many questions and informed the framework for the use of videos in the novel.

Radio Free Europe/Radio Liberty and Voice of America deserve a novel all their own—and I hope to write one. In countries where freedom of the press does not exist or is restricted by the government, Radio Free Europe/Radio Liberty provides uncensored news, discussion, and debate. Emil Hurezeanu is a journalist and writer who worked in the Romanian department of Radio Free Europe in Munich from 1983 to 1994. While I was writing the novel, he was serving as the Romanian ambassador to Germany and, despite his incredibly busy schedule, took time to assist my research and thoughtfully answer my long list of questions.

Nadia Comăneci is not only a legendary Olympic gymnast, she is a well of generosity. During our interview, Nadia continually emphasized perspective and the importance of focusing on what average Romanian citizens endured for so many years and their heroic courage while doing so. Her affection and sincere admiration for her fellow Romanians was so moving and highlighted the beautiful bond of the Romanian diaspora worldwide.

I'm very grateful to the elderly residents of Bucharest who welcomed me into their homes. They shared many details, vintage items, and examples that helped me research the structure and layout of the apartment blocks. As I've expressed, Romanian generosity is unending.

Claus Pedersen has been a longtime friend and steadfast research partner for several novels, and this was no exception. He embraces "peace, love, and good happiness stuff."

There were people who provided detailed information and heartfelt testimonies about the history and time period but for various reasons have requested to remain anonymous. I acknowledge them here and send them my love and sincere gratitude.

While writing and researching, I returned constantly to reference the invaluable works of Ana Blandiana, Paul Goma, Dennis Deletant, Katherine Verdery, Herta Müller, Mihai Eminescu, Gail Kligman, and others. A full reference list of sources follows.

I also thank the following for their generous assistance and inspiration:

The Association for Diplomatic Studies and Training, ASTRA Museum Sibiu, Andrei Bersan, Dr. Murray Bessette, the Brașov County Museum of History, the Bucharest Palace of Parliament, Adrian Bulgaru, the Ceaușescu Mansion, Laura Gabrielaitytė-Kazulėnienė, the Gerald R. Ford Presidential Library, Arnas Gužėnas, Octavian Haragos, the Institute for the Investigation of the Crimes of Communism and the Memory of the Romanian Exile, Ms. Mancea Ioncea, the Jimmy Carter Presidential Library and Museum, Ambassador Rolandas Krisciunas, Alexandra Loewy, MF3 High School, Peleș Castle, Adina Pintea, Ambassador Arvydas Pocius, the Radio Free Europe/Radio Liberty Historical Collection at the Hoover Institution Library and Archives housed at Stanford University, the Richard Nixon Presidential Library and Museum, the Romanian Institute for Human Rights, the Ronald Reagan Presidential Library, the Sighet Museum, Manuela Tabac, the Victims of Communism Memorial Foundation, and Victoria Brașov County.

SOURCES

I Must Betray You was built with bricks from the following books, academic papers, articles, films, and resources.

1989 Libertate Roumanie by Denoël Paris

"23 Years of Ceaușescu: Romania—Tight Rule of a 'Deity'" by Charles T. Powers, *Los Angeles Times*

Abandoned for Life: The Incredible Story of One Romanian Orphan Hidden from the World, His Life, His Words by Izidor Ruckel

"After the Revolution: The American Library of Bucharest Enters a New Era" by Mary Ann Ignatius

"Alternative Images: The '50s in Romania through Jokes Broadcasted by Radio Free Europe" by Gabriel Stelian Manea

At Home There's Only Speaking in a Whisper: File and Diary Recording the Late Years of the Romanian Dictatorship by Stelian Tănase

Authoritarianism: What Everyone Needs to Know by Erica Frantz

Betrayals: The Unpredictability of Human Relations by Gabriella Turnaturi, translated by Lydia G. Cochrane

Bottled Goods by Sophie van Llewyn

Broadcasting Freedom: The Cold War Triumph of Radio Free Europe and Radio Liberty by Arch Puddington

"Bucharest Journal; To Rumanians, It Just Feels Like the Third World" by Craig R. Whitney, *The New York Times*

"Bullets, Lies, and Videotape: The Amazing, Disappearing Romanian Counter-Revolution of December 1989" by Richard Andrew Hall

Burying the Typewriter: A Memoir by Carmen Bugan

The Captive Nations; Eastern Europe: 1945–1990: From the Defeat of Hitler to the Fall of Communism by Patrick Brogan

Ceaușescu and the Securitate: Coercion and Dissent in Romania, 1965–89 by Dennis Deletant

"Ceauşescu Palace Rises as Monument to Greed" by Joseph A. Reaves,
    Chicago Tribune

"Ceauşescu Regime Used Children as Police Spies" by Daniel
    McLaughlin, *The Guardian*

Checkmate: Strategy of a Revolution, documentary film directed by
    Susanne Brandstätter

The Christmas Gift, film written and directed by Bogdan Muresanu

Chuck Norris vs. Communism, documentary film written and directed by
    Ilinca Călugăreanu

Communism: Its Ideology, Its History and Its Legacy, curriculum created by
    the Victims of Communism Memorial Foundation

*Contemporary History Romania: A Guide through Archives, Research
    Institutions, Libraries, Societies, Museums and Memorial Places* by
    Stejărel Olaru and Georg Herbstritt

The Day We Won't Forget: 15 November 1987, Brasov by Alex Oprea and
    Stejărel Olaru

The Dean's December by Saul Bellow

"Doina Cornea's Doll" by Cristina Petrescu, Cultural-Opposition.eu

"The Enduring Legacy of Romania's Securitate" by Paul Hockenos, PRI

"Ex-Ambassador Says Washington Would Hear No Evil About
    Ceauşescu" by Mike Feinsilber, *Associated Press*

*Explaining the Romanian Revolution of 1989: Culture, Structure, and
    Contingency* by Dragoş Petrescu

"Fall of Ceauşescu: When Romanians Stood Up to Tyranny," *BBC News*

"Finally, We Called It Christmas Again: My Role in Romania's
    Revolution" by Eugen Tomiuc, Radio Free Europe/Radio Liberty

*Fodor's '89 Eastern Europe: Poland, Hungary, Czechoslovakia, Bulgaria,
    Romania, East Germany*

"Freedom!" by George J. Church, *TIME*

"The Great Escape: How Bucharest Rolled Entire Churches to Safety" by
    Kit Gillet, *The Guardian*

Handling the Truth: On the Writing of Memoir by Beth Kephart

The Hole in the Flag: A Romanian Exile's Story of Return and Revolution
    by Andrei Codrescu

The Hour of Sand: Selected Poems 1969–1989 by Ana Blandiana, translated
    by Peter Jay and Anca Cristofovici

"In Bucharest, Tears and Prayers for the Fallen" by Blaine Harden, *The
    Washington Post*

"In Romania, Kents as Currency" by Gary Lee, *The Washington Post*

"In Romania, Smoking a Kent Cigarette Is Like Burning Money" by
    Roger Thurow, *The Wall Street Journal*

"In Rumania, All Hail the Chief, and Dracula, Too" by John Kifner, *The
    New York Times*

Kiss the Hand You Cannot Bite: The Rise and Fall of the Ceauşescus by
    Edward Behr

Let's Go: The Budget Guide to Europe, 1989

Letters from a Stoic by Seneca

Letters to a Young Gymnast by Nadia Comăneci

Lines Poems Poetry by Mircea Ivănescu, translated by Adam J. Sorkin and
    Lidia Vianu

Memorialul Durerii, documentary television series created by Lucia
    Hossu-Longin

My Childhood at the Gate of Unrest by Paul Goma

My Life as a Spy: Investigations in a Secret Police File by Katherine Verdery

My Native Land A4 by Ana Blandiana, translated by Paul Scott Derrick
    and Viorica Patea

Nadia Comăneci: The Gymnast and the Dictator, film written and directed
    by Pola Rapaport

*National Ideology under Socialism: Identity and Cultural Politics in
    Ceauşescu's Romania* by Katherine Verdery

Peregrina: Unexpected Adventures of an American Consul by Ginny Carson
    Young

Pinstripes and Reds: An American Ambassador Caught between the State Department and the Romanian Communists, 1981–85 by David B. Funderburk

A Poetry Handbook by Mary Oliver

The Politics of Authenticity: Countercultures and Radical Movements across the Iron Curtain, 1968–1989 by Joachim C. Häberlen, Mark Keck-Szajbel, and Kate Mahoney

The Politics of Duplicity: Controlling Reproduction in Ceaușescu's Romania by Gail Kligman

"The Power of Touch" by Maria Konnikova, *The New Yorker*

"Radio Free Europe and the 1989 Fall of Communism in Romania" by Anamaria Neag

"Radio Waves, Memories, and the Politics of Everyday Life in Socialist Romania: The Case of Radio Free Europe" by Ruxandra Petrinca, *Centaurus*

Raggle Taggle by Walter Starkie

Red Horizons: The True Story of Nicolae and Elena Ceaușescus' Crimes, Lifestyle, and Corruption by Lt. Gen. Ion Mihai Pacepa

"The Rise, Fall, and Rebirth(s) of Steaua Bucharest" by Ryan Ferguson

"Romania: Human Rights Violations in the Eighties," Amnesty International

Romanian Journey by Andrew MacKenzie

The Romanian Revolution of December 1989 by Peter Siani-Davies

"Romania's Revolution of 1989: An Enduring Enigma" by Donald G. McNeil Jr., *The New York Times*

"Romania's Revolution: The Day I Read My Secret Police File" by Oana Lungescu, *Independent*

"Romania's 'Ungentle' Revolution 30 Years Later: 'Still No Prosecutions,'" Ziarul de Gardă

The Rough Guide to Eastern Europe, Romania and Bulgaria, 1988 by Dan Richardson and Jill Denton

"Ruling Romania: A Family Job" by Michael Dobbs, *The Washington Post*

"Rumours in Socialist Romania" by Steven Sampson, *Survey: A Journal of East & West Studies*

"Scenes from a Revolution: Romania after the Fall" by Dick Virden, *American Diplomacy*

"The Spies Who Defended Us: Spy Stories and Legitimating Discourses in Ceauşescu's Romania, 1965–77" by Dragoş Petrescu, *Romanian Intelligence Studies Review*

"Thirtieth Anniversary of the Fall of Communism in Romania" by Tammy Cario, DLIFLC

"Uses and Misuses of Memory: Dealing with the Communist Past in Postcommunist Bulgaria and Romania" by Claudia-Florentina Dobre, *European Memory: Eastern Perspectives*

The Voices of Silence by Bel Mooney

"Women as Anti-Communist Dissidents and Secret Police Collaborators" by Lavinia Stan

"Yes, He's for Real" by Walter Isaacson, *TIME*

"Youth and Politics in Communist Romania 1980–1989" by Veronica Szabo

ACKNOWLEDGMENTS

Completing a novel during a global pandemic proved to be extremely challenging. I have never been more grateful for the generosity, patience, and assistance of those so dear to me.

My incredible agent, Steven Malk, has guided my steps since 2007. Kacie Wheeler and Jeffrey Kirkland manage my days and events with loving care. My brilliant and tireless editor, Liza Kaplan, is my creative copilot and champion. Ken Wright and Shanta Newlin have stood beside me since the very first book. I am so grateful to Jen Loja, Jill Santopolo, Talia Benamy, Kaitlin Kneafsey, Kim Ryan, Felicia Frazier, Emily Romero, Carmela Iaria, Trevor Ingerson, Felicity Vallence, Krista Ahlberg, Ellice Lee, Theresa Evangelista, Christina Colangelo, Alex Garber, Venessa Carson, Helen Boomer, Bri Lockhart, Tomislav Tomic, and my Philomel family for giving history a voice and my stories a home.

Behind the scenes are all of the beautiful people at Penguin Young Readers, all of the Penguin field reps, Penguin subsidiary rights, Writers House, Marks Law Group, UTA, Luum, Penguin Audio, and SCBWI. I'm so grateful to all of my wonderful foreign publishers, subagents, and translators for sharing my words in over sixty countries.

Sharon Cameron, Amy Eytchison, Angelika Stegmann, Howard Shirley, Court Stevens, Beth Kephart, Claus Pedersen, Niels Bye Nielsen, Marius Markevicius, Yvonne Seivertson, Mike Cortese, Jason Richman, Steve Vai, Ruta Allen, JW Scott, Sean Marks, Genetta

Adair, Meg Fleming, Keith Ryan Cartwright, Mary Tucker, Noah and Andrew Faber, the Baysons, the Rockets, the Peales, the Smiths, the Brodds, the Myers, and the Schefskys have all supported me on the journey of this novel.

Deepest gratitude to my biggest supporters: the teachers, librarians, and booksellers. And most of all—the readers. I appreciate each and every one of you.

My parents taught me to dream big and love even bigger. John and Kristina are my heroes and the best friends a little sis could ask for.

And Michael, whose love gives me the courage and the wings. He is my everything.

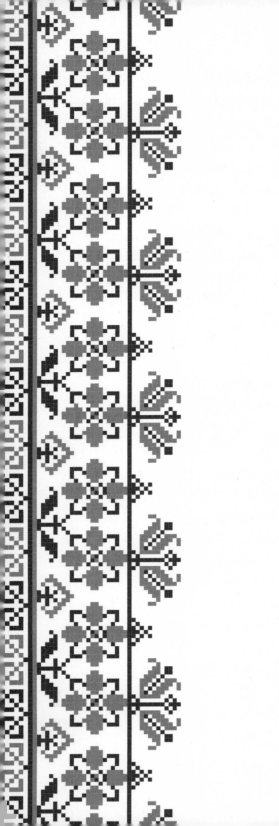